The Visitor

ALSO BY JOANNE DEMAIO

The Seaside Saga

Blue Jeans and Coffee Beans
The Denim Blue Sea
Beach Blues
Beach Breeze
The Beach Inn
Beach Bliss
Castaway Cottage
Night Beach
Little Beach Bungalow
Every Summer
Salt Air Secrets
Stony Point Summer
The Beachgoers
Shore Road
The Wait
The Goodbye
The Barlows
The Visitor
Stairway to the Sea
–And More Seaside Saga Books–

ALSO BY JOANNE DEMAIO

Beach Cottage Series

The Beach Cottage
Back to the Beach Cottage

Standalone Novels

True Blend
Whole Latte Life

The Winter Series

Snowflakes and Coffee Cakes
Snow Deer and Cocoa Cheer
Cardinal Cabin
First Flurries
Eighteen Winters
Winter House
–And More Winter Books–

This is a work of fiction. Names, characters, places, and incidents are either the product of the author's imagination or are used fictitiously. Any resemblance to actual persons, living or dead, events, or locales is entirely coincidental.

No part of this book may be reproduced, or stored in a retrieval system, or transmitted in any form or by any means, electronic, mechanical, photocopying, recording, or otherwise, now known or hereinafter invented, without express written permission of the copyright owner.

Copyright © 2023 Joanne DeMaio
All rights reserved.

ISBN: 9798364604859

Joannedemaio.com

the visitor

the seaside saga

BOOK 18

JOANNE DEMAIO

one

WHAT WAS HE THINKING?

Calling people at the end of the day. Intruding on their lives, their home—right at the dinner hour. When they're tired and maybe eating supper. When they're hundreds of miles away. Did he think that they could help? That they could change the course of the past few hours?

Pacing now, Shane nearly trips on the toppled chair at his kitchen table. He circles around it while holding his cell phone to his ear. A bead of perspiration moves down his temple, his face. He looks this way, that way. Darkness presses at the window, at the back door. In the dimly lit kitchen, the walls are closing in. Again, there's that breathing thing. The air just won't fill his lungs.

"*Forget it, Barlow,*" he practically whispers into the phone. "*I got to go.*"

"No! No, guy," Jason insists. There's a moment's pause, then, "Listen. Hey. Do *not* hang up, Shane. It's going to be all right."

"No. No, it's not."

"Well, I'm *here*."

There's some impatience in Jason's voice now; Shane hears it over the phone. Or some anger, even.

"And I want to talk to you, man," Jason's saying. "But you've *got* to stay with me, okay? So slow down, take a breath, and tell me what the *hell* happened."

Tell him what the hell happened—as if there's a way. If Shane could laugh, wouldn't he now at the futility of Jason's order.

But Shane doesn't laugh.

Can't.

Won't.

If he laughed now, he'd choke on the sob it would turn into. So instead? With a knot in his throat, Shane paces the shadowed kitchen. His booted feet are heavy as he walks around the wooden table. He bends to right that toppled chair—then changes his mind and walks past it. His fingers run along the planked-and-notched tabletop. A lifetime ago, he and his father built that table with their very own hands. They used lumber from a dilapidated barn a local family dismantled on their property. That slab of reclaimed wood made a beautiful table.

And Shane knows. On the lobster boat, no gripes are *brought* to the table. Below deck, the table's almost a sacred place, sacred *time*, as the boys just eat there and bullshit some.

But the boat rule is: *No gripes*.

Oh, but Shane's *got* a gripe tonight. Got one *hell* of a gripe eating him up.

Beyond the kitchen, the rest of his house is in shadow. There's only a lamp shining in the front window.

"Is it Celia?" Jason presses him then. "Did something happen with Celia?"

"Don't bother Celia."

"But maybe she—"

"Just leave her be, you hear me?"

"Okay, I hear you. So what is it, then? Lay it on me, because I can't read your God damn mind, Shane."

"*Ach*, listen." Shane still paces. Drags a hand through his hair. Nearly trips on that toppled chair again. "I really shouldn't have called."

"But you *did* call. So you owe me some answers."

"Yeah. I'm trying to figure them for myself."

"Well, let me help."

"Help? Shit. You have your own busy life to live," Shane says, turning toward the kitchen counter. His key ring is there, the keys glistening on the gray-and-black quartz countertop. "Sorry, Jason, for bothering you. I'm sorry, really."

And before the words are completely out of his mouth, Shane disconnects. Just clicks off the call. He holds the phone for a long second, though. Finally, in one fell swoop, he tosses that phone on the counter and scoops up his keys. Locks up the house, too. Back door closed. Windows shut. There's no more talking to be had, no more thinking. Keys in hand, he just walks directly to his front door, goes outside and gets in his pickup truck in the driveway.

Nine, maybe ten seconds pass when he takes in the sight of his shingled, harborside house. Only one light is on—that lamp in the front window. The rest—the kitchen lights, the outdoor front light—he'd snapped off on his way out. The sun's set, and damp sea air makes its way into his pickup as he backs out of the driveway then. His truck's tires crunch over the gravel. His headlights sweep the narrow road ahead as he drives off.

⁓

"Son of a bitch." Jason gives his cell phone a shake.

"What happened?" Maris asks from where she's sitting at the table in the kitchen nook.

"The call disconnected."

"What do you mean … *disconnected*?"

Jason shakes his head with a small laugh. "I think Shane just hung up. Gave me some vague apology and—that's it. Hung up."

"Was someone there with him?"

"Don't know."

"Well, try him again. Hurry up."

Jason crosses the kitchen and sits with her at the table. After cuffing back his denim shirtsleeves, he makes the call to Shane. "Nothing," he says with the phone to his ear. "It just goes to voicemail. He's not answering."

"Hang up and try *again*," Maris quickly insists, leaning close. "He'll pick up."

Jason right away does, but there's no answer. "Shane. Come *on*," he says in a voicemail instead. "We … Maris and I … we just want to be sure everything's okay. Call me back, guy."

Maris reaches for his phone and tries it for herself, giving up when the call goes to voicemail again. "Well, what did he say *before*? When he first called?"

"That he was pretty fucked up." Jason looks at her

sitting there in her knit shrug over a black V-neck tee and faded jeans. "Said he was going to lose it."

"*What?* Are you kidding?"

"No, I'm not."

"Oh my God."

Jason turns up his hands. "And *whatever* happened, he did say it's bad. Kept repeating that, actually."

"And for *him* to say that? Shane *Bradford*? Well. It must be really bad."

"Seems it." Jason drags a hand along his jaw. "But he never said what *exactly* was the matter. It's like he was in shock or something. He just rambled a lot. Said this stuff can't keep happening. That he couldn't change things. Can't change *anything* in his life. That nothing works." Jason pauses, looks toward the dark window, then back at Maris across from him. "He was *shot*. Not sure I've ever heard him like this."

"Was he drunk?"

"No. No, he wasn't. But he made mention of going out for a drink."

"Not good, Jason."

"No."

At the table, Maris takes Jason's hands in hers. A wide strand of hair escapes from her low ponytail. Her voice is soft in the kitchen as she squints at him for a long second. "Do you think he and Celia broke up or something? To be *that* upset?"

"Couldn't tell."

"So what should we do now? *Call* Celia? Or I can text her."

"No." Jason sits back in his chair. "Shane said—*insisted*, really—that we not. Said to leave her alone."

5

"Well, I don't know about that. This seems pretty serious." Maris checks her watch. "Look. It's seven already, and Celia will be busy with the baby, I'm sure." Maris stands and walks around the table. With her hand on Jason's shoulder, she bends and kisses his cheek. "But how about if we at least drive by her house? Just to be sure things look okay there."

Like clockwork, sea damp arrives in the evening.

Maris sees it, feels it, as Jason drives her golf cart along the gritty beach roads. She pulls her knit shrug close around her shoulders. Some of the cottages they pass are dark and empty—already buttoned up for the long winter season ahead. But lanterns glow on the porches of others. And there it is, that sea damp rising in a mist. It's almost magical, the way the mist blurs the lamplight shining in cottages still occupied.

She and Jason don't talk much as he steers the golf cart along the winding roads. There's just an occasional remark, a shake of the head as they try to figure out what happened to Shane. Every now and then, Jason tells her something he remembered from his phone call. But he's still at a loss. Did Shane get in a fight with someone? Is he in some kind of trouble? Get his heart broken?

As Maris listens, and looks at the tucked-away cottages, Jason veers the golf cart around a curve and heads toward Elsa's Ocean Star Inn. It rises stately against the night sky. Starlight shines above; solar garden lights glimmer on the inn's pristine grounds.

But the inn isn't their destination.

Celia's gingerbread house behind it is. Moonlight shines on her little shingled cottage sitting on a stone foundation. Wide white trim edges the windows. Windows that let in gentle sea breezes and quiet birdsong. There's an open front porch, too, and a diamond-shaped stained-glass window in a gabled peak.

And Maris thinks all looks at ease. Peaceful. Celia's car is there. Lights are on in the living room windows. In the nursery windows over on the side, lamplight also glows.

At the curb, Jason slows the golf cart to a stop. "Should we go in?"

"No, I don't think so," Maris says, still studying Celia's cottage. "Everything looks okay here. If there were a problem, I feel like the place would be more lit up or something. The outside porch light on, maybe." She looks past Jason to Celia's house. "*Something.*"

"You sure you don't want to just check in?"

"And say what?"

"I don't know." Looking at the cottage, Jason's quiet a moment. "Shit. What could we even say?"

Maris nods. "Celia's with the baby. I can see the light's on in the nursery. And I don't want to upset her, or frighten her, as she's putting Aria to bed. Hopefully, Shane will call her once he calms down." Maris leans low to better see the little shingled home. "*He's got to,*" she whispers.

So Jason slowly cruises the golf cart past Celia's cottage. Its cedar shingles have a golden hue beneath the misty moonlight. Beyond, the cottage's sloping side yard leads to the secret dune-grass path to the beach and Long Island Sound.

Maris looks over her shoulder as Jason drives on. Oh,

life, life. It's so deceptive. Because there's Celia in some sweet, oblivious fairy tale—content and happy in her gingerbread cottage by the sea. She's surely cooing to her baby. Getting her dressed in snuggly pajamas. Is winding up a tinkling music box. Windows are open to the sweet salt air. Maybe she'll sing Aria a soft lullaby.

And all the while, Celia's blissfully unaware that at this very moment? The love of her life is coming absolutely undone.

two

THE ROADSIDE BARBECUE JOINT IS practically empty this Monday night. Square tables covered with red-and-white checked vinyl tablecloths fill the dining space. The tables are small, seating only four. A handful of families eat and talk. One family pushed two tables together to fit everyone in. Near the door, a young couple leans close while waiting for their meal. Laminated menus are propped behind stuffed napkin dispensers on the tables. Framed vintage *Reward* posters of outlaws—Jesse James and Butch Cassidy and such—hang on the dark walls. The day's specials are chalked on a big blackboard mounted over the counter. Dinner platters are served on dull and dinged silver trays. Old venetian blinds hang on the wall of windows. The restaurant's showing its age.

Shane takes it all in as he sits alone at a window table. The slatted blinds beside him open to the dark parking lot outside. A streetlight drops misty light on the pavement there. The place is a few towns over from where he lives, but feels a world away. A world away from the day, from how it went down, from everything that happened. Shane glances out, then picks at his glazed spare ribs, side of mac and cheese and square of garlic bread.

"Something wrong with the food?"

"What?" Shane looks up at the heavy guy who stopped short as he was walking past. He's about forty and wears a chef apron over navy twill trousers and a tee. His hair is shorn close; a pencil rests behind an ear.

"Barely touched your plate," the guy says, nodding to Shane's half-eaten dinner.

"Oh, no." Shane sits back in the straight wood chair. "Food's fine," he says, then sips from his coffee cup.

The guy crosses his arms and squints at him. "Waiting for someone?"

"No. Just passing through."

"Gotcha. Well, name's Doug. I own this joint, wanted to be sure your meal was palatable."

"It is."

"So, where you from … ?"

The way his question dangles there, Shane knows. The dude's waiting for Shane to fill in the blank. To tell his name. Waiting to bullshit and kill some time on this slow night at the restaurant. Shane looks up at him. "Name's Vance," he says. Because hell, the *last* person he wants to be right now is Shane Bradford. Doesn't want Shane's life. Doesn't want his lot in it. Doesn't want this place. "From New Hampshire," he tells Doug.

"Oh. The Granite State."

"Funny you should say that," Shane goes on while lifting

a forkful of mac and cheese. "I work in a granite quarry there, actually," he lies. "Manage a small crew."

"No shit." Doug pulls out a chair from the table, clasps his hands and leans his arms over the chairback. "Tough line of work. Dangerous, too."

"Tell me about it. Cutting massive blocks right from the rock face in the pit?"

"Takes a lot of skill, I imagine."

"And strength. Our main quarry is over two hundred feet down in the earth. Actually spooks some guys."

"Yeah, I'll bet. So what brings you this way, to Maine?"

"Job fair," Shane lies again as he drags his garlic bread through dregs of barbecue sauce on his plate. "We're looking for workers. Laborers. Heavy-equipment operators. You know, wire saws. Cranes," he adds around a mouthful of the bread. "To extract stone for processing in our plant. Entry-level opportunities. But with company training, the guys can work their way up to foreman. Supervisor."

Work your way up.

Shit. Shane can't help but think of his own life, and what he worked *his* way up to. Graduated high school and did stints in juvie that landed him on a lobster boat. That's it. He never got off those boats since then.

No working his way up.

No climbing a ladder.

Never got off the Atlantic Ocean.

And here he is, denying all of it with a stinkin' lie. Denying all of his life.

"Well," Doug says, straightening that chair he leaned on and pushing it back to the table. "Not a bad gig, having a business trip here in Maine this time of year. September's a nice month to visit. Less crowds, some foliage."

"Yeah." Shane looks across the dimly lit dining area to the counter—where take-out containers and paper napkins are stacked high beside the register. Finally, he slides his empty mug across the table. "How about a refill on the coffee?"

"Sure thing, Vance. I'll get that for you."

Shane nods and turns to the window. Cuffs back his khaki shirtsleeves. Vance, Steve, Vic. Hell, any name'll do. Any line of work will do.

Just to have ten minutes to be someone else, he thinks. *To be out of my God damn life.*

three

"I WAS THINKING," JASON SAYS.

"About what?" Maris hands him a clean plate from the dishwasher later that evening.

Jason opens a pale gray Shaker cabinet and sets the dish on a stack there. "That maybe I should go check on Shane."

"What?"

"Go to Maine," Jason explains while taking more cleaned dishes from Maris and setting them in the cabinet.

"You mean … *tonight*?" she asks, handing him the dishwasher's silverware caddy now.

"Yeah. We went by Celia's, and everything looks okay as far as we can tell. But we still have no answers. And I've got a bad feeling about what I heard on that call from Shane."

Then? Only quiet in the kitchen. The crystal pendant chandeliers glimmer over the denim-blue island. The dog dozes in front of the slider screen. And the talking stops.

There's just the clinking sound of forks and knives and spoons that Jason sets in the silverware drawer. Maris stands in the shadows nearby. She's bent over the dishwasher and lifting out clean coffee cups.

"It's too much," she eventually says while putting the cups on a shelf in another cabinet.

Jason only looks at her. When she glances at him over her shoulder, he's finishing up with the silverware. But says nothing.

So she keeps talking. "First? It's too far away."

"I could make good time, driving at night."

"But what about work tomorrow? You can't bail on the TV crew like that. What would you tell Trent?"

"I don't know yet."

Maris puts the last of the coffee mugs away and waits at the dishwasher for Jason to return the silverware caddy. "It's not like there's a family emergency that Trent would be obligated to honor," she tells him.

"But it *could* be an emergency," Jason says, fitting the caddy onto the bottom rack.

Maris closes the dishwasher and dries off the countertop with a paper towel. "Well, there are way too many unanswered questions for you to make the trip—just to find out."

"Unanswered questions? Like what?"

"Like would you have to pack? And ... and how long would you stay there? And what if Shane doesn't even *want* you at his house?"

Jason crosses his arms and leans against the counter near where she wipes. "Answers. One, yes, I have to pack a duffel. Two? I stay for a day. One overnight. And three."

When Maris looks over at him, he just shrugs. "Doesn't matter what Shane wants. I'll already be there."

So Maris pulls out a stool and sits at the island now. "Do you think it's something with his brother? That something happened between them?"

"With Kyle? No way. If it were, Kyle would be live-texting me. Or sitting in this kitchen right now. No." Jason glances outside through the slider. "It's not Kyle."

When Maris gets up to freshen Maddy's water bowl, Jason closes the kitchen windows. Outside, night has settled. It's dark; the air's cooled down some. So he draws the blinds and heads to the living room. "Well, I'm going to put on the TV, then. Catch the weather for tomorrow's filming," he calls back on the way there.

And says no more.

⁓

"*Ooh*," Maris whispers under her breath in the kitchen. She stamps a foot, too. "I know *just* what you're doing."

And it's enough. Enough to get her standing and marching to the living room. She stops in the doorway and squints at Jason through the shadows. He's sitting on the sofa, but leaning forward, elbows on his knees. He's also watching some meteorologist click through a weather map of the East Coast.

"You are *not* watching that forecast for tomorrow's *Castaway Cottage* filming, Jason Barlow."

"What?"

"Don't give me that. You're watching the weather to see if you'll have clear sailing three hundred miles north. To drive to Maine … *tonight*."

Jason just flops back on the couch and tosses his hands in his lap. In other words, she's right.

"Jason," Maris persists from the doorway—where she crosses *her* arms now. "Are you *kidding* me?"

"I'm not, Maris."

"But you're *exhausted*. You just came home last week—after three weeks away at Ted Sullivan's. Three weeks of our marriage *separation*, Jason, which was very stressful. Then Friday night was the whole deer thing when I almost got in a really bad accident. And Saturday you were up so late with everyone being here to check on me. Then you worked *all* day today. You have a busy schedule. A busy week. Not to mention, you *can't* leave the CT-TV crew in the lurch."

"I wouldn't."

"Of *course* you would. And Trent will *fire* you, he'll be so pissed."

"No. I'll explain things to him."

Maris walks into the living room. She sits beside Jason on the couch. Touches the back of her fingers to his scruffy jaw. "*Jason, come on,*" she whispers. "What are you going to say to Trent? There's not a death in the family. So I don't think he'll really let you off easy."

"There's *not* a death in the family, true. But I don't know *what* kind of talk that was from Shane earlier. I don't know if he's going off on a bender. If he'll land himself in jail. Harm himself, even. And we're just going to sit around here and wait to see?"

"Not sit around, Jason. Like Shane said, we have busy lives. And you just *can't* fit this in to yours. Your hands are tied."

"But it *felt* like he was calling for help."

Maris quickly shakes her head. "Listen. Shane's *not* at that rented bungalow here. He's five. *Hours.* Away."

"I know. Three hundred miles." Jason turns to her on the couch. Touches her half-undone low ponytail. "And that's what Shane drove Saturday—three *hundred* miles—to be sure *we* were okay."

Maris does it. She takes a long breath that says it. That says, *Fine. You win.*

And Jason knows it—she can tell—because he gives a slow nod.

"All right. Go." Maris leans close and points a rigid finger at him. "But at the *very* least, you have to sleep a few hours *first. And* make all your business calls *before* sleeping. Because you have a serious responsibility to Trent and the crew."

⁓

She's right.

Jason knows she is. And she loves him—he knows that, too—or else she wouldn't give a damn.

So he makes it quick. For her. He gets back to the kitchen—where his phone is charging. Grabs up the phone and goes outside on the deck. Waves splash down on the bluff. The night's sea air is damp on his skin.

And the clock is ticking.

So sitting at the patio table, he flicks on the lights strung around the umbrella spokes and gets to it.

Texts his clients Austin and Nina. Tells them he'll have the final blueprint for the new porch on their shotgun cottage by week's end.

Leaves detailed voicemails for two of his contractors: Tanner at Beach Box, first. He asks if the beadboard's up yet on the newly vaulted kitchen ceiling. Cody, second—at the White Sands shotgun. He checks with Cody on the status of the navy vinyl siding order. Mentions they might have to adjust to accommodate a new front-porch add-on.

Texts Mitch Fenwick he'll be out of town for a couple of days, and will see him midweek for filming.

Then, Trent. Trent, Jason actually calls.

And Maris was right. His producer doesn't like the sound of his disappearing act, not one whit. He lets Jason know it, too.

"Time is money," Trent shoots back at him. "And money is budget. And I can't be blowing that budget with idle time, Barlow. You want the plug pulled on your show?"

But ... they work it out. They go back and forth until minutes later, Jason finds Maris still in the living room. She's watching the news, but shuts off the TV and turns to Jason in the doorway.

"Trent told me that if I'm bailing—"

"Oh, Jason. *Bailing?*"

"Hang on. He said that if I'm bailing on *Castaway Cottage* for a *day* or two, I better damn well do something to make it worth the station's while. He wants me to grab footage of something—*anything*—they can use on the show. Some mini segment. This way, I'll be in Maine kind of on CT-TV's time clock."

"That's a lot of pressure for you. On top of everything else, you'll have to find something to film?"

"Yep. Worry about that when I'm there." Jason leans back from the doorway and glances down the dark, paneled hallway behind him. "Where's that gear CT-TV gave me when I signed on last year? The tripod and lighting to have on hand."

"I think it's in the coat closet. In the back," Maris says.

"Give me a hand packing it up?"

"Okay." She stands and walks to him. "But then? Sleep, mister."

"No, sweetheart. No time." Jason cradles her face and lightly kisses her. "I'll be all right and want to hit the road."

Maris pulls quickly back.

Quickly enough that he knows. *This* battle is hers to win. It's in her fierce brown eyes. In the determined set of her beautiful jaw. She will not lose.

"Jason Barlow?" Maris goes on, taking his whiskered chin firmly in her hand. "You are *not* running up to Maine on fumes, you hear me? You're grabbing three to four hours of sleep—which will put you on the road at midnight. So you'll be in Maine by sunrise. Take it or leave it."

Take it, no question. He'll sacrifice the win for the greater gain—making sure their old beach friend is okay.

four

WHAT SHOULD BE BEAUTIFUL, ISN'T.

Not tonight.

What should be peaceful is troubling.

What should be comforting is enraging.

What should give Shane answers instead deeply challenges him.

It's all wrong. Everything's wrong. His faith isn't doing anything it should be.

It's silent here at this open-air chapel nestled on a hilltop in the woods. But thoughts swirl in Shane's mind, questions begging to be spoken. To be *answered*, damn it.

Driving the coastal road back home from the restaurant, he veered onto the turnoff here—to the outdoor chapel he's visited from time to time. Two weeks ago with Celia and the baby, even. Tonight, he drove a ways into the wooded area, parked and carefully walked through the garden and around moss-covered granite ledges. Dew, thick salt-air dew, covered everything. His boots slipped over it. Finally, he climbed stone stairs to this rustic wood-framed chapel sitting atop an ancient stone foundation.

Maybe he knew all along—even when he drove to that barbecue joint—that *this* was his ultimate destination.

That there was actually nowhere else to turn.

The chapel's empty at this late hour, so he sits alone on one of the few sparse wooden benches. A stone floor is hard beneath his booted feet. Wide, peaked cutouts in the wooden side walls look out onto the night. Onto trees and gardens and stone walls and stone staircases surrounding the chapel.

But it's the altar Shane faces. At least he *considers* it an altar. The entire front wall of this simple wood-framed chapel is a soaring open-air arch. A tall, narrow cross is mounted on a high beam there, fitting into the curve of the solemn arch.

And that one open, arched wall gives a wide view of the distant sea. His altar tonight.

Sitting in the dark on the wooden bench, Shane lifts his head and looks at that coastal sight. A waning full moon hangs low in the sky. The only lightness in the night, that heavy moon drops a swath of gold on the black water.

"Why didn't You listen to me?" he asks the sky above.

Shane pauses then, as if there will be an answer.

But what happens instead is that he remembers being on the lobster boat only this morning. Remembers the vessel motoring through the harbor as the captain made for open water. The engine chugged; the boat left a frothy white wake in the harbor behind it. And all was *good*. Shane, as always, gave one last look toward his diminishing harborside home. The bell buoy clanged; the air was clear. And he knew. He hadn't felt *that* good heading out to sea in a long, long time. But he felt good only because of everything that recently came into his life. Celia. His long-estranged brother, Kyle. Old friends at Stony Point.

Yes, his life was filled to sweet capacity, and so Shane did it. Standing on the lobster boat, he tipped up his newsboy cap and thanked the Lord. Problem is, it's those very words haunting him now. *Thanks anyway*, he'd murmured on the boat's stern. *But give any more good to someone else—someone who needs it.*

Come to find out? No one was listening.

"I *told* You," Shane utters now in the dark night. "I *just* told You this morning to give *any* more good to someone else. To give *my* good away, damn it," he says, his voice rising as he stands and paces the empty chapel. "And You just wouldn't do it, would You?" He stops and leans his hands on one of the open-air window ledges. His head drops for a long second before he throws up his arms in anger. Throws them to the black sky.

Which is when Shane realizes something. His face is wet. His eyes sting with tears running down his cheeks, dripping from his jaw. Burning tears that he fought all blessed day. That effort exhausted him until he can't fight those tears anymore.

So he lets his words rip with the tears. "You're all bullshit, You know that?" he manages around some pained sob. "Everything about You. Would it have killed You to just *listen* to me? To do me *one* God damn favor in this lousy life? To give *my* good away—to someone who *desperately* needed it today? *Desperately*." Swiping at his wet face, Shane walks to the open-air altar facing the glory of the sea.

And just breathes. His chest heaves. His shoulders shake.

"No. You wouldn't do it. Instead You tuned me right out and wreaked awful hell on earth. *Hell.*" When he looks up at the sky, the moonlight, the stars, it's all a blur behind his tears. "You happy now, God?" There's a silence, a long silence. "Answer me!" Shane finally yells into the night.

After he does, there's only that vast silence. He shakes his head; looks around in a panic; in the dark, walks back to the pew-like straight benches. At the first one, he doesn't sit. Instead, he sinks to his knees on the stone floor, leans his arms on the bench and drops his head, his shaking shoulders.

Oh, his mind … it hurts from the searching it does right now. But he comes upon it, the psalm he hasn't recited in many long years. Kneeling alone in faint moonlight at this open-air chapel, Shane falls into deep prayer as he whispers, over and over and over again, the lines. His words are halting. And interrupted with restraint—utter restraint. But the words manage to pass over his lips and into the night.

"*Save me, O God; for the waters are come in unto my soul.*" He's drowning in those waters, actually. Shane knows it. Drowning in grief. In rage. In disbelief. But he manages a shuddering breath and goes on. "*I sink in deep mire, where there is no standing: I am come into deep waters, where the floods overflow me.*"

five

JASON'S BREATHING GIVES IT AWAY.

When Maris stops in their bedroom doorway and looks in on him an hour later, he's lying on his side in bed. An arm is crooked beneath his pillow. And his breathing comes steady. He's asleep.

Her relief is huge. *Some* sleep, even for a few hours, is far better than none.

So she tiptoes into the bedroom and grabs Jason's extra pair of forearm crutches from the closet. Gets her pajamas—plum floral-print tank top with matching drawstring pants—from her dresser, too. So as not to wake Jason, she changes in the bathroom before bringing his crutches downstairs.

In the kitchen, Maris gets methodical. If Jason's going to do this, she's going to help him do it right. So she lines the island with a small cooler, Jason's lunch sack, bottles of water, snacks, rinsed fruit. Next up? Food prep. Her hands keep moving, putting together cold-cut sandwiches topped with mayo, cheese and slabs of Elsa's fresh tomatoes—all on crusty, whole-grain bread. Everything gets wrapped, labeled and chilled in the fridge.

Coffee next. She sets the coffeepot timer to begin brewing in a couple of hours. Puts Jason's big thermos beside it, too. Anything to help keep his road trip running smoothly.

And oh, the dog's onto her. Maddy picks right up on any anxiety, or worry, in the house. She circles Maris; nudges her hand; whines some. So Maris calms the German shepherd, petting her head, giving her a biscuit, talking softly.

With everything prepped, wrapped and ready to roll then, there's only one thing left. Maris puts Jason's forearm crutches right at the slider to the deck. The last thing he needs to do is hit the road without those in the vehicle. Whatever lies ahead won't be easy as it is. And there will come a time when he'll *have* to remove his prosthesis. Without those crutches, well, that'd be a nightmare for him. She folds his black zip sweatshirt and leaves it on the counter there, too.

His house is barely distinguishable from the night.

The one lamp he'd left on in the front window doesn't much help. Once Shane's home from the chapel, he walks through the dark rooms. The only sound is of his booted feet on the wood floors. Problem is, the rooms are as dark as the night pressing against the windows. As dark as the streets he'd just driven. As dark as the harbor waters off in the distance. As dark as his sadness.

Usually, Shane welcomes darkness. Sleeps well in it.

Tonight, the darkness will only keep him awake. Because he doesn't want what comes with darkness. Doesn't want the silence of it. The solitary feel of it. The aloneness. Today, it's just too much to take.

Lightness helps him deny the day. Deny what happened.

So Shane starts in the kitchen. There, he flicks on every light. The ceiling light, sink light, under-cabinet lights. And they help, the lights. The black-and-gray quartz countertop glimmers beneath them. The lights illuminate the dishes stacked on an open shelf near the sink. Shine light on more dishes leaning in the dish rack. Show the pieces of mail tucked against the napkin holder on the rustic wooden table. He opens the door to the deck outside. The clear bulb lights strung around the deck? *On.* And right away, he sees memories. Sees visions of him and Celia sitting out there ... talking. Celia writing music. Sees visions of easy suppers with his buddy, Shiloh. Of making plans with him to shop for lobster gear.

Shane keeps going. Back in the kitchen, he opens a door there to the side yard. Standing at the screen door, he looks out onto the black night and watches it happen. Watches light pour forth like a wave when he flicks on the wall lantern mounted outside, beside the screen door.

So he leaves the wood door open, letting that light and fresh salt air flood his home through even the screen.

And the flicking continues—into the living room, flick. Recessed lights, flick. Second table lamp, flick. Mantel lamp, flick. Everything. He sees now. Sees split wood stacked on narrow floor-to-ceiling shelves beside the brick fireplace. Sees his and Kyle's red toy sailboat leaning against a framed seascape painting on the mantel. A knitted throw tossed across an ottoman.

It's almost fluid, the way the house is lighting up. The way illumination is moving like a rolling wave from one room to the next. Hallway, flick. Aria's bedroom: ceiling light, dresser lamp—flick, flick. Even her nightlight gets the treatment.

Bathroom? Ceiling light, flick. Shower light, flick.

His own bedroom slows him some. But he continues. Ceiling light, flick. Dresser lamp, flick. He walks to one of the windows, where knotted jute rope holds back the long curtains. Standing there and looking out, he bends and throws open the window. The night outside is unusually quiet—as though it's mourning, too. No noises come from the distant harbor. No late lobster boat chugs into port. No bell buoy clangs. The foghorn is silent.

And it's almost more than Shane can take.

So he goes back to the living room, climbs the stairs to the loft and turns on the light there, too. Every single room of his shingled house is lit up now. Every paned window glows. Windows have been thrown open to the cool, damp air outside. It's about all he can do to give a sense of *life* to his still and hushed home.

A sense of living, breathing life.

Oh, there's one more thing. In the living room, Shane picks up the remote and turns on the TV. Some all-night news channel is on, and the voices—the ongoing, talking voices—suit him. So he sets the volume to low, grabs the knit throw off the ottoman, sinks onto the couch and takes off his boots. Stretching out there, he pulls that throw over himself, closes his eyes—and is done.

Every so often, Jason thinks, *time stops.*

Like now, in the middle of the night. As fast as things are happening—Maris nudging him and waking him up; taking a quick shower; having a coffee in the kitchen; putting on his prosthesis in the living room—the long, dark hours still stretch out before him.

"You going back to bed now?" Jason asks as he rolls the silicone liner up onto his leg stump, then adds a sock to it.

"I never went to bed."

He looks at Maris sitting on the sofa. She's in her pajamas, and he'd just assumed she'd been asleep. "Seriously?" he asks, then fusses with the liner and sock as he smoothes them up onto his thigh.

"Yes, seriously. I got everything ready for you, babe. Food, snacks. Water."

Jason nods, then presses his prosthetic limb onto his stump, too.

"You better call me along the way," Maris goes on.

"I will." Jason leans over and zips the long custom zipper in the inside seam of his jeans, right over his prosthetic leg, before standing.

They don't say much, then. Maris helps bring his crutches and bags to his SUV. Gives him a hug and kiss in the driveway.

"*Drive safe*," she whispers into the kiss.

"*Love you*," he whispers back. "And thanks. For everything." He lightly tosses up his hands. "Coming around to this. Packing."

"I know." When he gets into the driver's seat and closes the door, Maris leans in through the open window. "You call me, and take some breaks. It's a long ride," she says, touching a curl of his shower-damp hair.

He gets settled in as she goes up the deck stairs. Seatbelt on. Mirrors adjusted. Right away, Jason notices what she's done, too. Sandwiches are set up at the ready on the passenger seat. Bottled water is in the console. Snacks are on the passenger seat, too. Everything in easy reach as he drives.

When he looks up to the deck, Maris blows him a kiss right before he backs down the long, twig-strewn driveway. The SUV's headlights cut through the middle-of-night darkness. All the cottages are only shadows. Lampposts have been shut off. Porches are dark. Night has truly fallen.

And that clock *still* seems stopped as Jason approaches the stone train trestle.

Because even after all he just did, there are five long hours of darkness to drive through.

To God knows what awaits him.

⁓

Time is warped the whole way to Maine.

As the tires roll down the highway. As divided lines blur past. As forests hulk in shadow against the night sky. As one state morphs into another. As one exit sign nears and passes, then another. And another.

Two hours in, Jason stops at a scenic-view rest area just to get out and stretch his legs. To walk for a few minutes. From the lookout railing there, he calls Maris.

"Did you try reaching Shane again?" her sleepy voice asks.

"No. I'm not going to. I'm just showing up there."

More highway driving then. The air changes. The

temperature drops some, so there's a chill in it. The air's clearer, too, to breathe.

Another rest stop to top off his gas tank. To take a quick walk and work his leg muscles. A quick restroom pit stop. A quick coffee from his thermos as he sits in the driver's seat before the final few exits bring him to Rockport, Maine.

six

HE EXPECTED IT TO BE dark.

Jason slowly turns his SUV into Shane's gravel driveway. The tires crunch over the stones. But the surprise is that at this early hour, right before sunrise? Every single window of Shane's dockside home is lit up. Every one. Upstairs. Downstairs. Lights glow inside and out. At first, Jason thinks there must be people here. Visitors. Friends who spent the night, maybe. Because the house looks filled to capacity with all those lights shining.

But Shane's pickup is the only vehicle in the driveway.

And there's no noise coming from the house. No sounds. No talking voices carrying through the open windows.

Nothing.

After turning off his SUV, Jason sits back. Can't help it, actually. Because, hell, his preconceived notion of Shane living in some shabby seaside shanty is now debunked. He turns his architectural eye on the illuminated house, the details.

The weathered silver shingles.

The window and door trim painted the same blue as the Atlantic waters.

The tended geraniums spilling from window boxes.

The substantial granite step at the blue front door.

The peaked roof.

The visual lines of the shingled cottage tuck it naturally into its coastal environment. The harbor is off in the distance beyond it. In the pale light of early dawn, Jason can make out lobster traps stacked on the docks there. Against the blue-gray sky, there's also a tree somewhere behind Shane's house. The tree's spread of dark green leafy branches partially frames the roofline.

Getting out of his vehicle now, Jason steps back to better see the house. He leans this way. Steps that way. A few straggly shrubs hug the front of Shane's home. But the front entrance is closed. He spots a side door, though, on a wing off the back of the house. Could be a kitchen door. On a shingle beside it, an old seashell wind chime dangles from a nail. There's a copper caged lantern mounted on the shingles there, too. The lantern illuminates a screen door with a painted frame. When Jason sees that an interior door is *open* behind that screen, he heads in that direction.

Shane's heard voices all night.

Lying on the sofa in his work clothes, his sleep was fitful. He tossed and turned. The knit throw tangled up around him.

His eyes opened to yesterday's memories—to panic. Urgency. He sweat. But every time he woke up, other voices were talking, too. The newscasters on the TV droned on and on, keeping some humanity in his awareness.

Except those voices weren't like the one calling out now.

"Open the God damn door, Shane! You've got a visitor."

There's a harsh sound then, too. The screen door in the kitchen is being repeatedly rattled against its lock.

It takes a few seconds for Shane to come to. To fully wake up. To realize just who's agitated at his door and calling inside through that screen. When he recognizes the voice, he throws off the knitted throw, gets up and heads to the kitchen.

"Jesus Christ, Jason," he says while crossing the kitchen floor in his stocking feet.

"Jesus yourself. Open the fucking *door.*"

Jason stands just outside that door. He's got on some black sweatshirt over jeans, and steps closer to the screen. Squinting into the kitchen, he gives the wood-framed door another good yank against the lock, too.

Doesn't waste any time, either, lacing into him once Shane unlatches the door.

"I've been on a wild-goose chase for *hours* because *you* decided to hang up the phone last night," Jason informs him before he's even fully inside.

Shane veers to the sink, pours a glass of water and downs half of it before turning to Jason—who's still at him. Still telling him how he packed a bag and hit the highway to be sure Shane wasn't in some sort of trouble.

Shane only motions to the table. "Have a seat," he says.

Jason crosses the kitchen—looking back when his feet

crunch pieces of that shattered coffee mug on the floor. "What the hell's going on with you?" he asks while pulling out a chair. "Straight up this time."

"Straight up."

"Yeah. None of that mumbo-jumbo bullshit you gave me earlier."

Shane shifts. Folds his arms in front of him. Waits a second, then spills it. Carefully says the words. "I lost my best friend yesterday, Jason. And I'm beside myself. Don't know what to do."

"What?"

"You heard me. I lost my best friend on the boat. Best friend here in Maine. He died suddenly. He's just gone."

"Oh, shit, man." Jason drags a hand through his unkempt hair, then pushes up out of his chair. He walks over and gives Shane a hug, clapping him on the back while telling him, "I didn't know."

"Yeah." Shane turns up his hands. "I called you, last night. Figured you'd be the only one to really understand. But I just couldn't get the words … couldn't go there. It was too fresh. Couldn't even think anymore. Hell, it's been a tough twenty-four hours. Really tough."

Jason looks around the kitchen. And Shane sees what he sees. Sees the evidence of a day gone completely wrong. Every light burning bright to stave off the darkness. Chair toppled on the floor. Mug smashed to smithereens. And when Jason looks at him, Shane *feels* the utter wreck Jason must see.

Jason doesn't mention it, though. "Help me bring in my things, would you?" he only asks while turning to the side door. "Then we'll talk."

"All right." Shane throws on his unlaced work boots and follows him through the squeaking screen door. The outside light is still on. The sky's some shade of dark silver as sunrise nears. They go down two wooden steps to the gravel driveway—where Jason's SUV is parked behind his truck. "You drove all this fuckin' way?" Shane asks him.

"Yep," Jason tosses over his shoulder, right before lifting a duffel off the SUV's front passenger seat. "You bet I did."

seven

M AYBE SHANE WAS AFRAID.

That's all Jason can figure once his bags are inside and he heads out to the deck. It's a massive one, too, with a custom built-in bench facing the distant harbor. Clear bulb lights are strung around the deck—each one of those lights also shining bright—just like in the rest of the house.

So maybe it's true. Maybe Shane was afraid of the dark. With every bulb on the entire property illuminated, what else can Jason think? Not that Shane's actually afraid of the *dark*, but afraid of the thoughts darkness will elicit. Because if you know better—which apparently Shane does— darkness isn't always a comfort. Sometimes it's a ruse. Hell, the dark has you *believing* it'll hide everything—even your pain. Lures you with that assurance. Makes you *think* you'll feel better in it. Doze off in it. Escape. Leave your troubles behind. The soft quiet of it draws you in, gets you to lie down. Close your eyes.

As if darkness *is* the place to ease your conflicted mind.

And once you're in that snare of darkness, the demons come out.

Jason knows. He's been there. He's landed in that darkness where the soft quiet becomes the playground for every anxiety, every regretful memory, every fear. They spin and chant and get you lurching from a restless sleep covered in sweat. Get you to a sink and splashing water on your face. Get you to a window, or door, gasping a breath.

Yeah. Jason's turned on the lights in his time, too.

Sitting at the deck table now, he looks over to the door when Shane comes out carrying two bottles of beer. The breakfast of surrender. The white flag of giving in to hell.

"All your lights were on when I got here," Jason says when Shane gives him a bottle opener and sets down the beer. "In the whole house. Every room." Jason lifts the bottle opener and pries off the beer caps. "Have company last night?"

"No."

"Looked it."

"No company. Just couldn't be in the darkness." Shane sits and takes a swig of the beer. "That's where my friend is now," he says.

"Tell me about him."

When Shane just nods, Jason takes a long swallow of the brew, too. Eyes Shane across the table. He's obviously shot. Unshaven. Shadows on his face. Day-old shirt and jeans hanging on him.

"Name's Shiloh," Shane begins. "Twenty-six years old. Worked with me the past five years, ever since he started lobstering. Really, I couldn't ask for a better crewmate—a better friend—here in Maine." Shane taps one of the bottle caps on the table. "Shit, man. Still can't believe he's dead."

"So what happened?"

Shane takes another swig of his beer. Toys with that bottle cap.

And once he begins talking, Jason hears the depth of yesterday. Hears how far it reached into Shane's life. Jason hears the hoarse fatigue in his voice. The grief. The raspy result of some weeping that happened while the clock ticked away those long, dark hours. Hears it when Shane tells him that the wrongness of the whole death is that it happened *so* randomly. During such monotonous routine.

Sitting there on the deck, Shane's low, even voice winds through the damp morning air like a wisp of fog. It just unrolls. Unfurls until it overtakes everything.

"Boat was about twelve, maybe fifteen miles offshore yesterday. Captain's regular territory. He was in the wheelhouse. Three-man crew was working the deck. Been hard at it since we started dropping pots at sunrise," Shane tells Jason as today's sun rises over the harbor beyond them. "Only difference in our routine was that usually we're lifting *out* a string to start the day. Legal starting time to do *that* is four a.m. Typically we'll haul up the pots, empty out the lobsters, measure them for keepers, rebait the traps, give them a once-over for any damage and then set them right back out. But yesterday? Yesterday was our first day on the water after the busted fuel pump fiasco. So because of those two weeks off, captain had no pots in the water. Nothing to haul."

Shane stands then. He walks to the deck railing facing the harbor. The sound of a chugging diesel engine reaches them—a lobster boat heading out. He stands silently there, as though listening. As though picturing just twenty-four short hours ago. Eventually he turns, leans on the railing behind him and picks up his story. His voice comes monotone as he relays simple details.

"On the boat, we were doing different tasks on deck. Shiloh was on the stern. Was chipping crusty barnacles off some of the traps. He's meticulous like that. I was at the rail with Hunter—the other crewmate. He and I were setting up the next string of traps, you know? Baiting them, lining them up till captain gives the signal." Shane shakes his head with a regretful laugh. "Weather was good. We'd been at it for hours and almost ready for lunch break. I turned around at one point and didn't see Shiloh. A moment later, I looked again—and saw him flat out on deck. Hell, we dropped everything—me and Hunter—and got right over to him. I didn't know how long Shiloh'd been down, but already he was in and out of it."

"You didn't hear him fall? Trip?" Jason asks. "Something?"

Shane looks at him. Seconds pass. Jason sees his weary eyes. Not much sleep happened the night before. And the clothes—that wrinkled long-sleeve khaki shirt loose over a ratty tee and tired jeans? They're so obviously clothes never changed out of since that one moment. Since he turned around and saw Shiloh had fallen.

"No. Heard nothing," Shane answers. "I was talking with Hunter. And captain was motoring along, so the engine drowned out any sound of Shiloh's fall. Well. We got down on our knees beside him once we saw him there. *Open your eyes, Shiloh*, I told him, nudging his shoulder. *Open your eyes*. Captain came out, but it wasn't good. We could tell right away. Shiloh's coloring was off. His eyes, unfocused. Captain called the Coast Guard, quick. But me and Hunter, hell, we didn't leave Shi. Didn't leave his side. At any response from him, we'd encourage him to stay with us. He was pretty motionless there on the hard deck, so I folded up my sweatshirt like a pillow and put it under his head."

Shane quiets and sits at the table again. He fidgets with that beer bottle cap. And Jason knows. He's in yesterday's tragedy all over again.

"*Open your eyes. Open your eyes, buddy*, I kept saying. *Stay with us, man.*" Shane pauses, shakes his head. "Coast Guard response boat was there in no time. Checked him out on deck, then transported him ashore to a waiting ambulance. Time was critical. So I went with Shiloh, you know? On the Coast Guard vessel. Answered any questions for them, best I could. Once back at the docks, I followed in my truck to the hospital. Guess they worked on Shiloh more in the ambulance. He'd come to, I was told, then just went out." Shane pauses to sip his beer. "Fast, fast, too damn fast," he says, his voice so low it's almost indecipherable. "Shit, like a bolt of lightning came out of the sky with no notice—that's how fast time passed by. One second I was on my knees on the boat, next I was in the waiting room at the hospital. Tammy and Keith—Shiloh's parents—arrived, too. Captain had contacted them directly from the wheelhouse, then he brought the boat back to harbor and came to the hospital himself. With Hunter. But an hour, or two—Jesus, everything happened in a flash—we knew. Captain and I. All of us. A doctor had brought Shiloh's parents to his room. A while later, Keith invited me to go in and see Shiloh. To say goodbye."

"Oh, man."

Shane nods. His voice is calculated and tight now, no doubt working its way around a hard knot in his throat. "Then he was gone. Just like that."

"Well what the hell happened?" Jason asks. "What brought it on?"

Shane turns up his hands. "Never going to know for sure, I suppose. But I'll tell you this. The ocean can mess with your whole body. Knock your balance for a loop sometimes, mess with the inner ear and get you weaving. Seriously. And we'd been off the water for two *weeks*—what with delays to the boat repair, wrong part coming in. So was Shiloh's equilibrium off after all that downtime? Because, hell, he took a hard fall, apparently. Went down and suffered a blow to his head that knocked him right out. Traps were stacked five-high when we set out that morning, and plenty were still left on deck. Did he hit one just so? He was practically unconscious when I found him there, so whatever happened was quick. *Quick*. But, you know. Which came first? Did he fall *first*? Or did he pass out from something else first, and *that* caused the fall? Doctor said it could have even been something he ate. His sugar levels. Or he could've been dehydrated. Or that equilibrium thing, you know, being off-kilter out on the waters again."

"I'm sure Shiloh's family will work with the doctors to get answers."

"No God damn answer's going to bring him back."

"No."

"Well," Shane says, rubbing a thumb over that ridged bottle cap. "All *I* know for sure is this. Had dinner with Shiloh Sunday night. Right *here*, where we're sitting. Ate those gourmet tomato sandwiches Elsa sent me home with.

Saw Shi again yesterday morning before dawn. Had coffee on the docks. And by three o'clock?" Shane snaps his fingers. "He was gone."

"Shit."

"Yeah. He was alive, drinking coffee, smelling that sweet salt air. Doing what he loved all morning—setting out pots. Bullshitting. Working hard as the captain steered us out to sea. Waves lapping at the hull. Morning sunlight breaking through the sea mist. And by midafternoon, his life was over."

"I'm really sorry, Shane," Jason tells him. "Look. It's no consolation, but I know everything you're feeling. Losing someone so sudden like that ... it's tough, man."

"Shiloh was like my kid brother."

Jason only nods, then finishes what's left in his beer bottle.

"I looked after him," Shane explains. "And he looked up to me. I got him through his greenhorn days—which is no easy feat. And his parents? They were *so* proud of him; he was such a hard worker. Real good person, too. Avoided the trouble. Sidestepped the riffraff. The temptations. The drink. Drugs. You name it. Shiloh was clean and kept his nose to the grindstone—a rarity. And today he's *gone*? I just don't get it. With a finger snap?"

"Was there *any* warning, Shane? Was he ... off at all?"

"Been wracking my brain on that one. Only thing I come up with is this. At his parents' barn brunch Saturday, when I asked him if he was ready to hit the high seas? Maybe he was a little leery. Said he had to get his sea legs back. But hell, he was more worried about *me* than himself."

"You?"

"Yep. Wanted to be sure I had my head on straight."

"What do you mean?"

"That, as he put it, I'd be *focused* aboard ship, and that Celia wasn't taking up valuable real estate in my mind."

"Huh. And what *about* Celia? She know all of this?"

"No. Nothing." Again, Shane toys with that bottle cap, turning it in his hand. "Listen," he goes on, turning that cap again and again. "I don't want Celia coming here. It's too much with the baby. And sneaking here behind Elsa's back—because Elsa would *know* she'd left for *somewhere*. So Celia doesn't know about Shiloh yet. Last thing I want is her hauling herself and Aria on a secret five-hour trek. It's not good—driving on the highway like that. Distracted. Upset. Things on your mind. No."

"Shane, come on—"

"I want to be alone anyway," Shane interrupts him.

"But Celia should at least *know*. You can't keep Shiloh's death from her."

"I won't. Just not telling her *yet*. Not putting this on her. Because, shit. She met Shiloh when she was up here. And he texted her this weekend. They got along. So she'll be devastated, too. For Shiloh *and* me. And to tell you the truth? I can't face that with everything else." Shane gets up then and crosses the deck. Behind him, the sun's rising over Rockport Harbor. Lobster boats are docked there. The empty masts of moored sailboats reach to a pale blue sky laced with pink. Calm. Calm as can be. A far cry from Shane's demeanor when he turns to Jason from the railing. "Actually, Barlow?" he says. "I don't even know how I'll get through the day myself."

"With a second beer to start. Hold on." Jason gets up,

goes in through the screen door and brings out two more bottles. Back on the deck, he opens them with that bottle opener and gives one to Shane. He's sitting on that custom bench now. One leg is drawn up on the seat; an arm is wrapped around the bent knee. He takes the beer as Jason goes on with his talk. "How do you get through the day? I'll tell you how," he says, leaning on the railing and facing that picturesque harbor. "You don't think that far ahead."

"You don't think of the day?"

"No, man. That's shooting yourself in the foot. Thinking of the whole day ahead is too big. Too much. You have to go hour by hour, you hear me?"

Shane nods and slightly raises his bottle to Jason.

"My father taught me that, and he oughta know," Jason tells him, swigging from his own beer. He still leans against that deck railing as he talks. "You know how many friends he lost in the jungles of 'Nam? Too many, right in front of his eyes." Jason drags over a chair from the patio table. He sets it near Shane, sits and leans his elbows on his knees. Now his voice is as low, as straight-line, as Shane's had been. "Listen. After the bike accident ten years ago, I was a *wreck*. My leg was gone. My brother gone. It all happened like you said, with a snap of the fingers. Out of the blue. Just gone. Believe me, I went down some dark roads in my mind back then. Wasn't easy to be with—sitting around in my wheelchair with a bandaged stump and a fucked-up head. Making it through most days was a challenge that I wasn't handling well."

Shane says nothing. He just drinks that beer and listens as the day takes hold. As the sky lightens.

"My father tried to help," Jason says. "Dad had this

pewter hourglass that my mother gave him when he came home from the war. An hourglass is all about time passing, and she said this one—filled with Stony Point sand—would signify every minute they'd finally be together at the beach, by the sea. So anyway, one day early on after the crash, I was sitting in the kitchen. In my wheelchair. And my prescription meds were lined up on the table. Left to my own devices, *some* of those meds I'd chase down with a shot of liquor. And my father knew it. Knew how I'd be spending the day. Wasted. Dad came in holding that hourglass and sat there at the table. Talked to me some. Told me he'd been on plenty hard roads, himself. In 'Nam. So he knew what I was facing every day. *And there's only one way to travel that hard road, son. Hour by hour*, he said then. His voice, I'll never forget it. It was just ragged. Exhausted with me. With losing Neil. With the way it seemed that God damn war followed him right into his home. *Hour by hour, Jason. You reach for this every hour, on the hour. This and this alone*, he said, nudging that hourglass closer to me. *Pick it up, flip it over and get through the next hour.*"

"Did it work?"

"Sometimes. Sometimes not. But Dad never gave up on me."

"Shit, man. Tough guy," Shane says.

"Yeah. Great one, too. Miss the hell out of him. My father and I had some precarious moments during my recovery, I'll tell you that. But he knew damn well what he was doing." Jason stands now and crosses the deck. Opens the screen door and motions Shane inside. "So that's how you'll get through the day too, my friend. An hour at a time. And we just got through one."

"Son of a bitch, we did," Shane says, standing and finishing the last of that beer.

"And you're going to get through the *next* few with your eyes closed," Jason tells him. "Fatigue's no joke, and makes everything a hundred times worse. You've got to get some serious shut-eye," he insists, motioning Shane and his weary body and fatigued thoughts through the door. "Go."

—⁓—

Fifteen minutes later, Jason calls Maris from out on Shane's deck. He sits on that custom bench that affords a clear view to the harbor. The salt air is pungent here, straight off the Atlantic Ocean. He takes a long breath of it while waiting for Maris to pick up. When she does, he fills her in. Explains how Shane lost a friend yesterday. His name was Shiloh, and he took a bad fall working on the lobster boat. Jason tells her about the shock of the sudden death. How it unhinged Shane.

"Oh my God, Jason. Is he okay?" Maris asks.

"He's getting there. Sleeping some of it off right now. But when he called me yesterday, when he was a wreck, the death had *just* happened. And he really had no one to turn to. Nobody." Jason looks out toward the harbor. The sun's rising higher, dropping ocean stars on the water. They sparkle on the distant view of blue.

"So it was worth the trip, then," Maris says. "You're glad you went?"

"It was a haul getting here. But, yeah. Because I'm really seeing something I'd *never* have known otherwise."

"What's that?"

"How alone Shane is here. I mean, he has friends, yeah.

Crewmates. Neighbors. But, hell. There's no brother here. No family."

"No Celia."

"No. And after what I saw in Shane? I mean, he's *devastated*, Maris, with the way he lost his friend."

"I'm sure he is—it must've been awful for him. The whole situation is just so incredibly sad." Maris pauses a moment. "Is there anything *I* can do?" she asks then.

"Yeah. You need to go see Celia. And tell her about Shiloh. But make it clear to her, too. She's *not* to come here. Shane won't stand for it. For putting her and the baby through that five-hour ordeal."

"Are you *sure* I should talk to her, then?"

"I am. Because if she even *calls* him, it'll help. Celia's *everything* to the guy. I could see that when he wouldn't subject her to the trip north. To the secrecy the trip would entail. Through all that's going on here, he just wants to protect her."

"All right," Maris assures him. "I'll see if I can track her down."

When they end the call, Jason picks up the few empty beer bottles on the deck, the napkins and bottle caps and brings it all inside. Shane's house is quiet. No doubt he didn't get *any* rest last night. The house is so still, he must be sound asleep now. So Jason leaves the bottles on the kitchen counter and tosses out the trash. When he looks for a utility closet, he notices an impressive collection of framed paintings hanging on the walls. There are oils and watercolors. Dark landscapes and portraits that look historical. He walks past them in a small hallway connecting the kitchen to the living room. The walls are covered floor-to-ceiling with paintings of all sizes. Some miniscule in thick, heavy frames; some massive. He touches the canvas on one, the frames of others.

And again notices the quiet of this shingled harbor house. Other than the cry of seagulls carrying in through some open windows, there's not much else. It's a peaceful, coastal spot. When he comes across a small closet in an alcove, he finds a broom and dustpan that he brings to the kitchen. There, he carefully sweeps up the shards of a smashed coffee mug. Sharp ceramic pieces tumble beneath the broom bristles. He reaches the broom to the corner, beneath cabinets, under the low radiator. Every piece of shattered cup—of Shane's anger—is pushed into a pile that Jason sweeps onto the dustpan and dumps in the trash. He lifts a fallen chair at the wooden table, too. The planked wood of that table is old but smoothed. It looks similar to the barnwood of his studio back home.

Finally, Jason turns into the bathroom and tosses some cold water on his face. Does more exploring then, too. In a second bedroom off the hallway, an unexpected sight stops him. Aria's baby things are in that spare room. There's a portable crib there. A plush animal mobile above it. A music box on a dresser. A sunbonnet and package of disposable diapers on a shelf. All of it neatly set in place. All of it a part of Shane's life now.

There's also a bed in that room. So after getting his forearm crutches from where they lean in the living room near the front door, Jason returns to that spare bedroom. Walks to that bed, too. A twin bed upon which he sits, bends over and takes off his prosthetic left leg. Setting the limb aside, he lies back on the bed, rests his head on the pillow and tosses an arm over his tired eyes.

eight

*W*HERE ARE YOU?

Standing in the kitchen, Celia reads the text message from Maris again. Something's up. She looks from the phone back to the inn's living room nook. Early sunshine drops in through the windows this Tuesday morning. It glints off the decorative white starfish propped in the panes. Elsa's there, too, holding a framed baby portrait to one of the taped squares on the wall. Aria's lying in her play yard beside Elsa. The baby's dressed in a bright yellow top over black shorts covered in a sunflower print. The shorts are sashed with a wide bow at the waist; a matching yellow bow is in Aria's dark hair. She's cooing, too, and pumping her arms as Elsa says sweet nothings to her.

"Oh, yes, little love," Elsa's soft voice goes on. "Your mommy says we're grabbing a beach day later, it's so warm out today!"

Celia lifts her phone and quickly types an answer to

Maris. *At Elsa's. Why?*

"Who's on the phone?" Elsa calls to Celia in the kitchen.

"Maris!" Celia calls back when another text dings. She reads Maris' message there. *Can you get away? Really need to talk. Important.*

And the day changes.

Eight-thirty in the morning, and Celia's easy feelings are gone. Evaporated like a sea mist—right before her eyes. The light talk and coffee she and Elsa had while hanging formal portraits? Done. Celia knows it from Maris' message. Something's wrong.

Hanging baby pictures, Celia types now on her phone. *Can take Aria for walk in hour. Meet me on boardwalk.*

"Celia?" Elsa calls from the living room. "Everything okay?"

"What?" Celia vaguely asks, glancing up from her phone. "Oh, yes," she answers, setting down her phone and adjusting the chambray shirt half-tucked into her frayed black shorts.

And so it begins again.

The lies.

Because everything's *not* okay. Celia just doesn't know what's wrong yet. But with a smile on her face, she sort of bustles back into the living room.

"What did Maris want?" Elsa asks while lining up the portraits still to be hung. One is of Aria in a basket on the sand earlier in the summer. Another is Celia wading in Long Island Sound. Gentle waves lap at her ankles; Aria's in her arms. The last is Elsa laughing and lifting Aria to the sky on that same sunny day.

"Maris?" Celia repeats. And stalls. "Oh. She's … stuck on a chapter." Truth, all true. Because surely Maris gets stuck with her writing. It goes with the territory, no? Celia turns to the blue taped squares still on the walls from their unfinished portrait-hanging session last week. "Maris wants to talk out a plot point with an unbiased ear over morning coffee," Celia continues while eyeing those empty blue squares. Partial truth, she convinces herself. Because Maris *does* want to talk. About what? That's questionable. "We do that sometimes," Celia says with an airy tone as she picks up the portrait of Aria in a basket.

But what Elsa *can't* see is how shocked Celia is. Shocked at the way the lies just keep rolling out. Because Celia's *never* before talked out a chapter of a novel.

She's certainly learned something this summer, though. While sidestepping questions and evading looks to keep her relationship with Shane Bradford a secret, oh, she's learned it well.

If all else fails, lie.

So she does.

Celia tells lies.

Tiny white lies mixed with some truth as she and Elsa finish hanging the framed summer portraits in Elsa's living room nook. Even an hour later, Celia still lies. The secret situation with Maris is fudged over when she wheels Aria down the inn's walkway. When she waves to Elsa watching from the front porch. When she calls out that they'll meet up for their beach time once Maris is squared away with her chapter.

But the lies stop cold when she meets Maris on the boardwalk.

When Maris squeezes her hand and says, "Let's walk to my house, okay?"

When Maris' serious voice tells her, "We'll talk there."

Walking the cottage-lined streets then, Celia worries. Because she knows. In the midmorning sunlight, as she wheels Aria's stroller down the gritty beach road, she just knows.

This is going to be bad.

And talk Maris does.

She thinks it best if they sit on the stone bench out on the bluff. Wild grasses edge the view of Long Island Sound. A sea breeze blows, too, rustling those grasses. Celia, holding Aria in her lap, sits beside Maris on the bench. And Celia doesn't really move. She's riveted to Maris' every word, especially when Maris lets on about Shane's phone call last night. And talks about his distress. And how Jason drove to Maine to check up on him. That Jason's there now, and got the story out of Shane this morning. No, Celia's eyes never leave hers as Maris explains what happened out on the Atlantic yesterday.

It's Shiloh ... Working on the boat. Out to sea ... took a fall. Hit his head ... Not good ... Shane found him on deck. In and out of consciousness ... Coast Guard ... Hospital ... Shiloh didn't make it.

"Wait." Celia squints at Maris then. "He *died?*" she asks.

Maris nods. "I'm *so* sorry, Celia."

"Oh my God. I can't *believe* this. Shiloh's really gone?" She looks out to the Sound in the distance, then back to Maris. "I have to talk to Shane."

"I know. But listen to me first. Please."

Celia only nods.

"Shane. Well, he's taking Shiloh's death really hard."

"I'm not surprised," Celia says as she shifts Aria in her

lap. She lightly kisses the top of the baby's head, too. "Shiloh was such a good friend to Shane. They did so much together. Hanging out. Shopping for lobster gear. I think Shane was truly a big brother figure to him. He loved the kid, and vice versa. I mean, Shiloh was his best friend there."

"But Shane never let on what exactly happened when he called last night," Maris says. "He was *that* upset, and ... and rambling. Then when Jason *finally* got the story this morning, well, he thought I should tell you."

"Oh, thank you, Maris. My God, Shane. The loss. He must be *devastated*. But ... " Celia lifts Aria. "Can you hold the baby for a sec? Please?" When Maris takes her, Celia pulls her cell phone from her purse. She checks her voicemails, her text messages, then looks up at Maris. "Shane never called me."

"No, Celia. But please understand. He told Jason he *intends* to tell you, just not yet. He's *so* afraid you'll try to make the trip to Maine and says it's too much."

"But I *want* to see him. To be with him."

"And he knew you would. Which is why he insisted to Jason that you not know yet. But, well, Jason thought otherwise. *Not* for you to go to Maine. But to just *call* Shane. Help him through this."

"Maris. This is ridiculous. *Jason's* up there—and I'm not?"

To which Maris slowly shakes her head.

Celia's eyes fill with desperate tears as she considers this. And thinks of Shane. And of losing Shiloh. "*Look, look*," she whispers then, scrolling on her phone. "I texted Shane just Sunday night. Shiloh was there having dinner on the deck with him. And Shiloh took his phone at one point and had this to say to me."

When Celia holds out the phone, Maris shifts the baby in her lap and reads the phone screen.

Celia: *Hope you had a good drive home. Just had a cloudburst here, then a rainbow.*

Shane: *No rain here. Sun's about to set, clear sky. Having tomato sandwiches with Shiloh out on deck.*

Then: *Hello, Celia. Shiloh here. And don't you be distracting my boy on deck Monday, you hear?*

Celia: *I won't bother you guys. I promise, Shiloh. Safe travels to you both.*

"*Safe travels,*" Maris whispers, then gives Celia a sad smile. "That just breaks my heart."

"I'm sure Shane's is in a *million* pieces right now." Celia looks at the text messages, then back to Maris. "Would you do me a favor?"

"Anything."

"Can you take Aria while I call Shane from here?"

⁓

Celia sits alone on that stone bench for a minute. Just sits and looks out at Long Island Sound. The sun's rising higher in the sky. Ripples of seawater glisten beneath it. The sense she gets, sitting alone here, is this: This beautiful bench is surely the place of many heavy talks. Words no doubt get said beside the sea. Hurt feelings get mended in the salt air drifting across the bluff. Arguments and apologies get made to the backdrop of waves breaking against the rocky ledge.

And now, this.

She calls Shane then. Listens to his low voice, to his *one* word, when he answers.

"Celia."

And it chokes her up. But she swallows that knot in her throat and goes on. Tells him she heard about Shiloh. That she's shocked at how suddenly it all happened. That she's *so* very sorry. Asks Shane if he's okay. If he needs anything.

"How'd you find out?" he asks instead of answering.

"From Maris," Celia tells him. "And don't you *dare* be mad at her—*or* Jason."

"I won't," Shane only says.

With the cell phone pressed to her ear, Celia bends into the call. That sea breeze blows her hair while she talks. "Maris filled me in with what she heard from Jason." Silence then, for a long moment. "*Shane*," Celia whispers. "*This is bullshit.*"

"Bullshit?"

"Yep." She takes a long breath against her surprising anger. "Because I don't want to be *hearing* things filtered like that through someone else. I want to hear it from *you*." Another pause, then, "Did you even plan on telling me?"

"Celia, of course. In time. Because, listen. I don't want you coming up here. That's *why* I didn't say anything."

"Shane—"

"No," he insists back, stopping her. "You have the *baby*. And then there's Elsa. You'd be keeping it secret that you'd be headed here. And it's too much. Too *much* to make up lies. Too *much* to pack and make the long road trip here *again*. And for what?"

"For *what*? To *be* there with you. Jesus, Shane."

"It's just not worth what comes with the trip. Not for a couple of days. Because I'm figuring the wake and funeral will be happening some time this week."

"So soon?"

"Everybody Shiloh knew is around here, so yeah. Then I'll be right back to work the next day. That's how it is on the water. You keep going. Captain's got to haul, got a quota to meet. And it'll be good for me to be busy."

"Maybe. But things had to be pretty bad when you called Jason if he got himself up there."

"I didn't ask him to come."

"I'm coming, too."

"Celia."

There's impatience in Shane's voice now. Celia imagines he's running a hand through his hair. Closing his eyes.

"Trust me," he's saying, his tone low and restrained. "I'm fine, and it's better this way. I just got caught up in really strong emotions yesterday. When I called Jason … Hell, it was only an hour or two after Shiloh passed." More silence, then, "So I'm asking you, Celia."

She stands now and walks along the bluff. "*Asking me what?*"

"Not to come up here."

That's it. Nothing else. Just more silence. And the wind blowing off the water. And a seagull flying low. Celia takes a step alongside the sweeping grasses atop the bluff. She sees some old stairway winding down it to the sea below.

"Where's Jason?" she asks Shane now.

"Went out for some food."

Standing there, Celia leans to the side and squints down that surprising stairway. It looks rotted through, the wood dark with sea damp and age. The rope handrails frayed and ripped. The steps misshapen, with blades of wild grass growing through them. She turns away, though, and brushes back her windblown hair. That wind ripples the fabric of her loose chambray shirt. "Are you *sure* you don't want me to come up? Maybe it'll help."

"I'm very sure. Stay home."

"But Shane—"

"No."

The way he cuts her off, she knows he doesn't want to hear her argument.

Or else it's something more.

Or else he doesn't want her to see his grief. His sadness.

"*Shane, please*," she whispers. Now? Now tears well in her eyes. Stinging tears that have her sit on the bench again. Sit and face the sea. Tears that keep her from saying more lest she sob on them.

"Don't do this, Celia. Don't make things harder." Shane's voice comes to her ear, close. His mouth is dry; she can tell. His voice, tired. "Stay there," he tells her, "and take care of yourself and the baby."

As if.

As if she's good to *anyone* when she can't reach, get through to, drive to, be with, talk to, hold, eat with, listen to, walk with, comfort—Shane.

When he just won't let her.

But her mind is made up—no matter what Shane Bradford says.

Celia, like it or not, *is* going to Maine.

But here's that lying thing again. This time, to Maris. Because after Celia's phone call to Shane devolves on the bluff, she has to get out of there.

Out of the Barlow house.

Out of Stony Point.

The clock is ticking.

So she finds Maris with the baby on the front porch. When Celia rounds the corner, Aria smiles and wiggles in Maris' hold.

"She wants her mama," Maris says, gently giving Celia the baby.

Cradling Aria then, Celia talks for just a few minutes—without letting on that she's *making* that trip to Maine. Because, oh, Celia may be new to the group here, but she's wise to their shifty ways. Telling Maris would go something like this: She mentions her trip to Maris; Maris relays the information to Jason; Jason reports in to Shane.

Uh-uh. No, no, no. Shane would then do his damnedest to stop her. Instead, Celia only tells Maris she *called* Shane. That everything's fine. "He's doing okay," Celia lies as she settles Aria in her stroller, gives a wave and heads back home.

nine

THEY'RE ALL ONE AND THE same, these roadside joints. Bars, taverns. Local dives. Jason stops in the propped-open doorway of this Red Boat Tavern and looks inside. With the dark paneled walls, square wooden tables, droning voice of some noontime news anchor on the mounted TVs, the low hum of folks bullshitting over lunch, the occasional laugh ringing out? He could just as easily be in The Sand Bar as in this Rockport watering hole.

The only difference here is the buccaneer statue right inside the door. The swashbuckling pirate is bearded, with a skull-and-crossbones hat, and a black patch over one eye. Wood-carved knives and a pistol are strapped over his black coat. One arm is hooked. Jason walks past the statue, crosses the dark tavern to the bar and grabs a stool.

"Hey there, sailor. What'll it be today?"

He turns to see a waitress standing beside him—Mandy, according to her name tag. This Mandy wears a fitted red tee over a black denim skirt. A half-apron is slung around her hips; her blonde hair is in a loose braid; a pencil's poised over a pad in her hand.

"How you doing. Takeout for me, if that's all right. I've got a list." Jason reaches to his pocket for a note that Shane had written and runs through the order. Meatloaf sandwiches and triple-decker turkey clubs. Philly-style steak-and-cheese subs. Extra melted cheddar on this; fried onions on that. Sides of crispy potato wedges and fried zucchini chips.

"Oh, and a double grilled cheese, heavy on the ..."

Mandy squints at him. "Tomato?"

"Yes," Jason says with a laugh. "That's it. Couldn't read the handwriting."

"No problem," Mandy tells him. "Let me get this order to the kitchen."

As she walks off, the bartender approaches. He's about fifty, with a shaved head and manicured beard. A full maroon apron is tied over his short-sleeve button-down and slacks. "Can I get you anything?" he asks. "While you wait?"

"Water. Ice water," Jason tells him.

"I'm Landon," the bartender says as he sets down the frosted glass, then eyes Jason. "I own the place here. And you? You must be from away."

"Come again?" Jason asks.

"From away. Not from around here."

"That's right, I'm not. From down the coast. Connecticut."

"Now that's a haul. And what brings you to these parts?"

"Visiting someone," Jason tells him, then takes a swallow of that cold water. "A friend."

"It's Shane, isn't it?" that Mandy asks as she returns to the bar.

Jason looks at her and only turns up his hands.

"I figured when you ordered that double grilled cheese sandwich," she explains. "Only Shane orders it heavy on the tomato."

"*And* Shane's talked some about his Connecticut crew these past few weeks," Landon goes on. He crosses his arms and leans against the bar. "Got a brother there, I hear? Some old friends, too?"

"Definitely," Jason tells them. "Shane's brother, Kyle, was best man at my wedding. We all go back many, many years. Grew up together. Shane, his brother and myself, at the same beach."

"Ayuh." Landon squints at him. "And you are?"

"Name's Barlow. Jason Barlow."

"Put it here," Landon says, extending a hand. "Good to meet you."

"Surprised you came all this way," Mandy adds.

Landon glances at the propped-open tavern door. "No one's seen Shane much since we lost one of our own yesterday."

"Heard about that." Jason nods. "Shiloh."

"That's right. And Shane's been keeping himself scarce," Landon quietly says.

Mandy sits on the stool beside Jason. "He's in a bad way, isn't he?"

"Little bit. You know."

"Honorable of you to say. Because I'm guessing if you dropped everything to be here?" Mandy goes on. "Shane's worse off than that."

A funny thing happens, then, as they're talking.

As Landon mentions that Shane and Shiloh were a

formidable team on that lobster boat.

As Jason's waiting for his take-out order to be delivered.

As he explains that Shane did everything he could to help Shiloh yesterday.

As Mandy says she hopes Shane's not going too hard on himself.

What happens is that a couple of the guys in the tavern mosey over. One—a grizzled older man—brings his beer from further down the bar. Another, a fisherman in his thirties maybe, lifts his lunch from a table and takes a seat at the bar, too. At the same time, a warm breeze carrying the scent of the sea drifts in the tavern's open door.

All the while, the voices around Jason are low. Concerned, even.

Everyone's worried about Shane here—it's obvious. Everyone likes him. So when Jason collects his order and pays Mandy, they *all* tell him to let Shane know they asked about him. To just give a shout if he needs *anything*. That they'll see him at the wake later in the week.

"The whole town will be there," Landon says. "It'll be quite a turnout for Shiloh, I'm sure."

"*Poor kid*," Jason sadly remarks.

"And his parents, too," Landon adds. "Oh, Lord have mercy on them. So that's the breaks, huh? *Awful, awful,*" Landon says almost to himself, then shakes Jason's hand. "But, hey. Really nice meeting *you*."

"Same here," Jason tells him, then gives a wave to everyone as he heads out.

THE VISITOR

Back at Shane's house, Jason stacks most of the packed-up meals neatly in the refrigerator. As he does, Shane sets up their take-out lunches and napkins and a jug of soda on the deck table.

"We'll stop at Keith and Tammy's after we eat," Shane mentions when Jason joins him outside. "Drop off those meals for Shiloh's parents."

"Sounds good." After setting down a second small food bag, Jason sits across from Shane and fills their cups with soda.

"What'd you order?" Shane asks as he lifts the top of his own double-decker grilled cheese.

"Toasted meatloaf sandwich. Cheddar cheese, little horseradish." Jason lifts half the sandwich from its wrapping and digs in.

"Shit, you Barlows are all the same."

"What?"

"Neil ordered that same damn thing, anytime he was here."

"No kidding."

Shane just nods. Lifts his soda cup and takes a swig. "To your brother."

Jason lifts his cup, too, before taking another bite of his amazing sandwich.

"So … talked to Celia," Shane lets on, digging into his monster grilled cheese.

"You did?"

"Yeah." Shane wipes a dribble of tomato off his chin. "She called. Thanks to you, man."

"What do you mean … *thanks to me?*"

"Appears you filled in Maris, and Maris filled in Celia."

"Ah, man. That's where you put me." Jason holds up his loaded meatloaf club. "Right in the middle."

"Damned if you say something, damned if you don't?" Shane swigs the soda. "Don't sweat it, Barlow. Celia and I talked, and she's going to stay put there."

"That's decent. And while *you* were talking to Celia, *I* was talking to a few people at the Red Boat," Jason says around a mouthful.

"That right?"

"Damn straight. The owner, Landon. There was a waitress, too, by the name of Mandy? An old-timer having a brew joined in. And a younger fisherman. Alex, I think he said?"

"Sure. Sure." Shane drags a potato wedge through some ketchup on his plate. "Good folks there. All good folks. Most of them, anyway."

"Well, they're upset about Shiloh," Jason tells him while chewing. "But really worried about *you*, man."

"Eh." Shane waves him off.

"No, seriously. They all wanted to be sure you're okay." As he's talking, Jason reaches into a take-out bag he'd brought onto the deck. "Which means," he says while setting out two fruit-oozing pieces of pastry, "they threw in a couple of *loaded* blueberry pie slices. On the house."

⁓

Right after Celia left, the day took a turn—one Maris *never* saw coming.

A turn that has her changing her outfit before lunch. That has her fingers buttoning up her fitted black denim sheath. That has her pulling her hair back in a low twist—right as her cell phone dings with a text from Jason. She picks up the phone and scans his message.

Having early lunch.

With Shane? Maris texts back, then sets the phone on her bedroom dresser. She leans close to her dresser mirror, too, glancing at her phone when it dings again.

Yeah. Out on his deck.

How is he? she thumb-types, then gets back to that mirror and puts on thin silver hoop earrings. After the second one is in, her phone dings again.

Hanging in there. He's getting more forks inside.

Okay. Talked to Celia. Guess she called him after, Maris types. She takes the phone to the bed, where she sits and pulls on her Western-style black boots. Glances at the dinging phone beside her, too.

Yeah, he told me.

What're you up to this afternoon? she thumb-types again before heading to the scarf rack in her closet. There, Maris lifts a black-and-white paisley scarf, wraps it twice around her neck and ties the ends in a loose knot at her throat. When she hurries to her dinging phone on the bed, she groans when she sees Jason's question.

Actually headed to Shiloh's parents' place. Dropping off take-out dinners there. You?

"Hmm. What am I doing today?" Maris whispers. "Oh, he's going to kill me," she then says to herself before texting Jason back. *Okay. Okay, well. Um*, she types while saying the words, too. *I'm actually filling in for you?*

⁓

Jason flops back in his chair at the deck table. Sits back and drags a hand along his jaw. "*What the hell?*" he whispers, then actually *calls* Maris. Her phone rings right as Shane's coming out the door with clean forks for the pie. Jason holds up a finger while on the phone, so Shane slowly sits—and pays attention.

But that pie's too much temptation for Jason. He takes one of the clean forks, puts his phone on speaker and sets it down on the table. Digs into his slice of blueberry pie, too. "Get a load of this, guy," he tells Shane, nodding at the phone.

"Jason?" Maris' voice comes through the speaker. "Why aren't you texting me?"

"Spill it, sweetheart."

"*Oh, this should be good,*" Shane quietly says, dropping a fork through his own pie.

"Well," Maris is saying. "I didn't want to bother you. You have a lot going—"

"*Maris ...*"

"Okay, *okay*. Trent has a tight schedule and he actually *just* called me." There's a pause then, as though she's doing something. Putting on lip gloss, maybe? Or a bracelet. "To host?" she finally comes back with.

"*What?*"

"Well, Jason. The weather's perfect," Maris' words come rapid-fire now. "And you never know how long it'll last. It *could* rain again and throw production off. So Trent said I did really well when I cut my finger during filming with you? And I guess some window people need to finish up *today* at the Fenwicks'—but *you're* not available? And that's the beauty of writing, Jason. I'm so accessible to anyone needing my assistance. My aunt, or sister. You. Even *Trent*." That word, Trent, she says with a lift in her voice.

"You mean, you're taking *my* job?" Jason asks while lifting a hunk of blueberry-dripping pie. "Next thing you know—"

"Got to go, hon. Can't be late. You know Trent's motto. A-B-F!"

"Yeah, yeah. Wait—good luck!" Jason calls toward the phone, but it's no use. The phone's gone silent. His whirlwind wife must be spinning down the stairs and out the door right about now.

"A-B-F?" Shane asks.

"Always. Be. Filming. Trent—that's my producer—it's his catchphrase."

"That right?"

"You bet. If he's not filming enough, projects can get slashed." Jason lifts another overloaded forkful of pie, letting the fork hover there as he talks. "Which is apparently why Maris just took over today's *Castaway Cottage* gig. To keep the cameras rolling."

"No shit." Shane fork-slices another piece of pie. "So are you in serious hot water for coming here? With your TV show?"

"Maybe. A little," Jason says around a mouthful of pie. A salty breeze lifting off the nearby harbor reaches them at the table. "Don't worry about it, though," Jason tells Shane.

As he does, Jason sees something, too. There's a change in Shane. A grin as he goes at that pie slice of his. So maybe Shane's *welcoming* hearing something else. *Something not sad,* Jason thinks. *Something as random as Maris doing some filming and stealing my job.*

ten

AFTER LEAVING MARIS' PLACE, CELIA had to catch her breath.

Think.

Process all that's happened with Shiloh.

With Shane.

So half an hour later, she's sitting beneath the shade pavilion on the boardwalk. Gently, she moves Aria's stroller back and forth along the sandy planks as the baby dozes. That easy motion belies the turmoil Celia feels. Because there's another difficult phone call to make. This one's to her father. Finally, she reaches for her cell phone, presses his number and waits for him to pick up.

"Dad," she says right away when he does. She keeps the call brief, telling him something happened to Shane and that she has to go to Maine. "Can you take care of Aria for a few days?" she asks. "I'll explain more when I'm in Addison later." Relief, then. Instant relief when he *warily* agrees.

The Visitor

And here comes the hardest part—Elsa.

Elsa's waiting to have a late beach morning with her and Aria. While walking back home down the sandy road, Celia spots her. She's sitting on the inn's porch swing. Sand chairs are leaning against a beach wagon on the lawn. When Elsa stands, Celia sees she's wearing her bathing suit, too—a jet-black halter-top one-piece. Her gold chain necklaces glimmer; a green sarong lined with fringed tassels is tied around her waist.

"Oh, *Elsa*," Celia begins as she wheels the stroller closer. And there it is—Elsa's disappointment. Her smile fading as soon as Celia says she has to cancel. "I was at Maris'," Celia says. Truth, all true. "And checked my calendar for something. On my phone?"

Elsa only nods.

"And saw I have another commitment." More truth—a commitment to getting to Rockport, Maine.

"Why didn't you say something earlier?" Elsa asks. "When we hung the pictures?"

"I'd completely forgotten all about it." Okay, a lie here, damn it.

Which is when their talk took a turn and went downhill.

"*Ach*," Celia's saying fifteen minutes later as she tosses an overnight bag on her bed back at her gingerbread cottage. "Lies, *lies*." She has just enough time to pack while Aria finishes her nap. The poor baby was tired from all the attention this morning—earlier from Elsa, then from Maris—not to mention the sunshine and fresh air.

69

So the baby's nap buys Celia packing time.

In her bedroom, she unzips her luggage, pulls open sticking dresser drawers, puts her hands on her hips and wonders what to bring. Too much, or not enough? It's hard to think straight while replaying all the damn lies she just told Elsa.

One lie has her slamming a drawer. *There's a birthday party back in Addison. My good friend Amy's daughter.*

Another lie has Celia stomping across the bedroom. *Her little Grace is turning five ... I'll be staying at my dad's a few days ... With Aria.*

A third lie has Celia shoving some piece of clothing or another into her overnight bag. *He hasn't seen her much lately.*

Making the lies even *worse* was Elsa's sympathetic way. Her small smile that came when she told Celia she understood. That these things happen.

Which only amped up Celia's guilt. Amped up more lies trying to justify letting Elsa down. *I'm going to work on my staging class lessons there*, Celia told her while slowly backing away. *Maybe write a song in Dad's big backyard, too.*

And now, the visual. The image in her mind of Elsa waving her off. Telling her to give her best to Gavin. Calling out not to worry.

And Celia calling back, *I'll make it up! We'll grab another beach day.*

All those lies dumped Celia into this packing *mania* now. Piles of clothes are on her bed as she chooses what to bring. What not. It's a funny time of year. Could be warm in Maine, or cool.

Meanwhile, her worry grows, too. By leaps and bounds. Should she have just sat with Elsa on the beach for an hour? Just told her *not* to talk as she came clean about her and Shane's relationship?

"*Don't know, don't know,*" Celia whispers now while shoving pajamas—one summer pair, one fall—into her bag.

Shorts *and* cropped jeans go in that overnight bag next. A couple of tees, a sweater. Shoes *and* sandals. A little summer, a little fall. Undergarments, too.

But there just wasn't time to talk more with Elsa. Celia tucks her hair behind an ear. No time. *Tick, tick.* She can almost hear that clock ticking down.

Because I need to get to Shane, she thinks while brushing through her bedroom closet.

And need something to wear for the funeral.

And need to get to Addison.

Need to explain yet another situation to my father.

"Need life to get easier," she tells herself while considering her half-packed overnight bag. How many days will she be away? The baby needs clothes packed, too. And it'll be so hard leaving Aria—*again*. But Celia can't bring her to Maine. Not this trip.

Finally, after tossing a little of this and some of that in her luggage, and dropping her hair dryer and toiletries and shampoo into a small duffel, she's done. While wheeling her suitcase and lugging her bags into the living room, she catches sight of Elsa outside. An umbrella and sand chair are in the little beach wagon she's pulling along as she heads, alone, to the beach.

Celia stands near her window and watches. And wonders if she should've fessed up.

Oh, who knows.

But what Celia *does* know? She's gotten really damn good at something this summer.

Lying.

―⌒―

It's just not the same.

There's no one to ask, *Here? Is this a good spot for the beach umbrella?* No reason to put a finger to chin and say, *Hmm. How about over there?*

Instead, Elsa surveys the beach alone. She passes a few late-season stragglers. People reading a book in the sunshine. Or wading in the shallows. She walks about halfway down the beach and contemplates where to sit.

"Oh, what does it matter?" Elsa quietly asks herself, then drops her wagon handle, shoves her umbrella pole into the sand and twists it in deep. But she doesn't open the umbrella yet. Some warm sunshine would feel good first. That, and a nice sigh feels good, too, when she sits in her sand chair beside the closed umbrella.

A genuine sigh … okay, one she *might've* dragged out. But it *did* feel good. Sometimes a smidge of self-pity is comforting. She reclines her chair, leans back and closes her eyes behind her sunglasses. A little morning snooze is in order, too. You can do that when you're alone on the beach. Heck, there's no one to talk to, anyway.

Well. Not until footsteps shuffle closer in the sand and a shadow falls over her sun-warmed skin.

"What are you doing here?" a familiar voice asks.

"Cliff?" Elsa peers over her sunglasses, then raises her sand chair. Cliff's approaching, wearing his full beach commissioner regalia—black polo shirt, khaki uniform pants, gold-stitched *Commissioner* cap. "I'm on a solo beach outing," she tells him. "*And* feeling sorry for myself," she admits, looking over her shoulder.

"*Sorry?* Why?"

"Was supposed to be here with the girls."

"Girls?"

"Celia and Aria. But something came up with Celia. Some obligation in Addison."

"Well, I'll keep you company." Cliff drops a messenger bag that was looped over his shoulder. He also lifts a beach towel from Elsa's wagon and sets it out beside her chair, then opens her umbrella, too. "I just put sawhorses around the Fenwick place. *Castaway Cottage* filming is going on later. Don't like onlookers getting too close. It's a liability thing, you know." He sits on that towel now, not wasting any time either. As soon as he's sitting, he's handing over paint chips for the guard shack.

"*Aha!* I was *hoping* to have a look at these." Elsa takes the paint chips and fans them out in her hand. "Hmm. I like the blues instead of the grays. But it would be nice to see something more of a ... blue-*green*. Like ... like the *sea*," she says, pointing a chip toward the lapping water.

Cliff grabs back the paint chips. "*Eh*. There'll never be a consensus," he mutters. "Blue-green like the sea. Blue like the sky. Gray like fog. *Light* gray like a seagull. Tan like the sand. Oh, I've heard it *all*." After he tucks those color samples back in his messenger bag, he pulls out something else. "Check this out, too," he says, handing it over.

Elsa takes what looks like a poster and reads aloud the announcement on it. "Reward offered for any information leading to the identity and BOG conviction of the Stony Point moose-napper." With a raised eyebrow, she eyes the photograph on the poster, too. It's a full-color picture of the mounted moose head now hanging in *her* inn. "Are you *kidding* me?"

"No, I'm not. Jason emailed me the details yesterday morning," Cliff explains. "So I designed that reward flyer for him. Going to hang some on the bulletin boards, utility poles. Let me tell you, Jason's really determined to have justice served. Hell-bent, actually, on finding the culprit who took that moose from his studio—once and for all."

Elsa looks at Cliff sitting on the sand beside her. *Oh, you're looking at the culprit*, she thinks. *Right now, mister. So tell me, what do you think of having a criminal girlfriend, neighbor, lover—who's a hot mess of a woman?* But she doesn't say *any* of that.

"What's the point of the reward?" Elsa asks instead. "It's not like he can have the moose head back."

"He can't?"

"No. Legend has it that whoever *steals* the moose head ... keeps it."

"Now, Elsa. Jason—and everyone else—knows that *you* are behind the theft. That poor moose landed at *your* place, after all—"

"Where it rightfully belongs."

"But you could *never* have lifted that behemoth." Cliff pauses, leans closer and lowers his voice. "So ... just between you and me—you have my word—who *did* you hoodwink into your crime? Because Kyle was stationed at his hot plates that night. And Shane was driving down from Maine. So I'm wondering *whose* strong arms did that heavy lifting for you."

"Clifton!" Elsa swats him. "You conniver! You're just angling for that reward money!"

"No! No, I just thought, well, you know. We share certain intimacies ... and this secret could be one of them."

Elsa watches Cliff through her squinted eyes. She leans even closer, too, and takes hold of his arm as she whispers, "*A woman never reveals her secrets.*" But as the words leave her lips, she maybe wishes she could take them back. Because as she and Cliff silently challenge each other with their looks alone, the moment turns more serious than she intended. Oh, the midday sun shines down just the same, and small waves lap at her feet, but does something change between them? Is Cliff thinking of the *other* secret that she's keeping? A romantic one, in particular? By the name of Mitch? Is Cliff wanting *that* secret revealed? In their long silence, Elsa can't tell.

"Well," Cliff quietly says while pulling away now, "Jason's willing to pay one *hundred* dollars just to know *who* stole it." Cliff points to the poster in Elsa's hands. "It's all there, the reward info. On the bottom."

"The old moose means *that* much to Jason?" Elsa asks.

"Oh, he means business. And wants answers." Cliff takes the poster back from her. "I wouldn't mind knowing myself, either," he adds, his voice low.

Swell, Elsa thinks. *I'm doomed. Everyone's onto me, in every way.* After a glance over at the Fenwick cottage—then back to Cliff—she shifts in her sand chair. *Doomed in more ways than one. Because there are only a few hours until my tomato-sauce lesson—with Mitch.*

Cliff's standing now and sliding that poster securely back into his messenger bag. He's also mentioning something about seeing his son, Denny, that night. "Bowling leagues are starting up. Thought we'd try a game. Decide if we want to join a league this fall." Cliff tips up his brimmed *Commissioner* cap and looks down at Elsa in her sand chair. After another long moment, his blue eyes twinkle again. And there's that dimple in his smile as he tips his head. "I'd invite you, Mrs. DeLuca, but I can already hear what you'd have to say about renting bowling shoes."

When Elsa waves him off, he turns to leave. But he surprises her when he backtracks, bends down and kisses her cheek.

It actually leaves her a little speechless as she brushes her fingers over her cheek and watches him hurry down the sunny beach with his moose-napper posters.

And she sighs again. Okay, she *wanted* to make a late-summer memory this morning—sitting with her granddaughter on the beach. And she still misses that one.

But she got this memory in its place: hanging out with Cliff seaside, complete with a simple calling-your-bluff kiss.

As Cliff walks across the sand, he looks over his shoulder at Elsa sitting, knees pulled up, beneath her umbrella. Looks over his shoulder two times.

Huh. And both times, she's actually looking *his* way—peering over the frame of her big cat-eye sunglasses. The second time he looks at her sitting alone on the beach, she gives him a finger-wave, too.

Oh, Celia knows the folklore well. Anyone leaving Stony Point beneath the stone train trestle departs with one of

THE VISITOR

three things: a ring, a baby, or a broken heart.

After packing up her car and giving Aria her lunch bottle, Celia's leaving, too—heading to Addison. Then on to Maine.

But first? She has to get through the train trestle.

And today? Today it's with a broken heart. For Shane. For Shiloh. For lying to Elsa, even.

Oh, a broken heart on *so* many levels.

Which is why, before heading down Shore Road toward the highway, Celia pulls into the Scoop Shop parking lot just past the trestle. The emotion of it all—of her sad broken heart—makes it too hard to drive.

Here she is, feeling so blue, all while happy Aria's cooing in her baby seat in the back.

And here's this beautiful September day, while Celia's stopped and choked up on tears in a convenience store *parking* lot. A minute later, she's aggressively putting down her window, too.

Because yes, she's sad.

But hell, she's *mad*, too. Mad at herself. Mad at situations. Mad that Shane won't hear of her trip there. Mad at the secrets in her life. "*Ooh*," she says under her breath, all while slapping the steering wheel. Darn it, she *lied* to Elsa after they just fixed *everything*. After their mounted moose head hijinks sealed the deal—the two of them were once again thick as thieves.

Elsa even tried to reassure her when Celia *lied* to her today. "That's okay," Elsa had said, her voice soothing. "I'll go to the beach for a bit myself. I'm meeting up with a neighbor later on anyway."

Sitting in her car, in this dingy parking lot, with her trunk packed with luggage and baby gear, Celia pictures Elsa alone on the beach. Umbrella open. Quiet. No chitchat. No doting over Aria, her *little love*.

Swiping a tear off her face as she pulls herself together, Celia's actually overcome by the seriousness of ... well, of *everything*.

Of Shiloh's death.

Of holding back from Elsa.

Of Shane's frame of mind. He doesn't want Celia there—but she's going, anyway.

The seriousness of imposing on her father.

Of driving to Maine tomorrow.

Of *lying* to Elsa—especially when Elsa didn't bat an eye.

Celia doesn't *want* to lie. She so badly wants to confide in Elsa.

Oh, maybe it's all of the above that has Celia frazzled.

Or maybe it's only this, she thinks as she puts her car in gear and heads out.

It's that she knows, Lord does she know, that what's ahead of her the next few days is going to be long. Tiring. Hard.

eleven

AFTER LUNCH, AND AFTER LOADING Shane's pickup with coolers of prepared meals from the Red Boat Tavern, they hit the road. For a few miles, Shane drives winding streets hugging the coastline. They pass shingled homes, some with lobster traps stacked in the front yards. But Shane eventually veers inland. The views are more country-rural here. The streets, more wooded. The yards, spread out.

Jason takes it all in—the way the landscape changes, and the way the architecture changes along with it. Because when Shane finally turns onto a large property, it's anchored by an old white clapboard farmhouse. The roof is steep-pitched with angular lines. There's an open front porch with rockers and a wicker settee. A few steps off the side of the house, on a slightly sloping hill, a long, narrow shed sits in the shade of leafy maple trees.

Except, Jason notices, it's not a shed. It's a little white farm stand selling berries—though its shelves are empty today. A roof overhang gives the shed an open front porch matching that of the main house. Potted geraniums hang from that overhang. So do a cluster of faded lobster buoys. A hand-painted *Blueberries* sign dangles there, too.

"This is it," Shane says, pulling over on the long driveway. The early afternoon sun shines bright. A few other cars are parked askew; one there, a couple here.

"Shiloh's parents are farmers?" Jason asks, bending to get a better look at the farmhouse before them.

"Little bit. They're more gentlemen farmers. Which means they lease most of their land to local farmers, but tend to a small plot themselves. Just for pleasure."

"Not a bad gig." Jason gets out and lifts a tote filled with food from a cooler in the truck bed. As he does, he looks over to the house. A man and woman are walking down the porch steps. The couple is middle-aged and dressed casual in light sweaters and jeans. The man calls out Shane's name, so he hurries to them.

And Jason knows. Knows by the hug Shane gives to both of them—a long hug ending with comforting pats on the back. Jason knows by the woman—with tears in her eyes—touching Shane's cheek. Knows by the fatigue on their faces, the shadows beneath the sad eyes, that these two people are Shiloh's parents. The mother is more distressed right now than Shiloh's father. She presses a hand to her mouth to quell a sob. Shakes her head while Shane leans close, talking to her.

Jason comes up behind them. "Shane," he says, hefting that tote on his shoulder. "Can I help bring in the food?"

"Oh, man. Jason." Shane nods to Shiloh's parents. "This here is Keith and Tammy. Shiloh's mom and dad."

Shane turns to them now. "Jason's got those meals from Red Boat Tavern I told you about."

"Really sorry to meet under these circumstances, Keith," Jason says, setting down the tote of food and shaking Keith's hand. "Please accept my deepest condolences," he tells Tammy, too, while giving her a light hug.

"Jason's a friend from Connecticut," Shane explains. "He's a coastal architect there, renovates and builds some incredible beach homes. Came north to Maine for a brief visit."

"Glad to meet you, Jason," Keith says, nodding. "Any friend of Shane's …"

"Appreciate that," Jason tells him when he sees that Keith can't continue. That his sentence drifted off, unfinished. Because *his* son was a friend of Shane's, too. "Shane speaks very highly of your son."

"Our Shiloh," Tammy says then. Her shoulder-length silvery-blonde hair is slipping from a low ponytail. A crumpled tissue is tucked into her jeans pocket, and she dabs that tissue at a tear on her face. "Shiloh loved Shane like a brother."

"I couldn't have asked for a better partner on the boats, either," Shane assures her.

"Jason." Tammy tips her head and softly asks, "What do you do in Connecticut?"

She asks this, even though Shane just told them both.

So Jason steps closer and kindly repeats it, talking briefly about his architecture work. As he does, he realizes something. It's something that actually fills in a missing piece in his life.

Yes, Jason realizes *this* is what he missed—ten years ago.

This is what he missed when he was laid up in the hospital after Neil's death. Tammy and Keith, here and talking—but not really hearing *anything*—would've been *his* parents back then. Not hearing. Not present. Utterly lost in grief.

This scene on the front lawn of an old Maine farmhouse played out on the front lawn of the Barlows' gabled house on the bluff. Words said but not heard. Comfort given, regardless. Caring hugs. Nods. Embraces and whispers.

All of this happened with his own mother and father.

But Jason never saw it. He was confined to a hospital bed. He never saw the visitors who stopped by the house. Never heard the stifled sobs. The murmurs of longing. Never saw the tired eyes. The haggard bodies.

He never saw what a child's death immediately does to the parents.

Now, he's witnessing it.

"Why don't you take the food Shane brought, Tammy," Keith says, "and bring it inside?"

Tammy nods and lifts the tote off the lawn. "We were at the funeral home this morning," she tells Shane and Jason, then backs up a step toward the house while lifting the tote strap to her shoulder. "We don't want to prolong things. So Shiloh's wake," she goes on, then swallows a difficult knot in her throat, "will be tomorrow."

"If there's anything I can do, Tammy," Shane tells her, "to help. You be sure to let me know. *Anything*."

Tammy only nods before turning and climbing the porch steps.

"Funeral's Thursday morning," Keith continues to Jason and Shane, then looks to the driveway when more people arrive—this time a young couple. Their car doors slam before they walk across the lawn. When the man clasps Keith's shoulder, Keith points to the house. "Tammy's inside. Why don't you stop in there? She's got some food that needs tending to."

"Keith," Shane says then. "I just wanted to drop off those meals for you and Tammy so you don't have to worry about having something to eat. But we won't keep you now."

"Wait." Keith hooks an arm through Shane's while motioning for Jason to follow as he walks to the side yard. A couple of farm dogs lift themselves off the sunny lawn and tag along behind them. Keith stops beneath the shade of a towering maple tree. The dogs sniff around and settle near him on the cool grass.

"What's up?" Shane asks him.

"Shane. Jason. Listen," Keith says with a glance back toward his house. "Tammy's really torn up."

"Understandably," Shane says.

"No, no." Keith looks to them both. "The thing is … *huh*. How do I even put this? We have no clothes for Shiloh. You know, for tomorrow."

"What do you mean?" Shane asks.

"Well, the funeral director asked us to bring in an outfit that we'd like for Shiloh to be wearing. You know. For in the casket. And … *hell*. Shiloh was a twenty-six-year-old kid. He has halibut tees and lobster gear and … and cargo shorts. But …" Keith stops and blinks back tears that look to sting. "Nothing to be laid to rest in. Who does, at twenty-six?"

Jason right away elbows Shane. "We're on it, no?"

"Definitely," Shane tells him with a quick glance before turning to Keith. "Listen. You tell Tammy *not* to worry. Let us take *that* load off you, at the very least."

"Well, I don't know. I mean, there's the matter of Shiloh's sizes."

"I got a pretty good idea," Shane insists. "Been shopping with Shiloh many times. Here," Shane goes on, pulling his cell phone from his pocket. "You fill me in on the particulars, regardless. Shirt size. Pants. Shoes."

As Keith does, as his low voice relays measurements and style preferences and asks that they get something suitable for his boy, Shane types the notes on his cell phone.

He also tells Keith again it's the least they can do to help. "Don't you worry," Shane says. "We'll swing back with a nice suit for your son."

⁓

An hour later, they're in a men's clothing store a few towns over. It's in a low brick building on a downtown street, and a long striped awning extends over the store's display windows. Shane parked in a space at the curb. The afternoon sun shines bright, but it's darker inside the specialty store.

"This feels wrong," Shane's saying as he lifts a navy suit jacket off the ready-made rack.

"Sure does," Jason agrees. "You never fathom these kinds of days."

"A suit for a twenty-six-year-old should be a job-interview suit. Or a wedding suit. Not a suit for a casket."

"No shit," Jason says, brushing through a rack of pima

cotton tees. "This suit will be filled with all the life that *wasn't* lived. What a sad shame."

"Well, I want to keep it top shelf for Shiloh, you know? And I like this navy suit because the jacket and pants are the color of the ocean. The deep blue sea. A color familiar to Shiloh, and it's the finest fabric. But … what to go with it." Shane turns to the button-downs and picks up a crisp white one. "What do you think? Navy suit with this shirt? Maybe with a silk tie?"

"Eh. I don't know, Shane."

"Yeah. That's what I was thinking. Because I mean," Shane says, holding the formal button-down against the navy suit jacket. "Where's *Shi* in this getup?"

"How about something more like this?" Jason asks from a T-shirt rack. He lifts a hanger with a trim black tee on it. "It's got that modern fit and if Shiloh wears *this* beneath the suit jacket, it'll keep the look more youthful. Because hell, he *was* young, man. Let's dress him that way."

"Shit, yeah. I like that. Okay." Shane grabs the jacket and pants. "We'll keep it formal with the suit, for the seriousness of this all. But young."

Jason takes that pima cotton black tee and walks over to Shane. "We're good, then. Let's grab a pocket square, too."

"Pocket square, right. Mix in some more formal. Formal is the right tone, can't go wrong," Shane says as he thumbs through the silk pocket squares.

"His parents will appreciate it, man. Just think of Tammy and Keith."

Shane chooses a red pocket square, then shakes his head.

"What's the matter?" Jason asks, taking the pocket square from him.

"I don't know." Shane holds up the suit jacket and gives it a long look. "I really want to do right by Shiloh."

"Looks like you are, guy," Jason tells him. "Those are all really nice threads."

"They are. But I've got something else in mind, too. We need to get shoes after this, then there's one item I want to pick up special on the way to his parents'."

"All right. Now listen, you pay here and I'll meet you outside. I'm going to call Maris, so I'll meet you at your truck."

Jason heads out. But on his way through the store, as he walks along the wood-planked floors and through the muffled quiet of racks of fine clothes, as he passes long rows of button-downs evenly hung and spaced, and an endless collection of suit jackets sorted by color and hung side by side in another row, and stacks of casual trousers neatly folded on wood shelves, he gets sidetracked.

Legitimately sidetracked … enough to veer deeper into the store to an accessories department. There's a display of men's watches that catches his eye—and gives him an idea. So Jason spends a few minutes inspecting them. He eyes the sport watches and dress watches. Military styles and solar styles. Metal banded and leather.

But while alone at the men's jewelry case, he's doing some thinking, too. And remembering. Jason looks long at the display of watches, but then lifts one. Only one. The color of the watch's band is what gets his attention. The metal band is the same dull silver color as his father's pewter hourglass. Exactly the same.

And that does it.

He looks no more, but instead buys that one watch on the spot.

⁓

In the fine clothing department, Shane sets Shiloh's burial outfit on the checkout counter. Racks of silk ties are behind it. There's a wood spindle-back bench off to the side, too—a seat for waiting customers.

"Will that be all, sir?" a saleswoman asks from behind the counter.

"Yes. That's it," Shane says, nodding to the suit jacket, pants and tee, the pocket square. And the leather shoes he picked up last minute.

"I'll put everything together on a proper hanger for you," she tells him, then lifts a contoured wood hanger and folds Shiloh's navy suit pants onto the trouser bar. After hooking that suit hanger on a garment rack behind the register, she turns to the suit jacket still on the counter. "It's really a beautiful suit," she says. "Special occasion?"

Shane looks at her. Looks at her and thinks, *Yeah. Damn special occasion, all right. My best friend's going six feet under the earth in that suit. He had nothing to wear, so I'm stepping up for him.* But he doesn't say any of that. Doesn't even come close.

"Yeah," Shane says instead. "Really special occasion. Outdoor wedding," he lies—for Shiloh's sake. Because damn it, that fine suit *should* be for a nice occasion—even if Shane can only find *nice* in his mind. Ten minutes of *nice* as he's rung out and the receipt printed, and as the tee is wrapped in tissue paper and bagged along with the shoes. Ten minutes of what that special suit really *should* be for.

After walking across the hushed store then, Shane pushes through the doors out onto the sidewalk. It's midafternoon and the daylight gets him squinting. A little nightmarish feeling comes over him, actually. And why wouldn't it—with all the death-planning going on inside the serious, quiet store countered by this bright September sunshine, the happy blue sky above. Darkness versus light. Good versus evil.

And then there's Jason. He's hours from home. *Hundreds* of miles away from the life he *should* be living back in Stony Point right now. Shane glances down the sidewalk and spots him leaning against his pickup. He's got on a zip sweatshirt over his shirt and jeans and is finishing up talking to Maris. As Shane hangs Shiloh's suit on a hook behind the driver's seat, Jason swigs from a bottled water he snagged from inside the truck.

"Got everything?" Jason asks when Shane walks around to the sidewalk again.

"Yeah. So far."

Jason caps his water bottle and hands Shane a small bag from the clothing store. "Open it," he tells him.

Standing there on the sidewalk, Shane pulls a significant men's wristwatch from the bag. The watch is really impressive with a silver-gray titanium band and black face with simple cream numbers circling it. Shane lets out a low whistle, then squints through the sunlight at Jason. "This for Shiloh?"

"No, man. It's for you."

"Me?"

Jason nods. "Help you get through, remember? Hour by hour. We just got through one," he says, opening the truck passenger door and climbing in. "Now we're going to try for another."

―~―

And Shane thinks it's a tough hour.

At the end of the next sixty minutes, after stopping at a specialty boutique, they're dropping off Shiloh's suit. Delivering it to a father and mother who tragically lost their only son. Shane and Jason don't stay long. They know Shiloh's parents have to get that suit to the funeral home.

Shane gives Tammy and Keith a small box before they leave. "This goes with the suit," he says. "Something I picked up to give it a little more meaning."

Shiloh's parents don't say much. It's apparent they're out of words. There's only grief right now.

"From what I've heard about Shiloh?" Jason tells them. "I think he would've really appreciated that," Jason says, nodding to that box as he does.

twelve

THE DRIVE TO ADDISON FELT long, but Celia's finally here. The baby was fussy the whole trip, no doubt picking up on Celia's worry. It's late afternoon now. Celia's sitting on a slatted-wood chair on the front porch of her father's yellow bungalow. Aria's napping inside.

"I want some answers, Celia." Her father, Gavin, wears a light flannel shirt with brown denim jeans and is leaning against the porch railing. His sneakered feet are crossed; his expression, cautious. He's fiddling with a blade of grass as he waits for her answers. When those don't come soon enough, he brings that blade of grass to his mouth, all while squinting at her.

Celia looks at her father and hesitates.

"I like Shane," Gavin says around that piece of grass now. "But I *don't* like what I'm seeing. What comes with him. The lies. The secrecy—"

"That's not Shane's doing," Celia interrupts. "That's mine.

Shane would announce our relationship on a *billboard* if it were up to him."

"And it's not?"

"No."

"You must have doubts then, that the relationship can hold water."

"I have doubts about *everything*, Dad." Celia stands and leans both her hands on the porch railing. She looks down the country lane to the wispy top of a lush cornfield golden at summer's end. A crumbling stone wall reaches down the winding street, too. She turns then, crosses her arms and leans against the railing beside her father. "That's what the past year did to me. Cast doubt on everything. Where I live—on the grounds of Elsa's inn. What I do."

"Assistant innkeeper?"

Celia nods. "Should I just get back to staging homes fulltime? Like I did when I lived here? Before I sold you the place? I've even doubted that—living *anywhere* in Stony Point. *Is* it the right place for me to raise Aria alone? Am I doing right by my daughter, and filling her life with good people? People who love her? And *you're* farther away now. So why didn't I stay here—in my own house? With my own independence. Did I jump the gun uprooting? Oh, sometimes the doubts just keep rolling. But. *But*, but, but, Dad. I do *not* have doubts about Shane Bradford."

"And he wouldn't be *in* your life if you didn't do all those things you doubted."

To which Celia just tosses up her hands.

"So set yourself at ease and tell people about him," her father says while shifting that blade of grass between his teeth. "What's the big deal?"

"The big deal? It's Elsa. The big deal *is* my four-month-old daughter. Four *months*! The big deal is the tangled mess of all my friends in Stony Point—who didn't accept Shane for a long time."

"So now you're just running up to Maine ... on a whim?"

"*Not* a whim, Dad." Still leaning on the porch railing, Celia looks at him beside her. "Shane's best friend just died. Shiloh. Shiloh was his name. He somehow got hurt out on the lobster boat yesterday and *died* hours later. And Shane was *right* there."

"Well, now," Gavin says. "That throws new light on the situation."

"Yes, it does. Shane even went on the Coast Guard rescue boat with Shiloh. And was at the hospital. And after Shiloh died, Shane must've been *devastated*, Dad. Because he reached out to Jason—who's in Maine with him as we speak."

"So your friends stand behind Shane now?"

"They do! But Jason and Maris are the only ones who *know* about me and Shane."

"And Elsa? What does she think about your absence?"

"Elsa." Celia pushes off the railing, sits in that slatted-wood chair again and turns back the sleeves of her chambray shirt. "Elsa thinks I'm with you for a few days. And visiting Amy and Grace next door for Grace's birthday party."

"I don't like the lies, Celia. The way they're building." Gavin crosses his arms. "You don't even know *how* Elsa would react to learning the truth. To learning about you and Shane. What she'd say. In time, she might be very happy for you. That you found someone who really cares about you and your daughter. So *what* would be wrong with Elsa knowing about Shane? And that he lost his good friend. And that you're seeing him and are worried sick about him. Damn it, with knowing … *all* of it?"

"I'll tell you, Dad. It would feel like an arrow to her heart, okay? After losing her son. Because she'll think Aria and I will be out the door to Maine. That I'll move on with my life and we'll leave her behind."

"Will you?"

"No. Shane and I are just seeing each other—"

"It's more than that, and you know it."

"And *you* know that Elsa *will* have those sad thoughts that me and Aria are leaving her for good—and right now?" Celia toys with a turquoise pendant at her neck. "Right now it feels cruel to put that all on her."

"Put what on her?"

"That I did move on—from Sal. That I *might* one day leave and take her only grandchild far away." Celia pauses, then. The late-afternoon sun sinks lower behind the distant cornfield. Shadows are growing longer. When Celia looks at her father again, tears pool in her eyes—tears she fights. "*That for Elsa? This will erase Sal, somewhat,*" she nearly whispers. "*Me and Shane.*"

For a quiet moment, her father watches her struggle with those tears. "Maybe not just for Elsa, Celia."

"Right. For me, too." Celia swipes at an escaped tear. "And I struggle with *that* sometimes."

"*Ach.*" Gavin takes that blade of grass from his mouth and tosses it over the porch railing. "I don't like it. Don't like the lies." His voice drops, but is dead serious. "Those lies are a distraction as you're driving hundreds of miles *alone*. A new mother." He looks at Celia, then paces the front porch. "I'm leery," he says, sitting in a chair beside hers. "I'll do it *this* time. I'll cover for you—under the circumstances. Doing it for Shane, mostly." He reaches over and clasps Celia's arm. "But I *won't* support this secrecy going forward. This is it."

"I get it, Dad," Celia says before leaning over and hugging him. "But thank you. For this time. You know that means a lot to me."

Gavin gives a single nod. "As sad as the situation is, I'm glad you're not just going north on some whim."

"It wasn't a whim last time, and it's not a whim now."

"Well," Gavin says, somewhat at a loss. "I'll watch Aria for these few days. But I want you to rest here first. Sleep over. Have a good breakfast in the morning before you go."

"I will." Celia tucks back her hair. "You ought to know something else, Dad. Because I have to be straight with you."

"Huh. What now?"

"Shane told me *not* to come. Insisted, actually."

Again, her father looks cautiously at her. "So he has no idea you'll be there?"

"No." Celia's voice is quiet, but matter-of-fact. "He'd just try to stop me."

Gavin raises an eyebrow. Then gives a small laugh. "I'm not surprised you didn't listen. Not from what I've seen of you two."

"But I *am* a little scared going up there, Dad. I don't know what I'll find. What Shane will say."

"You sure about going, then?"

She nods. "I love him."

"Oh, I figured as much." Her father, he sits back in his chair then. Crosses his arms again and looks out over the green front lawn. "Call me when you get there tomorrow."

"I will."

"Okay." Gavin claps his hands on his legs as though about to stand—but he doesn't. "I'll go get the grill ready. Got some fresh burgers today. We'll have a little cookout."

"If you don't mind? I think I'll set the table in the kitchen. It's kind of cool outdoors for the baby." Celia reaches over and briefly squeezes her father's hand. "I'll get a bottle ready for Aria, too."

For a few minutes then—before life goes and turns on end tomorrow—they just sit there on the front porch. Neither one stands; neither one leaves. A lone robin holds on to its song as the afternoon wanes. The bird's clear melody lifts through the air. Low sunlight glints off the old red barn at the end of the street. She and her father say some quiet words about the day, the weather.

Eventually, when Celia just gives her father a sad smile, he pats her leg, silently stands and heads around back to start the grill.

thirteen

NEIGHBORLY COOKING LESSON VERSUS NEIGHBORLY date—that's the conundrum.

Closing her closet Tuesday afternoon, Elsa realizes what she did. Realizes how she answered that particular riddle.

Oh, she played it safe.

That's evident in her choice of outfit: deep tan utility jumpsuit with a long dark-olive zipper. Sure, she *zhuzhed* up the jumpsuit with a wide brown leather belt and a thick gold-link bracelet. Popped her collar and rolled up the short sleeves. Double cuffed the jumpsuit's pant legs, too, above, okay, above sleek high-heeled black pumps. Gold stud earrings glimmer beneath her brown hair—which she wears in a low chignon.

But, still. It's obvious she dressed tonight for a fun *cooking* lesson. To be neighborly.

Not for a date.

Elsa is cinched, zipped, and in ready-to-cook mode. At

her full-length mirror now, she texts her Milan friend Concetta her pasta-sauce plans with Mitch, as well as a photo of her outfit.

Concetta instantly shoots back: *A zipped-up-tight, belted jumpsuit? More like a modern-day chastity belt!*

Elsa gives a little huff, stamps a high-heeled foot—then ever so slightly tugs down that jumpsuit zipper. *Well, that's what I'm wearing to Mitch's*, Elsa types back. *No time to fuss.*

From Concetta then: *Pray tell, amica, if that ensemble drives the man wild. I want details on this cooking DATE later. (And oh yes, it's a date.)*

Elsa's not so sure about that.

Because it's obvious by *Mitch's* fashion choices that he played it safe today, too. His clothes—brown cardigan open over a loose, untucked tan V-neck tee and dark green sporty trousers—say the same thing her clothes do. Casual. Cooking lesson between neighbors. Nothing really ... *special.* Nothing date-ish.

"I know you offered to supply the aprons," Elsa says later, glancing at Mitch in his cottage kitchen. He's leaning against an old butcher-block counter. She reaches for her tote on the table. "But I'm particular about my aprons. They're all a part of the cooking ... *ambiance*, I suppose. A part of the ... *experience*."

"The *experience*," Mitch repeats, running a hand down his goatee. "Now I like the sound of that."

"Yes. Cooking is never *just* about the cooking. There's so much more going on. And I use certain aprons for certain occasions. Thus, one for you." Elsa pulls a gray half-apron from the tote. "A basic apron. It's waxed canvas, nice and sturdy. And it has a patch pocket on the front where you can keep your recipe card as you cook. Or a small notepad and pen to write notes about the meal you're preparing." She reaches into the tote again and pulls out a full denim apron. "And one for me," she says, holding it up. "Maris made this for me last year."

"Harkening back to her denim-design days?"

"Yes! She's never stopped dabbling with her denim, actually." Elsa slips the faded denim apron over her shoulders. "It even has belt loops on the front—to hang utensils that I need close at hand. So ..." She lifts his half-apron. "Here you go."

"Why thank you, Elsa," Mitch tells her, taking the half-apron she holds his way. "I'm rather enjoying this cooking lesson already."

They're quiet, then, putting on their aprons in the shabby, ready-for-reno kitchen. Quiet until Elsa meets Mitch's eyes. Meets his eyes all a-twinkle as he reaches behind his back to tie his apron, and she straightens her apron over her utility jumpsuit.

And in that quiet, connected moment, it begins. Oh, yes it does.

"So, needless to say, this apron's a favorite of mine and is well worn now," Elsa starts, well, starts *blathering*. "I've cooked *many* family recipes in it this past year, here at Stony Point. Big Sunday dinners. Meals for Jason and Maris. Special occasions—like when Jason signed on with CT-TV for *Castaway Cottage*. Kyle and Lauren's vow renewal, too," Elsa goes on, *and on*, all while reaching behind and giving her apron's threadbare ties a good hard tug before knotting them. "*And*," she continues, "we don't want to get any tomato sauce on our clothes now."

"Absolutely not," Mitch agrees, adjusting his own half-apron. He looks over his shoulder while still manipulating the apron strings—but his fingers fumble in their attempt.

"Here." Elsa hurries across the gray-painted, wood-planked floor. "Let me get that for you."

"I surely appreciate that," Mitch says as he turns around.

Gingerly, Elsa picks up the apron strings and ties a bow—keeping her touch light and quick. "There you go! Ready to cook," she says then—a little breathless—before *click-clicking* those high heels of hers straight back across the kitchen to her tote on the table. She ... well, she *collects* herself there, all while lifting out several jars of her canned tomatoes, and small plastic containers of oregano and basil.

"Did I mention Maris was actually here with the film crew today?" Mitch asks as Elsa lines up her sauce ingredients.

"Maris was?"

Mitch nods. "Carol told me when I got home from my class at the college. I guess Trent had Maris host one of the show's window segments."

"Wait. Maris ... *hosted*? What about Jason?"

"Not sure," Mitch says with a shrug. "All I know is he texted me he would be out today. But anyway, when I got home? Maris was already gone. *So* ... I proceeded on my merry way, setting things up here as I presumed would be necessary for sauce-making." Mitch nods to the counter. "Dishes, knives. Olive oil. A couple of pots on the stove. Figured *you* could use one pot, and I'd follow your lead in the other."

"Perfect." Elsa glances around the room. The cottage *is* undergoing a partial reno for *Castaway Cottage*, but the kitchen is still intact enough for cooking. The white cabinets are a little dingy. The gray-painted floor's seen better days, too. *But there's enough space at that butcher-block countertop for sauce prep.*

If they squeeze in close.

"*Hmm*," Elsa muses now, eyeing their cozy workstations. "Is your daughter around tonight? Will she be joining us?"

"Not tonight. She's actually working at Kyle's diner."

"*Carol* is? She's waitressing?"

"No, no. Her summer flowers are waning now, but she booked a fall event at the diner. It's Kyle's Harvest Night. He's serving up special early-fall recipes. Has some fall decorations." Mitch sets a couple of beat-up wooden spoons beside the stovetop. "And Carol's hawking her autumn wares on the outside patio. Picking up the end-of-summer slack."

"Wonderful! She still has flowers to cut?"

"Fall blossoms. Some black-eyed Susans. Sedum. Faded hydrangeas. Asters. Makes her bouquets in little baskets, or in tin cans wrapped with *autumn* ribbons. Why, I believe she even has some early pumpkins," Mitch tells Elsa. He returns to his prep station at the counter and continues. "Carol doesn't say much about her *winter* plans, though—which probably means she *thinks* I won't approve."

"Oh, is she looking for work? Or between jobs?"

"What she's doing, actually, is floating. Been doing that ever since she lost her mother."

"I can understand that."

"But it's been five years now, Elsa. Five years of odd jobs. Of dog-walking. And temping. And driving for rideshare services. And delivering groceries to people's doorsteps. The only constant's been that flower cart of hers."

"Well … Carol's young. In her early thirties. Maybe she's just trying to figure herself out."

"I wish I saw it your way, but I'm worried about her." Mitch goes a little quiet, then.

Elsa looks across the kitchen at him. The ceiling light's on, as are the under-cabinet lights. Cooking supplies are set out: gray pots on stove; wood spoons; knives; cutting boards; a food processor. There's no denying that … it's go time. "Oh, kids," Elsa prattles on instead. "As soon as they come along, the worry never really stops, no? Carol's lucky to have a father concerned like that. And you're *probably* worrying about nothing. She's got a lot of spunk, that girl. And I'm sure you'll … well …" Elsa clears her throat. "Well, why don't we begin?"

Begin what? is the question.

Because as onions are chopped and garlic is minced at the countertop, their elbows bump. More than once.

And as olive oil is poured into respective pots, their talk lightens.

"*His*," Mitch says, turning on the flame beneath his pot. "And *hers*." He motions to the second pot on the burner beside his.

Their arms cross then—as they reach for respective plates of the chopped onion and garlic. And they get tangled up—*again*—lifting the long-handled wooden spoons from the counter.

There's more, too. As they go at Elsa's freshly canned tomatoes, slicing them in half and scooping out the seeds? Elbows bump once more. The late-afternoon sun sets lower over Long Island Sound outside the window, too. Which inspires a *prep* break—when Mitch takes her by an arm and leads her to the living room's expansive windows overlooking the Sound.

And overlooking that fireball of a sun sinking into the sea.

Oh, then there's the wine. Back in the kitchen, Mitch opens a delicious bottle of Italian rosé and half fills two goblets. That partially poured bottle sits on the cluttered table beside now-empty canning jars and sampling spoons and napkins and a recipe card Elsa wrote out for Mitch.

But it's the laughs and easy talk that make the neighborly *cooking* lesson something more.

Especially once the prepared tomatoes and pinch of spices are added to the sautéed onions and garlic.

And once the stove flames are lowered and the spaghetti sauce simmers.

And once Elsa leans close to Mitch to look into *his* saucepot on the stove. She tells him then, her voice soft, "This has to cook for a couple of hours maybe. So the sauce can nicely thicken."

"Couple of hours, you say?" Mitch's low voice asks back.

The room gets quiet—noticeably so—until Elsa looks up at Mitch standing right there. She's close enough to see the metal pendant hanging from his two-strand rawhide choker. To reach up and brush a finger across it.

"*Well!*" she says instead, turning quickly toward the now-messy kitchen behind them. "Let me get your table cleaned up *while* that sauce simmers." She hurries across the gray-painted floor and starts bringing her empty, tomato-stained canning jars to the sink. Back and forth. *Clip-clip* go her shoes. More jars. Back and forth. Then spoons. Back and forth. *Clip-clip*, her pumps tap across the floor. "And remember to stir your sauce often," she tosses over her shoulder. "So it doesn't burn."

Mitch nods, reaches for one of the wooden spoons and turns to his bubbling pot of sauce. For a few moments, he simply stirs that tomato concoction. The sweet aroma is already filling the kitchen. The sun is dropping even lower now, casting its golden light in through the windows.

As Mitch stirs, Elsa straightens the napkins and a few potholders on the table. She sets her empty goblet beside the wine bottle still half-filled with that intoxicating rosé.

Or ... maybe it's the whole *room* that's intoxicating.

The close kitchen in the rambling old cottage.

The peeks of red-horizon-over-the-sea visible through the big windows.

The simmering, aromatic tomato sauce.

The company.

"Elsa DeLuca," Mitch says while he's at the stove. His back is still to her as he concentrates on making a *very* fine tomato sauce. Slowly and carefully, his arm is stirring those tomatoes. "I've actually already got salads put together. Didn't know if you'd stay on once the sauce was cooking," he admits, still intent on stirring. "But I'd be *awfully* pleased if you'd join me for a pasta dinner tonight."

Behind him at the table, Elsa throws a look his way—then turns back to the table. *And there's that pesky conundrum again.* Cooking lesson, date. Go home, lesson complete? Or ... stay for a romantic, seaside pasta dinner. Darn it if Concetta wasn't right.

Cooking lesson *versus* date.

Elsa does something else then, too. *Quick.* She tosses back a good swig of that Italian wine—straight from the bottle! Swallows and presses the back of her hand to a leftover drop of wine on her mouth. When Mitch glances over, she's *just* putting the wine bottle down.

But she manages a small smile, too. "Pasta dinner? I'd like that, Mitch," she tells him.

"Shall we, then?" After taking off his apron, he walks to the dining room.

Elsa follows and notices something rather sweet. The lovely white-painted dining room table is already set with two navy-colored cloth placemats. Silverware and napkins are also arranged there, as are water goblets. And the place settings? They're set side by side so that she and Mitch *sit* side by side—and face large windows. They'll have a water view as they dine. Then there's the centerpiece beneath the white chandelier—a navy glass vase holding late-summer golden marigolds. And are those photo albums? It looks like a couple of them are stacked on the side.

"Pictures?" Elsa asks. "We're looking at some family photos?"

Mitch nods. "Maybe after our salad. While the pasta water boils. Thought you might help me pick out some pictures for the rowboat shelf I'm having made."

"I remember you telling me about that. The old boat

your father-in-law went out in, searching for that little lost Sailor boy."

"That's right."

"How incredible that the forgotten rowboat will be back in this cottage. Have you and Carol narrowed down photos for it yet?"

"Hardly. Which is why I need your opinion. But first, please …" Mitch sweeps his hand toward the dining room table. "Make yourself at home."

Elsa takes it all in now—the set table, the view outside—then looks at Mitch just as he pulls out a white chair with a navy plaid cushion, steps back and motions for her to sit.

"Oh, wait," he says, stopping her. "Let me help you with your apron."

―⁓―

Cliff employs some fancy footwork.

Tuesday evening, he's light on his rented shoes as he relaxes his grip, thunders his spinning bowling ball down the alley and scores a strike. All around him, pins are clattering; balls hum down polished wood. His son, Denny, has a go at it, too. Just the two of them play this lane. Because it's decision night. And they're on a mission: Consider joining an existing league? Or don't commit and bowl just for the heck of it.

So there's no stress of competing within a league tonight. It's just easy fun. Just bowling, and sitting in those contoured plastic seats. Just having a beer; a side of nachos, too.

But it's busy here. Fall leagues *are* starting up. Nearly every lane is taken. Men, women. A high school team. Some bowlers are in serious league uniforms of reds, royal blues, greens. Each bowling tee is imprinted with fierce and quirky team names. Oh, the uniformed teams are ready to roll. Other bowlers are casual—in sweats or jeans. The competitiveness, and banter, and laughs are everywhere.

Cliff lifts his bowling ball from the return rack. While focusing on the ten pins again, Denny says something from a seat behind him. Problem is, Cliff misses it over the sound of crashing pins and booming ball drops. "You say something?" Cliff asks, turning around. His son's sitting there in his jeans, a light sweater and rented bowling shoes.

Denny nods, finishes a cheesy nacho, and repeats his question around a mouthful of that food. "You pop the question yet? To your lady, Elsa?"

"No." Bowling ball raised up to beneath his chin, Cliff looks at Denny a second more before turning back to those pins. He aims and gets a running start, but his stride is messed up this time. He's off-kilter. And when he rolls that bowling ball, it's the first *gutter* ball of the night. It barely wobbles down to the finish line, not even *close* to hitting a pin. Turning back to Denny then, he tells him, "Nope, my proposal plan was an *epic* fail." Pulling off his bowling glove, Cliff hitches his head to the ten still-standing pins. "Just like that."

The rest, the story of the Bradfords' date night undermining his proposal to Elsa ten days ago—that's right, he knows the exact number of days—gets told later at their bowling-alley dinner. Sitting at a small, metal-edged table, Cliff lays out his marriage woes over chicken tenders and curly fries. Denny pushes him, though, over his chili cheeseburger and tater tots, to try proposing again.

"Maybe you want to meet her first, son," Cliff suggests.

"Wish I could," Denny says. "But we're headed into fall landscape season. Overseeing lots of outdoor spaces in Addison—from the fountain green to Sycamore Square. It's a busy time … and *you're* procrastinating."

"Am not."

"Either that or you're losing your nerve."

"Won't fight you on that one."

"No worries, Pop. I'll meet Elsa once she says yes. Just don't wait too long," Denny cautions, raising his beer in a toast. "She seems like a keeper," he adds before they get up and bowl a second game.

With Jason in Maine, it's a good time to visit her aunt.

After parking her golf cart in Elsa's driveway, Maris knocks at the inn's door late that afternoon. She's still in the fitted black denim sheath and Western-style boots she wore filming for *Castaway Cottage* earlier. So maybe her aunt would like to go *out* for a bite to eat—since she's dressed for it.

Again, Maris knocks at the door. But there's no answer. She'd really like to tell Elsa about Shane, too. How he lost his friend, and how Jason went up there to check on him. "*Maybe she's in the yard*," Maris whispers, then walks along the side of the inn to the back. "Aunt Elsa?" she calls out from the veranda. Her eyes take in the grounds: the Adirondack chairs set out; the Sea Garden further in the back, near Elsa's stone garden shed; the sweeping dune grasses, where a secret path leads to the beach.

But not a single sign of Elsa. She's not bent over in the garden. Not watering her hydrangea bushes. Not chalking a message on her inn-spiration walkway.

There's not one sign of her around.

Maris sits on the veranda for a minute. Maybe Elsa stopped by a neighbor's. Or took a beach walk and is on her way back. "*Hmm*," Maris says. She walks around the side of the inn and spots Celia's cottage beyond the yard. But Celia's car is gone. Is Elsa out with her? After checking her watch, Maris gets in her golf cart and heads for home.

But she *really* feels like talking with her aunt. So she gives Elsa a little time. Hangs the tin sun Elsa gave her Saturday. There's a nice spot for it right outside the glass slider to the deck. Maris taps a thin nail into a weathered shingle there. Carefully then, she hooks the pretty painted sun with its gold wavy sunrays on that nail. Because seriously, can't they all use a little extra sunshine sometimes?

With that done, she feeds Maddy before heading in her golf cart to the inn again. Forty-five minutes have passed. It's well into the dinner hour now. Surely her aunt will be back.

But she's not.

Maris knocks on the side kitchen door, then goes around to the inn's main door and knocks there. No answer at either place. So this time? This time Maris sits on the porch swing, reaches into her purse and pulls out her cell phone. By hook or by crook, she's going to track Elsa down.

Elsa looks over her shoulder at Mitch standing behind her at his dining room table.

His beautifully set dining room table, where salads are waiting to be had. Where more wine is waiting to be sipped. Where the sun is *not* waiting to set outside the windows. Mitch is fussing with the full apron Elsa's wearing. She feels him trying to maybe lift it off with the strings still secured.

"Really, Mitch. I didn't think I tied my apron strings *that* tight!"

Mitch's hands move to those apron strings. Elsa feels him fussing with them, giving a tug or two. "Sheesh, Elsa. They're *really* knotted." His voice is vague as he's somewhat distracted by her knotted-up apron.

So she waits.

Which is when her cell phone dings with a text message. As Mitch tugs and twists her apron strings, Elsa precariously leans to the side. Her arm stretches toward her tote hanging on a chairback. A little more leaning in those black high heels and—*yes*—she lifts out the dinging phone.

"*Huh*," Mitch is quietly saying. He's bent close, and really focused on the task. "I'd hate to have to *cut* these to free you. Being that this is your *favorite* apron."

"It *is*." Still holding her phone, Elsa twists around to see over her shoulder again. "And the strings on this one *are* finicky. Because they're a little threadbare from so much use. Which is why I gave an extra tug before." Turning back to her phone, she silently reads the message from Maris now: *Have dinner with me? I'm waiting on your porch. Not around?*

"I guess you *did* tug them, darlin'," Mitch says with another string-pull. "They're tied extra tight. Were you, uh, a little tense about coming here?"

"What? No!" Elsa glances at the set table again. At those delicious-looking salads. At the lavender sky over the steel-gray water outside. "Oh, we'll just leave the apron on, Mitch. I *really* don't want the salads to sit long." Again, she looks at Maris' text.

"Nonsense. You can't *dine* wearing this apron. You won't *relax*." He reaches over for a fork on the table. "This'll do the trick, I'm sure of it."

Elsa peeks over her shoulder again to observe this untying procedure. Mitch, standing close, looks at her. Their faces are inches apart. Heck, Elsa could reach out and touch the silvery whiskers of that goatee. His easy smile can't be missed, either. Nor can the few moments' silence when they just lock eyes.

"I'll try sliding one of the fork's teeth into the *middle* of that knot," Mitch practically whispers. He looks down and does just that, wiggling the fork back and forth. "*Wait ... Wait*," he says under his breath, still fork-wiggling. "Shouldn't be long, Elsa, before these strings are loosened and I get them untied."

Oh, she thinks. *Heaven help her if the whole damn thing doesn't turn her on*. Mitch with those prying fork tines working her apron strings as she's snug up against him. Barely breaking from her reverie, Elsa—phone limp in hand—reads the next dinging message.

Elsa? is all Maris typed. She seems to *really* want an answer.

So Elsa obliges. She thumb-types a quick message back to her. *Visiting a neighbor right now. Kind of ... tied up. Talk tomorrow?*

The Visitor

A couple of hours later, Elsa's back at the inn. After changing into her turquoise caftan, she sits on the nautical-striped couch in the living room. Her hair is down. A cup of hot tea is on the end table. Her laptop is beside her.

But she just sips that tea for now. In front of her, lobster buoys hang on either side of the driftwood mantel. Two old rowboat oars are mounted with ropes over that mantel. The night is quiet. The hour, late.

Finally, she reaches for her laptop. "Every time I write you, my sea of troubles grows," Elsa quietly says, then clicks into her email and begins typing. Without hesitation. Without restraint.

Concetta, Concetta, her fingers quickly tap out. *I so badly want to pick up the phone and call you! But it's after 3 AM there in Italy. Anyway, you know it's been a crazy week here. First, Cliff's spontaneous Vespa ride and trailer-overnight. Now? This!* Elsa's fingers hover—typing paused—as she simply sighs. *Just got in from Mitch's cottage on the beach tonight. We were making spaghetti sauce,* she finally goes on. *Because you know what happens when you have surplus tomatoes. You stick them on anybody you know! Tonight, it was Mitch. And you were so right, Concetta. The evening leaned toward date. Because let me tell you—much more than tomatoes and sauce were simmering in that kitchen!*

"You're not kidding," Elsa tells herself.

Mitch had salads already made. Sliced, crusty bread, too. Wine. Oh, he knew we weren't going to just make sauce. Another pause before Elsa's fingers get typing again. *Hell, I knew it, too. Everything started out innocently enough, though. As we waited for the pasta water to boil, Mitch wanted help choosing photos to display in his renovated cottage. That was all fine. But, Concetta? Things first took a turn when my apron ties were stuck in a knot! Because once he loosened them, well, we both unloosened!*

"Did we ever," Elsa's monologue goes on as she thinks back on the evening.

On the grand, dimly lit cottage.

On that misty moon rising over the dark sea.

On the delicious food on the table, the fine wine, the talk and laughs.

Waving off some cozy feeling that overcomes her now, she resumes her typing.

I stayed for dinner ... and dessert. Not a food dessert, mind you, but a big smoocheroo. We were sitting close at the table, with the dishes pushed aside. And the wine poured. And that one big smooch melted into several more. I'm still fanning myself, actually. Well. It's either the heat of the kisses' passion getting to me—or it's the devil's wings beating hot on my shoulder.

A funny thing happens as Elsa wraps up her email. She doesn't feel as lighthearted as when she began it. *What am I doing?* she asks herself. And wonders why, for the life of her, she can't answer that question.

fourteen

EARLY WEDNESDAY MORNING, JASON'S SITTING on a low stone wall somewhere in rural Maine. He's far from the coast. In the Atlantic Ocean mist earlier, Shane drove his pickup along the shoreline before turning onto winding, forested roads. Eventually, he veered down a packed-dirt road nearly invisible to the naked eye—a road seemingly leading only deeper into the woods.

Until they came to a partial clearing. It's where they sit now, while having breakfast. They'd gotten out of the truck, brought cups of hot coffee and a sack of fresh-baked doughnuts, and settled on that stone wall. Some of the heavy stones are loose; moss and lichen cover others; tangled vines overtake entire sections of the wall. But he and Shane found a clear space, set their food on flat stones and dig into breakfast.

Jason downs a fruit-filled, powder-sprinkled doughnut,

drinks some coffee and starts on another. "What the hell *is* this delicacy?" he asks, ripping that second doughnut in half. It's all dark chocolate with a coffee glaze topped with toffee sprinkles.

"Mocha crunch," Shane says around a mouthful of some colossal iced cinnamon roll.

Well, the amazing Maine doughnuts are one thing. But the shocking *sight* before him is another.

A sight Jason can't stop looking at while he dines on this outdoor breakfast feast.

Hell, he'd thought he'd seen it all—until now.

An old abandoned mansion rises among the towering pine trees. The house is in ruins. Its shingles are more black than silver. All the paint—door trim, window trim—is peeling off in long curls, leaving behind mostly exposed and weathered wood. And in those windows with fading trim? If the glass panes aren't broken or gone, the tall double-hung windows have twenty-eight small-paned tops over plain lowers. More paned windows look out from the wood-shingled dormer-style roof. The house has strategically placed L-shaped additions—all of it over a massive stone foundation, which is also crumbling and lichen covered.

Yet the entire structure is a stunning work of art—soaring and expansive and imposing—even more so as it holds on in its abandoned demise.

While Jason tips up his take-out coffee cup and finishes the brew, he still eyes the house. Hell, if Trent wants a filmed segment to make this Maine trip worthwhile, this is surely the ticket.

"You ready?" Jason asks Shane.

Shane sets down his coffee, picks up the camera Jason brought and stands then. "That I am."

―――

Jason straightens his tan blazer over dark jeans and a long-sleeve button-down. When he takes his place in front of this abandoned old homestead, Shane gets that camera rolling.

"If you think of the state of Maine," Jason begins to the camera, "you might conjure images of its rugged coastline. Images of lobster boats. You might know that Maine's the largest of the New England states. That it's heavily forested, and the state animal is the moose. But there's another side to this state, too. One abandoned to time, and evolution, and nature itself." As he says it, Shane pans to the large but dilapidated mansion behind Jason.

Together then, they slowly walk up the steps to a pillared porch leading to the entryway. Jason ventures inside. Large windows allow in enough sunlight for Shane to continue filming. They tour an old kitchen, its floor slanted. A living room with the furniture left behind. Grit crunches beneath their booted feet. Upholstered chairs are blanketed in dust and cobwebs. Mold has taken over a large piano. There's a massive stone fireplace, partially caved in. A once-lavish dining room looks fitting for only spirits now—the grime-coated chairs and table still covered with place settings of dishes and tarnished silverware.

And everywhere they walk, the dampness is bone-chilling in this big decrepit house in the woods.

"The detritus of a life abandoned is within these walls," Jason explains to the rolling camera. "A family walked away from here for something else, leaving maybe when a logging camp closed, or the village became too remote and was cut off from civilization. The house itself was too remote to even *attempt* to remove its contents." The shadowy tour continues, with Shane filming the relics of furniture and dusty lamps and faded kitchenware left behind. As Jason narrates, he's also careful of his step—especially walking unstable floors with his prosthetic leg. He scopes out the spaces before entering any of the rooms.

Finally going outside again, Jason looks back in through the open front entranceway. That cavernous remnant of a home long abandoned really gets to him.

"Abandoned to ruin, and to destruction by nature, and to a bygone era. The entire historical house and its architecture? A lifestyle long lost."

But before he wraps this segment for *Castaway Cottage*, Shane stops him—and stops filming.

"Wait, *wait*," Shane says, setting down the camera. He's looking past Jason and squinting through the shadows to the inside of the house. His feet crunch over glass pieces as he hurries through that open doorway once more. "There's something over there I want to check out."

So Jason follows, watching as Shane tips back an old framed painting leaning against a dusty, wallpaper-peeling wall. The painting is of a wooded landscape. Though the scene beneath the filth covering it is hard to decipher, one thing's apparent. A little bit of a house—one that looks very much like this actual house—is visible through dark trees in the image.

Shane hefts up the large painting. "Taking this with me."

"Seriously?"

"Yeah. It's just going to rot here." Shane holds it at arm's length and eyes the framed artwork. Brushes dirt off the possibly gold frame—it's hard to tell *what's* beneath the dirt coating it. Then he tucks the painting beneath his arm and carefully walks over old plaster fallen from the walls. Walks around fallen furniture covered in grime, too. "I'll have the painting refurbished and hang it in my house."

Once they're back outside, Shane picks up the camera again so that Jason can close out his segment for Trent.

"Rolling," Shane quietly says.

In the front yard, Jason positions himself beside a lichen-covered stone planting urn. That abandoned shingled mansion rises up behind him. Some of the structure is only a skeleton in the parts where walls have caved in to time ... and rain ... and wind.

Jason half turns and takes in the sight of the sadly derelict, yet striking, house. "Haunting in so many ways," he says to the camera. "And the absolute *most* castaway cottage I'm sure I'll ever see."

Shane fiddles with the camera a moment longer after he pans out. "And that's a wrap," he calls, then gives the camera to Jason.

Before leaving, they head back to that crumbling stone wall to pick up their things—breakfast bags and napkins, a backpack Jason used for his filming gear. Trees rise around them. The gray stone wall weaves right into the woods, as far as Jason can see.

"I'm sure that wall once bordered the whole grand property here," Jason remarks. He looks from the wall settled into leaves and brush, to the long-empty shingled house.

"Still grand, don't you think?" Shane asks, motioning to the practically falling-down structure and timbers and foundation stones just fading into the woods. "In its own way?"

"Absolutely." As he says it, Jason turns from the house to Shane. And it's obvious. This outing was good for Shane. Gave him a purpose. Filming this segment actually kept Shane's head above water as he's still dealing with the sudden loss of his friend. "Thanks, Bradford. Really needed this for Trent," Jason tells him as they walk to Shane's truck now. "What a rad spot," he says, glancing at the house once again. "Pretty wild, man ... So you said you came out here with my brother—back in the day?"

"I did. A few times." Shane keeps walking, his booted feet crunching over sticks and leaves and stones. "Did some exploring at abandoned houses here in Maine. Abandoned buildings. A little chapel. A store. That's when I come across my paintings."

"No shit. All those pieces of artwork hanging in your house?"

"Yep. All came from places like this. Neil was my accomplice some of those times, too."

They walk away then, but Jason looks back—one last time—at the dreary abandoned mansion behind them in the woods. You could almost miss it, the way the house's gray shingles blend right in with the trees and stone walls and shadows of the forest.

And hell, if he squints just right into a glint of sunshine, can't he picture Neil exploring here—maybe sweeping brush aside, or stepping over fallen timbers—and loving the history of it all. The *story* of it all.

Jason can almost hear his brother's voice in the whisper of leaves and pine needles rustling in the soft breeze.

fifteen

Shane was glad to help.

He knows what a haul it is getting to Maine from Stony Point. Knows that Jason blew off his job to get here. Ditched work to be sure Shane was all right. So filming a *Castaway Cottage* segment at an abandoned Maine mansion was the least Shane could do to thank his old beach friend.

Now they're both packing up at Shane's house. As one goes out with Jason's things, the other comes in. They carry duffels, a cooler, a toiletries bag. Jason swaps his tan work blazer for his black zip sweatshirt, then hangs the blazer on a hook in the SUV. Anything he brought is packed back in that vehicle before he hits the road again.

Shane heads in now to grab the forearm crutches in the kitchen. Jason's thermos is on the counter; a fresh pot of coffee is brewing to fill it for the ride home. His cell phone is charging on the counter, too. Right as Shane picks up the crutches, that cell phone rings. With a quick glance, Shane can see it's Maris calling, so he answers for Jason.

"Maris," he says into the phone.

"Shane?" she asks back.

"Yeah. Your husband is loading up his vehicle. About to take off."

"Oh, okay, I was just checking in. But Shane? I'm glad you answered, actually," Maris goes on. "I wanted to tell you how very sorry I was to hear about your friend Shiloh."

"I know. It's a tough time here. For his family, especially. The town."

"I'm sure. But how're *you* doing?"

"I'm okay," Shane tells her. "Rough few days, though. You know, with the shock of it all."

"Understandably. Losing someone sudden like that. It's so sad. And hard."

"Well listen, Mare." Shane looks toward the open front door for Jason. "I know it wasn't easy for Jason to get up here. With work and, hell, with his whole life put on hold. And I won't soon forget it, what he did. Really got me through okay."

As he's talking, Shane hears Jason coming back inside. The front door closes; there are footsteps. At the same time, there's Maris' soft voice, too. Words assuring Shane that they'll be thinking of him these next few days. Words asking when he'll be back on the water. More words telling him to stay safe.

When Jason walks in the kitchen, Shane wraps up with Maris and gives Jason his phone. As Jason talks, Shane finally grabs up those forearm crutches and brings them out to the SUV. The morning sun is warming up the day and burning off a lingering ocean mist. He hears the chugging engine of a lobster boat moving through the distant harbor. A seagull swoops low, calling a plaintive cry as it does. The sea air is thick with salt. All sensations that comfort Shane in their familiarity. In their sense of home for him.

As he reaches for the open liftgate of Jason's SUV, though, there's something else.

Another send-off is coming.

Hell, just a few weeks back it was all he and Jason could do to not utter venomous words to each other. Just a few weeks back, Shane stood on Ted Sullivan's deck to talk some sense into Jason about his faltering marriage. Even when Jason told him to get his sorry ass out of there, Shane persisted. Told Jason to hold on to his marriage, to his solid life. Told him, *Don't fucking blow it.* Lord knows, Shane did just that a few times in his life—and regrets it still.

So after he closes that SUV liftgate, he shakes off a feeling. Stands there and breathes that salt air that supposedly cures what ails you.

Yep, he's going to miss Jason.

Miss having a friend around.

⁓

Jason pockets his cell phone, then lifts the coffeepot. As he's carefully filling his thermos for the trip home, Shane walks into the kitchen.

"Time to go," Shane says, spinning around a kitchen chair and sitting with his hands clasped over the chairback.

"Ten minutes, guy." Jason looks over his shoulder, then fills a mug from the counter with what's left of the coffee. "I'll have a quick cup on your deck first."

"Okay. That's decent." Shane stands, digs his harmonica out of a kitchen drawer and follows him out through the back screen door.

They talk some, then. Jason sits at the patio table and works on his coffee. Shane walks over to the white-planked bench built between the deck railings. Jason can see that the bench is positioned to give a clear view of the distant harbor waters.

"You all set for Shiloh's wake later this afternoon?" Jason asks.

"Yeah." Shane leans forward and drags closer an old wooden lobster trap. "I'll meet up with some of the guys there. Crewmates and shit." He props a booted foot on that lobster trap now, leans into his harmonica and lets a short riff rise. "You know, Shi actually helped make this bench here," Shane says then, patting the bench seat. "A few years back."

"That right?"

Shane nods. "Between lobster runs one summer, I built this seat plank by plank. Planned out its location. Its angle facing the water there." He points his harmonica toward the harbor. A few sailboats float in the morning sun. Beyond the distant docks, a rocky ledge is shaded by sugar maples. "Shiloh stopped by sometimes that summer. Swung a hammer for an hour or two. Bullshit over a beer. Helped paint the bench, too." Again, Shane lifts his harmonica and gets a sad riff going, the notes pulsating in the sea air. "I'll be spending some of the next few hours right here. On this very bench."

"Helluva nice one."

"And it's got a real purpose today. Sitting here? An hour

at a time, I'll try to make sense of it all. Of my life. Of the people in and out of it. An hour at a time, guy. Like you told me."

"That's all you can do. And hey, nothing like getting answers from the sea," Jason says, hitching his head to that harbor and the Atlantic Ocean beyond.

"No shit." Shane looks out at the blue waters then leans into his harmonica again—sending a soulful wail that way.

"You know," Jason goes on. "I remember one time, my brother was sitting out on the bluff back at Stony Point. Just sitting there all morning, watching Long Island Sound from my father's old stone bench."

"Neil was." Shane hooks his arm over that leg propped on the old lobster trap.

"Right. So I eventually went out and sat with him on that bench there. And you know what he asked me?"

"No."

Jason gives a short laugh. "If I knew the first thing God did when he made the earth. Any guesses?"

"Me?" Shane turns up his hands. "Not sure."

"My brother told me God got the seas moving *first*. That the waters of the earth had to be flowing before God could continue on to create sunlight and creatures and trees. And night and day. Life itself."

"I could get that," Shane says, glancing toward the distant sea. "The power of water."

"Neil said it was all about motion. God's way of *getting* things moving. Get those seas flowing to start the tides— the rhythm of the planet. Once that happened, God could move on. And you, my friend, have to do that, too," Jason says as he stands to leave. He walks over to Shane and slaps his shoulder. "Keep moving, Shane. You'll feel better that way after losing your friend."

Shane nods, then stands. Pockets his harmonica and leans on the deck railing. "Keep moving. Ain't that the truth."

"My drug of choice, anyway. Throwing myself into work. So stay busy," Jason says, standing there on the deck. Breathing the pungent air here. "Talk to people. Talk to *Celia*."

"I will." Shane turns around then. "Thanks, man. For everything. And I'll be busy enough, don't worry," he says as they step inside for Jason's thermos, then go out to his SUV in the driveway. "Captain's headed out again on Friday. Texted me and the boys to be ready. Got to set those traps. Haul those pots."

"That's good, man. That's good."

"Yeah, I know. Right back at it on the lobster boat."

Jason leans against his SUV a minute and just listens as Shane tells him his plans. Tells him his way of getting through the week. An hour at a time.

"After the funeral and all that? Hell, I'll work out the loss," Shane says when Jason opens the SUV driver's door. "Work out my head, right on the Atlantic."

Shane backs up a few steps as Jason climbs into his SUV and rolls down the driver-side window.

"Sorry I can't stay," Jason tells him as he puts on his sunglasses. "In another life? Hell, I'd go to that wake, the funeral."

"Enough that you got yourself up here." Shane salutes him and backs up another step.

Jason nods, then pulls out of the gravel driveway. His tires crunch over the stones. The sun glares off his windshield.

Watching, Shane shields his eyes, then gives a wave before turning to go inside.

"Yo, Bradford!" Jason yells a few moments later.

Shane turns around and steps closer. He watches again as Jason's pulling over roadside and getting out. The vehicle's open-door alarm is dinging as Jason reaches back in, stretching across the front seat for *something*.

"Heads up, you son of a bitch!" As Jason calls it out, he also whips Shane's red *Rockport* Frisbee across the front lawn and straight toward him.

And Shane does it, damn it. He squints into the bright morning sun while running after that spinning Frisbee for all he's worth. He barely catches it in a good leap, and laughs, too, as Jason drives off—his tires spinning some on the gritty pavement.

sixteen

TWO DAYS HAVE PASSED.

Two days since Maris has done any writing. The last time she walked across the backyard, opened the old wood-planked door and stepped into Neil's musty fishing shack was Monday.

After Friday's deer incident.

After her and Jason's bed-in on Saturday.

After all their friends crashed the house that day.

After their moose head was stolen.

After Maris got caught in a cloudburst Sunday.

After Jason tenderly towel-dried her off.

And *everything* that happened in those prior days fueled her writing Monday.

But by Wednesday morning? There's a different emotion in the air. *She* feels different—ever since Shane's desperate phone call Monday night. And ever since Jason made the trip north. Ever since he filled Maris in on what happened.

Oh, emotions run the gamut. How quickly life can turn on its heel. As sure as the earth spins on its axis, so do moods. So does state of mind. And Maris wants to inject some of that feeling—that emotional volatility—into the *Driftline* passage she last wrote.

She rereads those paragraphs. Her characters are holed up in the last-standing cottage on the beach. A hurricane is in full swing, roaring right outside the boarded-up windows. Seawater sloshes beneath the cottage-on-stilts. The wind whistles. The night is dark.

And a hurricane party is getting underway. The characters are settling in the candlelit living room. A hot-dog roast is happening at the fireplace. A joint is being passed around. Laughs are being had.

But the scene needs something more.

There needs to be a dark undercurrent in the room. The good times kicking in must be laced with danger. With some fear countering the carefree party vibe. Maybe it's a fear that the cottage will be washed right off its stilts. *Something.*

"Okay, girl," Maris says to Maddy now. The German shepherd's lying at the propped-open shack door and gnawing on a rawhide bone. Maris crouches down and gives the dog's head a rub. "Jason's coming home today, but I've got to get some work done first. Okay?"

The dog's happy tail slaps the floor with that little bit of attention.

"All right, then." Standing and heading to her laptop, Maris stops at one of Neil's dusty baskets on a shelf. She lifts out a few salt-coated seashells and shards of sea glass, then sprinkles the pieces around her manuscript notes.

Lights the tarnished hurricane lantern for atmosphere, too. Hangs her lacy cardigan on her chairback.

Rereads her Monday passage.

"*No, no,*" she whispers while deleting several paragraphs. Tension needs to be heightened in this scene. So after flipping Jason's pewter hourglass, Maris raises her hands to the keyboard. Channeling the past few days' angst, she begins typing ...

It's quiet as they wait for dinner now. Quiet except for the wind howling outside the plywood-covered windows. There's also the sound of splashing waves rolling in beneath the elevated cottage on the beach. That's a sound she still hasn't gotten used to. It unnerves her with the thought that the whole cottage might get washed out to sea. Another one of the guys saunters in and lands on the couch, too. He takes a hit of that joint going around the room. Right about then, the fireplace chef puts a few of the roasted hot dogs on a plate.

"That burned enough for you?" he asks, holding the plate out toward the woman still sitting cross-legged by the hearth.

"No," she says, shaking her head. "I like them ... charred."

"What about you, then?" the chef asks, standing and meeting her eye instead.

Walking to him, she holds up her glass. "Not right now. I'm drinking my wine."

"Okay, princess."

Princess? She dips her royal fingers into the dark wine and spritzes him with the liquor—right before he starts toasting the rolls.

"Any of that wine left?" one of the guys on the couch asks into the shadows.

She turns that way. "No. I killed the last bottle."

A clap of thunder rumbles outside. More seawater sloshes beneath the cottage, too. In the candlelit room, the sounds seem even more ominous. It feels like those roiling waters are reaching right up to the other side of the floorboards. She can almost feel the violent splashing beneath her feet. And there's that whistle again. The mighty wind is picking up speed, blowing debris—branches, leaves—against the cottage's shingled walls.

But another sudden noise gets her to actually jump. She squints through the shadowy room when the front door slams open against the inside wall. Someone's practically falling over as he comes in with the driving rain. He's got on a slicker with the hood pulled low over his head and face. The guys on the couch look back at him.

"Thought you left," one of them says. "Took off for good."

"Nah." The drenched guy manages to push the door closed against that wind. "Got us some liquor. Keep the party going, you know?"

"Right on, man," the hot-dog chef calls out.

The other guy on the couch stands and turns to face the rain-splattered punk. "Seriously? More alcohol?"

"Yeah."

"From where?"

"Pilfered it from the cottage three doors down." He holds up a few bottles wrapped in fishing net.

"Stole it? How'd you get in the cottage?" the other couch guy asks, standing in the dark and reaching for the netted booze.

The thief swipes rainwater off his face. "Jimmied the lock," he says. Funny, though. He's not looking at the guy bringing the liquor back to the living room.

No. As he says the words, and for a long moment afterward, he's looking through the shadows at only her—standing there as still as he is. Finally, he silently hitches his soaking-wet head toward the kitchen.

But she doesn't move. There's no denying, too, that she has only seconds to decide.

"*Oh, isn't that the way?*" Maris asks herself, sitting back and reading her own words. She's thinking of Shane's fraught phone call Monday night, too.

Thinking of Jason's quick decision to go and check up on their friend.

Thinking that you sometimes only have a moment to make up your mind.

Thinking of how a split-second decision like that can surely be one to change someone's life.

Nodding then, Maris lifts her hands and types her character's decision.

Wednesday morning, Celia's sitting on her father's front porch in Addison. It's early still; sunlight shimmers over the distant cornfield. The September day will be another warm one. But she has on a knit shrug over a dark-olive T-shirt maxi dress—for the trip north in her car. Her woven leather satchel is on the floor beside her, too. Painfully hard as it is to leave the baby, she's ready.

All Celia wants to do is go.

To leave.

To get on the highway.

To get to Shane.

THE VISITOR

But first, this. A bit of a front for Elsa so that she doesn't suspect anything.

With one arm holding Aria on her lap, Celia's other hand holds up her cell phone. She focuses it on the baby, too, during the video chat.

"I'm going to put together some things from my staging shed here later. For my class starting up soon," Celia lies to Elsa—instead of saying she'll be spending the next five hours behind the wheel of her car. That she'll be driving to see the man she's in love with.

"Have to get a birthday gift for my neighbor's daughter, too. Do a little shopping," Celia goes on—instead of saying half her closet is packed in her trunk. That she wasn't sure what the Maine weather will be for Shiloh's funeral. That the *only* shopping she'll be doing is maybe for flowers for his family.

Elsa listens, and coo-coos to her precious granddaughter, Aria. Tells her how pretty the polka-dot bow looks in her hair. That she misses her. The baby gurgles and smiles at the sound of her nonna's voice.

The whole time, though, Celia's doing something else. While chatting with Elsa, she's keeping an eye on the driveway. Her father should be back *any* second after gassing up her loaded car. Shifting Aria on her lap, Celia searches beyond the yard for any sign of him.

And when she sees her car approaching further down the street, Celia lifts Aria's little hand and waves it at Elsa's face on the phone screen. And says *bye-bye* when the car turns in the driveway. And when her father gets out of the car, Celia blows Elsa kisses to end the video call.

Lies, lies to Elsa.

More and more lies.

All while keeping a happy face to not raise any suspicion.

―⁓―

"Out of control," Cliff says. He steps back while eyeing the guard shack. Peel-and-stick paint swatches cover it.

"It's not out of control," Nick answers. "It's an organized grid."

"More like grid*lock*."

"No, boss." Nick leads Cliff around to the side of the guard shack. "Look. Blues are on front. Here, on the side, are greens and grays. And on the other side," he goes on, heading that way, "we have browns and wild cards."

"Wild cards?" Cliff tips up his *Commissioner* cap and studies the various paint color swatches stuck on the far side of the shack.

"Yeah, boss. People here are *into* it. They're actually dropping off extra paint swatches they have at their cottages. You have reds, there. A couple of yellows. And how about that beige? It's called *Summer Sand*. With maybe some dark brown shutters? Pretty sweet, no?"

Cliff shakes his head. "Like I said, out of control."

"But there's a system to it." Nick walks back to his guard station across the street and eyes the multicolored shack from a distance. "This paint color is a big decision, boss. The guard shack is the *first* thing your eyes see when you enter this beach community. So I'm keeping tabs, too."

"Tabs?"

"Sure. Because when people drive by, let me tell you, they *give* their opinions. It's like we're putting the color

THE VISITOR

choice to the vote. I was thinking that we can then take the *most* popular colors and paint bigger sections for the final tally."

"And which colors would those be?" Cliff asks as Matt drives up and pulls his car over.

"Mixed bag for now," Nick says. "Little of this, some of that." He salutes Matt, too. "Hey, Officer."

Matt gets out of his car. He's dressed in full state police uniform. "Put me on Team Navy," he tells Nick.

"What?" Cliff walks over and takes Nick's clipboard from him. "We have … *teams*?"

"Why not? Some people even want to get a wager going and place bets on their color."

"But that's gambling, Nicholas." Cliff shoves the clipboard back at him and turns to Matt. He's stepping closer to the shack for a better look. "Listen, Matt," Cliff says, following after him. "If you're on a team, that means you help paint once the decision's made."

"Sure, man." Matt tips his state police hat at Cliff, then turns back to his idling car. "I'm on my way to work now, but sign me up for weekend painting!" he calls out.

"On it!" Nick calls back, flipping to a new page on his clipboard.

As Matt drives under the trestle, another vehicle pulls in—this one a sedan.

"Hey, Walter," Nick says.

Walter rolls down his window and squints at the guard shack across the street. "I like that ocean-blue color. Third one down, on the left. Looks like the color of my cottage."

"All *right*," Nick notes down. "Color-coordinating the shades of blue with your home."

"Oh, boy," Cliff mutters. "Not sure if we're opening a can of paint—or a can of Stony Point worms."

⁓

After sitting alone outside on his deck bench for an hour or so, Shane goes inside.

And looks around.

And has a drink of water.

And walks to the front door.

And listens to … nothing. Nothing but quiet.

He finally lands in the kitchen, where he lifts that hefty painting he stole this morning. Setting it on his table, he carefully dabs a clean rag over the painting's frame. The soft swish of that rag is the only sound in his house now. There's no more talking with Jason. No food bags being dug into. No refrigerator opening and closing. No footsteps, or Maris ringing up Jason's phone.

There's only the rag sound—which is just a whisper, really, as Shane's hand works the fabric over the artwork. Bits of gold show through where some of the grime comes off the painting's frame. He uses a second clean rag to gently wipe the canvas itself. Though the landscape oil painting *looks* dark, he knows from past experience that it's not. Years of accumulated neglect obscure it with dust and dampness. Some of his most beautiful framed landscapes started out dark and dreary beneath the dirt. But once cleaned and restored, they're the most captivating.

So he just sits there at his kitchen table, checks the watch Jason gave him, and works the rags on the stolen painting. When another hour passes, Shane sets the painting aside, stands and walks through his house again. Sunlight comes in through the windows. The mail truck delivers his mail. An occasional car drives by. But he ends up in his bedroom, where he draws the blinds before lying down on his bed and closing his eyes for an hour or two. By then, it'll be time to shower and dress for Shiloh's wake later in the afternoon.

⁓

Kyle stands behind the big stove in his diner.

Good thing, too. Because the orders come steady from the waitresses. It's going to be a busy Wednesday lunch hour. He spins the order carousel for the next meal in line. A tuna melt on grilled whole-grain bread with tomato and American cheese.

Before getting that going, though, he steps away, wipes his hands on his chef apron and looks out into the diner. It's crowded, but no familiar faces are at the counter today.

No Jason—who was here Monday morning to start his workweek with a cinnamon cruller.

No Shane—who stopped in a few times last week. Most notably on Sunday morning after they hung that moose head at Elsa's. Over eggs and bacon here at the diner, he and Shane couldn't stop yakking about how they got away with stealing that damn mammal.

After giving a last look around at the tables and booths now, Kyle heads to the big stove again. Everyone's back to their workaday lives, he figures.

Jason must be giving some spiel to the camera for *Castaway Cottage*, or else is in his studio and drawing up detailed architectural plans.

No doubt, Matt's on duty keeping the roadways safe.

Maris would be writing away in her little shingled shack out behind the house.

Cliff—oh, Kyle's *sure* of this one—is mired somewhere in paint samples and ordinances.

Eva's probably selling cottages with her *By the Sea Realty*. And then there's Shane.

Kyle brushes butter on two slices of whole-grain bread and sets them sizzling on his grill. Shane right about now must be out on the Atlantic. Feeling the sea beneath him. Hauling pots while a salty breeze blows and the sea spray mists his face.

seventeen

BLACK.

That afternoon, Shane goes with his black suit. He'd considered his navy suit—the color of the Atlantic Ocean—but it didn't feel right. Not today. Not for him. Black is what Shane's heart feels. Black with sorrow. He lifts a burgundy pocket square from his dresser drawer, though. The touch of red will be his tip of the hat to what Shiloh loved—lobstering on that vast Atlantic.

After showering, Shane hangs his tailored suit on the closet door. Sets out his good shoes. Coils his black leather belt and puts it on his dresser. His watch is laid out there, too. His wallet. A burgundy silk tie with faint diagonal stripes. Silk pocket square. A soft-bristle brush to give his shoes a buff.

Everything top shelf. Only the best for his friend.

There's a mirror hooked over the back of his bedroom door. Standing in front of it, he gets ready. It's time now.

So he puts on a white tee, then his white dress shirt. Buttons it up. Tugs the sleeve cuffs. Gets the suit trousers off the hanger and puts those on, too.

And still can't believe it.

Can't believe that he's standing here getting dressed for a wake he never saw coming.

For Shiloh's wake.

Time, time.

Shit, it tricks you. Fools you. Messes with you. Because just last week? Shane was beating the crap out of some loser in a bar parking lot. Some loser bothering Jason about his missing leg. A lowlife calling him a *peg leg*. Shane and Kyle laced into the offensive guy. Left him with a limp he can think long and hard about. And hell, it felt *good*. Shane felt good about himself as he and his brother defended an old beach friend. Stood up for someone who deserved a hell of a lot better than the slurs tossed his way in The Sand Bar.

Yeah, he and Kyle had done right. Shane walked back into the bar that night with his shoulders back, his head held high.

And a week later, he's leveled. Just leveled.

Shane picks up his tie off the dresser now, returns to the mirror and lifts the tie. Slips it around his collar, then pauses. And steps closer to the mirror. The shadows on his face can't be missed.

"*Yep*," he whispers while knotting that tie then. "*Leveled*."

Once the tie's knotted, he tucks in his white button-down and belts his pants. Reaches for his suit jacket afterward and slips in one arm, then the other, before pulling the jacket up over his shoulders—tugging here, shifting there. Folds his silk pocket square into the jacket pocket. Pulls his shirt cuffs a half-inch lower than his jacket sleeves.

Steps back and looks at his reflection again.

He's clean-shaven, having thoroughly put the razor to his face after his shower. His hair is dried, brushed and a little spiked with some gel.

But nothing can change that one fact. He's *leveled*.

In one week's time.

Leveled. Brought from machismo—to his knees. The bluster and bravado of righting a wrong situation outside The Sand Bar last week is gone. Long gone. Because only days later, out on the lobster boat, something transpired *again* right over Shane's shoulder—just like it did in The Sand Bar. Except this time? He didn't even know it. Didn't see it happen.

Couldn't help *this* friend.

Couldn't right the situation.

Couldn't give someone his due.

Couldn't save a life.

Shane draws a hand over his jaw now.

For Shiloh, he'll do it, though. He'll find a way. He'll bring *back* the bravado—so proud of the fight *Shiloh* gave on the boat. In the hospital. Oh, he fought the fight, damn it.

So standing there in his black suit, Shane throws back his shoulders. Stands straight. Holds his head up. Nods to himself and walks to his dresser. He picks up the shoe brush there, grabs his freshly polished black wingtips off the floor and sits on the edge of his bed. One at a time then, he gives each shoe a good buffing. Works that brush over the leather of each one, back and forth, back and forth.

Again.

And again.

And he keeps at it, keeps buffing and brushing until he gets control of himself.

Until the hard knot in his throat subsides and the burning tears in his eyes fade as he shines those damn shoes to a fucking sheen.

eighteen

By MIDAFTERNOON WEDNESDAY, HE DID it. Jason's home. The many hours of highway pavement rolling beneath his SUV, and divided lines blurring past, and exit signs, and rest stops and passing cars are behind him. Forest gave way to towns and cities—which gave way, finally, to Connecticut's marshes and saltwater inlets. He turns into his long driveway now. Twigs crunch beneath the SUV's tires, and when they do, he sighs with relief. Loosens his grip on the steering wheel, too. And leans into the headrest behind him. By the time he gets the vehicle around back, Maris is stepping out onto the deck. And by the time he parks and shuts the engine off, she's gotten down the stone stairs and is hurrying to open his door for him. And is reaching in to hug him before he's even stepped out.

And he holds her—maybe a little bit longer than he typically would.

Yes, he holds her, strokes her hair, lightly kisses her and whispers how good it is to see her.

Then he laughs when he hears the dog whine. When Maris steps back, Maddy practically jumps into the SUV. Her front paws are on his lap; she's licking at his face and whining still while her tail swings.

"Okay, Madison! Okay, girl," Jason says, slapping the dog's shoulders before he gets himself out of the vehicle. "Good to see you, too."

"And how's Shane?" Maris asks from the driveway. "Better?"

"He's doing all right, considering. It'll be a long day for him, though, with the wake happening right about now."

"I'm sure. But I want to hear everything," Maris says as she lifts an overnight bag out of the cargo area. "Start to finish."

"You will. Let me get inside first."

Which she takes literally. Because as soon as they bring all his stuff and gear and things into the house, Maris is insistent. "Tell me *everything* now," she says in the kitchen.

And he does.

Over a late lunch of take-out grinders and chips and soda Maris picked up from Pizza Palace earlier, they sit on the deck and talk. About Shane. About Shiloh. About what went down Monday aboard ship. About how Shane and the crew did their best to help Shiloh. To keep him awake. Conscious. Keep him with them. He and Maris talk about regret and feelings and loneliness. About abandoned Maine mansions. About sensing Neil there. About Shane, ever the rebel, being an art thief. About Maris holding down the Stony Point fort and taking over Jason's TV gig while she was at it. About Shane's impressive home on the harbor—a far cry from the rundown, neglected fisherman's shack Jason expected. About sleeping like a little baby himself in the surprising guest-room-turned-nursery Shane's got going on for Aria. They talk about manuscript passages and filming schedules and waiting clients. About logging this lunch together in their lost-time log: grinders dressed with mayo and olive oil and stuffed with shredded lettuce, tomato, Genoa, and ham; September sun shining; salt air drifting over the bluff.

"It was a long haul back and forth to Maine," Maris says. "*Not* to mention dropping everything to do that." She reaches over the patio table and lightly strokes his hand. "So you've *got* to have an early night tonight, Jason."

"I will, sweetheart."

"Shane's lucky to have a friend like you." Maris pauses, holding Jason's hand in hers still. "*I'm lucky, too*," she says, quieter.

That gets to him, so he lifts her hand and leaves a kiss on the back of it. "It's really good to be home," he tells her. "Think I'll unpack now and lie low this afternoon. Crash here, catch up on some work stuff. Catch my *breath*."

"Okay, babe."

They both get up. Maddy—who'd been dozing in a sunny patch on the deck—does, too.

"Oh," Jason adds as he picks up their food wrappings. "There's one more thing I *have* to do after dinner later," he says, then tells Maris his plan. "So I'll be going out for a while."

"Not too long," she says back, opening the glass slider now. "But that *is* one visit you've got to make."

Celia's heart sinks.

After five hours of maneuvering highways and rest stops, of her foot pressing that gas pedal, she made it. She's in Rockport, Maine. She's at Shane's house.

And he's not here.

Right away, she knows this. His pickup isn't in the driveway. So he's out. Somewhere.

Well. She's not leaving, that's for sure. Instead, she opens her car door and gets out. The long folds of her T-shirt maxi dress brush her legs. The dress seemed the right choice for the trip, in case she could *somehow* get to Shiloh's wake today. But the air's cooler here, so she reaches back in the car for her knit shrug and puts that on, too. And takes a few steps to stretch her legs. And realizes how tense she's been just by walking around a little. Unknotting. Her leather sandals crunch over the driveway gravel as she slowly approaches Shane's silver-shingled house. Geraniums still spill from the window boxes. A few faded buoys hang beside the blue front door.

That's where she heads, even though Shane's out. She walks up the wide granite step and knocks on the screen door, anyway. Cups her face and peeks in a front window, too. The house is shadowy inside, but some things she makes out. The lamp on the window table. And Shane's happiness jar beside the lamp. The brick fireplace. A framed seascape painting over the mantel.

But no Shane. No shadow of him moving through the room, or hurrying around a corner. The house is clearly buttoned up and empty.

Which isn't much help to her. And she doesn't want to text him. Or call him. No, she wants him to see in person that she's here. She made the trip. She glances at her watch, then turns away from the window—right as someone calls her name.

"Celia?"

When she looks toward the next yard, Shane's neighbor is walking over. He's about forty with brown hair and wears a checked button-down over dark trousers. And he's met her both times she'd been to Shane's house. "Oh, Bruno!" she says, shielding her eyes from the sun.

"Good seeing you, Celia. You just get here?" Bruno asks her.

"I did. How've you been, Bruno? Okay?"

"Ayuh. Doin' fine. Given the circumstances. We lost a fine lad in town this week."

Celia nods. "Shiloh. That's why I'm here. To pay my respects. To see Shane."

"He expecting you?"

"No. He's not." She glances back toward Shane's house, then turns to Bruno again. "Do you know if he'll be back soon?"

"Shane? Doubt it very much, Celia. He left for Shiloh's wake a while ago. I'm headed there myself now."

"Oh." Celia gives a sad smile. "I looked online to see when the wake is, and figured Shane might be there. Just thought I'd get here in time to catch him first."

"He left early, I'm afraid. Because it'll be mobbed at that wake, for sure. Expecting hundreds of folks. The whole town's turning out."

"Oh, boy."

Bruno leans over and glances toward Celia's car in the driveway. "Did you bring the baby this trip?"

"Aria." Celia looks toward her car, too. She can't miss the luggage stuffed into the backseat. "No," she tells Bruno then. "Aria's spending some time with her grandpop. Back home."

"Probably better. She's a real sweetheart, but ... you know. It's not a place for the little ones at these occasions."

"No." Celia presses a wrinkle out of the long dress she's wearing. "Well, Bruno? By any chance, could you tell me where this funeral home is? Think I'll try heading over there."

Bruno takes a step toward the road and points left. "It's a couple of miles down that way apiece." He stops then. Stops and looks at Celia just standing alone in Shane's front yard. "Ah, heck. Why don't you come with me?"

"Really?" Celia looks again to her car, then to Bruno. "Are you *sure*? Because I don't want to inconvenience you."

Bruno waves away her words. "You just leave your car right where it is, and I'd be glad to drive you, dear. We'll go together."

"That's so nice of you."

"Ayuh. Got to grab my jacket and lock up first, so come on over." He motions for her to follow him. "Let me get you a glass of water after your trip. You can freshen up inside, too."

Grateful for the hospitality, Celia only nods. Her hand lightly goes to her limp hair, and to the shadows that are no doubt beneath her eyes. She grabs her purse next, anxious to run a comb through her hair and put on some makeup, too.

Bruno looks over his shoulder, then keeps walking to the neighboring home—its shingles painted a dark red.

"Here we are," he calls, stopping to hold the door open for her.

"Thank you," Celia says, stepping inside. "You *really* don't mind?"

"Not at all. Glad I noticed you as I was checking my mailbox."

They head toward the kitchen now. Bruno gets her that iced water before locking the back door. "Like I said," he tells her, "it's going to be wicked mobbed at the wake. But don't worry, I'll find Shane for you in the crowds."

nineteen

THERE'S A HUM IN THE funeral home's visitation room. A low hum that somewhat pulses. It's the sound of voices. So many voices, each one of them hushed so that they blur into that pervasive hum.

From where Shane sits on a padded wooden chair near the back of the room, he has a full view of the space. People line up along the side wall and all the way back out into the main lobby. That line doesn't stop moving, either. It's in constant, but slow, motion as the guests file to the front to view Shiloh's body, say a prayer, murmur a quiet goodbye. People are in suits, sport jackets, skirts and dresses. The air is serious, and somber. Many of the room's chairs are already filled. The captain and his wife sit to one side of Shane; a few local lobstermen sit behind him. Sometimes one will nudge him to point out a familiar face arriving. Or to mention something they remembered about Shiloh. Or only to say how sad it all is.

The Visitor

Shane just pretty much nods, whispers a few words back.

Mostly, though, he takes it all in. Sitting there in his black suit, he occasionally leans forward, elbows on his knees, and bows his head. Other times, he simply sits straight and is a part of the moment. He's one of hundreds of people heartbroken for Shiloh and his family. One of hundreds of people missing the guy. One still fighting some anger at it all. Anger that it had to be Shiloh who took that fall; that it had to even happen; that the Lord above wouldn't do it—wouldn't disperse *Shane's* good to the one who needed it most. To Shiloh.

Shane waits, too. He still hasn't walked to the kneeling bench to view the body. He's not ready to yet. Things need to settle down some—in the room, in his thoughts.

And so he just sits.

There's a tap on his back, then. A firm one-two cuff before the hand clasps his shoulder and the guy bends low to talk.

Shane looks up at him. "Hey, Bruno," he says to his neighbor.

"Shane." Bruno hitches his head to the door. "You've got a visitor outside."

Shane walks out into the afternoon sunlight. He stops just past the doorway and straightens his shirt cuffs, his tie. Tugs his jacket. The sidewalk is packed. A crowd of people works its way into the funeral home lobby, where an usher directs them. So Shane moves out of the way of the entrance. The parking lot is packed, too. Attendants there direct traffic. Those attendants motion drivers up one row, down another. They point to vacant parking spaces for the cars, and pickup trucks, and SUVs snaking along.

And that sun. Shane shields his eyes and steps to the curb. The low afternoon sunlight glares off all the vehicles. Bruno told him Celia's waiting in the parking lot. That he actually left her outside Shane's pickup.

Right away, Shane spots her. She's standing in front of his truck. Her long dress flutters around her legs. A wisp of auburn hair blows across her face. When he catches her eye as he walks toward her, she gives a sad smile. He hurries closer. She takes a step to him—just one. He waits for a few cars to pass, then maneuvers around a group of arriving people. She's standing still, waiting. When he nears her, Celia just silently turns up her hands.

The hard knot in his throat—the emotion at seeing her here—is almost more than Shane can bear. He takes Celia's hands in his, kisses them, closes his eyes and wordlessly pulls her into his arms.

And his world can stop spinning—right there, right then. Because he knows now. For the past few days, that world of his spun out of control. It revolved at a dizzying pace. Moved through mayhem. Tipped off-kilter. Leaned at a frightening angle.

Until Celia stepped directly into it. Into his arms.

They hug right there. Standing in front of his pickup, Shane holds her close. Envelops her in his arms. Cars are everywhere around them—pulling in, leaving. People walk past. Voices murmur.

But Shane just holds Celia. He presses her head to his shoulder and slightly rocks. Kisses the side of her head. Strokes her hair.

They don't talk.

Bent over her in that embrace, Shane fights tears, too. The same tears he successfully fought inside the funeral home? A few silently run down his face now.

He holds Celia even closer still.

Feels *all* of her in his arms. All that he has in his arms.

Whispers so quietly in her ear, *"Don't let go."*

Shane's ready now.

After briefly talking with her in the parking lot, he leads Celia inside the funeral home. They don't sit, though. Instead, after signing the guestbook, they join the line of people moving through the visitation room. A few chandeliers glimmer above the carpeted floor. Sofas line the side walls. The sofas are flanked by large lamps on mahogany end tables. There's that quiet hum of murmurs in the room, too. As he and Celia move through the line, a few lobstermen reach out from their seats and clasp Shane's arm, say their hellos. Shane nods and says a few words back.

But the closer he and Celia get to the front of the room, the quieter the people are. Now, not too many talk. Now, heads are dipped. Tears are wiped. When it's Shane's turn to approach the open casket, he motions Celia to the kneeler ahead of him, then kneels with her once she's settled there. She looks briefly at Shiloh before blessing herself and tipping her head down.

Shane knows that she's doing what he can't. Not right now, anyway. No prayers pass through his lips. His thoughts. No. He hasn't been able to pray in days. Can't summon the words. Not sure he believes in prayer anymore. Not after what happened to Shiloh. So instead of bowing his head in prayer, he looks at his friend laid out in a brand-new navy suit in an open coffin. At first Shane thinks, *No. That's not Shiloh. Not lifeless like that. Not still.*

But it *is* Shiloh.

It is.

Which is why Shane can't pray. He only looks at his friend. But his mind is hearing Shiloh's laugh. Hearing Shiloh tell him to scratch off his sale coupon with a penny he slid across Shane's patio table. Hearing Shiloh call him the lovesick loser when they talked about Celia. Hearing Shiloh tell him the captain was in a wicked bad mood when the fuel pump busted. Shiloh saying he has to get his sea legs back after being off the water for two weeks. That he never got a tattoo at his folks' barbecue. *Was a bummah you left—and I chickened out ... Jeezum Crow, boys gave me hell.*

Shane still looks at Shiloh's body there. Remembers one more thing, too. Remembers this past Sunday night when Shiloh came over for some of Elsa's specialty tomato sandwiches. Shane told him they'd have a good day tomorrow, finally back on the water. They'd get the job done for the captain.

Ayuh, Shiloh told him with a swig of beer. *You and me, bub.*

And neither of them could've been more wrong.

Monday was their day from hell.

So Shane? Yeah. He's pretty much stopped praying. Telling the Lord off? Giving Him a piece of his mind? Now that's another story.

But when he sees Celia bless herself beside him, he

nudges her arm. "*Look*," Shane quietly says, then points to a polished brass cuff showing beneath Shiloh's suit jacket sleeve.

Celia looks and nods.

"I'll tell you about that later." Shane takes her hand then as they stand from the kneeler.

Once they offer condolences to the family, once Shane hugs first Keith, then Tammy—who sobs into his shoulder—Shane leads Celia to empty seats in the back of the room. On the way there, again, many lobstermen reach out to Shane. Clasp his shoulder. Hug him. Talk some.

Finally, though, he sits with Celia. They're quiet for a few minutes. But then Shane leans close and talks. "You saw that brass cuff on Shiloh's wrist?"

"I did," Celia tells him.

"When Jason was here yesterday, we actually helped Shiloh's parents. Jason and I went out to a men's clothing store and bought the suit Shiloh's wearing now."

"*Oh, Shane*," Celia's voice quietly says as she squeezes his hand.

He nods. "But, you know … it wasn't enough. The suit. I wanted something more, something to make that formal suit personal to *Shiloh*. So me and Jason stopped at another shop in town, and I bought that brass cuff. It's made out of an actual lobster gauge—because Shiloh *loved* being a lobsterman." Shane's voice is low and steady now. The words come easy, talking to Celia. Explaining the polished brass cuff on Shiloh's wrist seems important, too. "Those gauges are used to measure the body shell of every lobster we catch. To be a keeper, the carapace legally can't be shorter than three-and-a-quarter inches, or longer than five.

The lobster also can't be an egg-bearing female—those all get returned to the sea, too. So, you know. We measure and toss either one direction, or the other. Keeper or not. It's a way to help sustain the lobster population."

Celia listens, reaches over and kind of loops her arm through his. Leans into him, too, while softly stroking his jacketed arm.

It's as if she knows, Shane thinks. Celia knows that his talking on and on about a lobster gauge is really something else. His detailing the technique of measuring, of hooking the gauge behind the eye socket and checking the distance to the start of the tail? Well, she knows. She knows this talking about a lobster gauge is letting him think of something other than everything *else* he's thought these days.

Talking about a lobster gauge is helping him get through all of this.

Get through the day, the night. The week.

Get through two days ago—which he's still in—when he turned around on the lobster boat and lost his friend.

twenty

FEW THINGS ARE FOOLPROOF IN this life. Very few.

Oh, doesn't Kyle Bradford know that. He can count on one hand the things that have *never* failed him. Never let him down. Never disappointed him.

Now, things that *have* failed him? Hell, that's a different kettle of fish. Might as well say the entire decade of his twenties failed him—what with the unsteady nature of his steelwork; and Neil going after his girl; and Kyle's cancelled wedding to Lauren *barely* on again; and the rift with his brother, Shane. Okay, that one Kyle can blame on his younger hotheaded self. But still, in his twenties? There were many days, weeks—months, even—that Kyle felt like he could never climb out of and breathe easy again.

But foolproof things in his life *now*? In his late thirties? Things that he can count on blindfolded, hands tied behind his back, no matter what?

That's easy. There's Lauren. His kids. Love them all to pieces. His diner—which is his world away from home. His best man, Jason Barlow.

And the seven-day weather forecast.

Which is why Kyle stations himself in the kitchen every single night. Sits at the table *alone*—insists on it—so as not to be distracted. If anyone talks to him, or walks into the room, or gets his attention away from the kitchen TV at just the right time, he misses the seven-day outlook and risks losing business at the diner. Knowing the weather *ahead* of time is actually an ace in the hole for his diner's success. Kyle swears by it. Sunny days? People are out. Sunny days are a twenty-four-hour vacation. Folks are driving. Walking. Sightseeing. And they want to treat themselves to a meal. The diner's packed. And cold, rainy days that keep them all home? He offers meals to *get* people out. Comfort foods. Stews. Soups. Warm sandwiches.

And it works, this weather strategy.

Forecast-watching has never really let Kyle down.

Yep. Foolproof.

So this Wednesday night finds him turning to the most valuable improvement he made to his and Lauren's new house this summer—the cabinet above the refrigerator. That now-customized cabinet holds a sleek twenty-seven-inch television. And right now, everything's just right. The kids are in bed. Lauren's reading in the living room. The house is quiet. So Kyle turns on that kitchen TV, tunes to the local news and waits for the weather.

Well, he doesn't just wait.

He also toasts two slices of whole-grain bread, plucking them out when the toaster pops.

THE VISITOR

"Are you having a snack?" Lauren calls out from the other room.

Standing there holding a butter knife, Kyle takes a long breath. "Yes, I am."

"Is that a sandwich you're making?"

"It is."

"Oh."

But nothing more from Lauren. Kyle looks at the news program on the TV, then glances over his shoulder. "Did you want one?" he calls out.

"Just a half, if it's not too much trouble," her distracted voice comes back to him.

So after glancing at his watch, he toasts another piece of bread, then halves and butters it. Slices a tomato, too. Shreds some lettuce; lays a few pieces of thin-sliced roasted deli chicken on the toast; adds cheese, tomato and lettuce. Slathers mayo and a drizzle of mustard on the other pieces of toast, tops those mega sandwiches and sets the plates on the table. Gets a sharp knife, drops it through his sandwich and moves Lauren's half-sandwich aside.

"Your snack is ready," he calls out, then sits at the table with his own. A little sandwich will definitely hit the spot tonight. It'd been a long day behind the big stove.

Lauren breezes in, takes her plate and a napkin, kisses the top of his head and breezes out.

She knows, Kyle thinks. *The weather's due on.* And he timed the snacks just right. As the meteorologist begins, so does Kyle. He lifts his toasted chicken sandwich and takes a hefty bite. Sips his seltzer water. Crunches a few veggie chips. The meteorologist gives all the stats, the temperature highs and lows, chances of precipitation, sunrise tomorrow, sunset. Some viewer photos. Kyle takes another bite of the sandwich. Dabs his mouth with a paper napkin. And finally sees the seven-day block of forecasted weather.

"Sunny day tomorrow," he calls out to Lauren.

But she doesn't answer.

"Be busy at the diner," he calls then. "Folks flock to the shore on a sunny day. Then they want something to eat, you know?"

Still nothing from the other room.

So Kyle turns in his seat and listens. He quickly grabs the remote, too, and turns down the TV volume. It sounds like Lauren's talking to someone. Her voice is muffled, like she's out on the enclosed porch and talking there.

"Hey, Kyle!" her voice carries through the house then. "Come out here. You've got a visitor."

⁓

When Jason told Maris he had one more thing to do today, it was this.

He's standing on Kyle's enclosed front porch now and chatting with Lauren. Tiny white lights strung around the windows twinkle in the dark night. A salty breeze drifts in from the bay across the street. It's a nice spot, the Bradford porch. Seashells line the window ledges. Lauren turned a tall, narrow piece of driftwood into a *Welcome* sign—the letters of the word painted vertically on the wood sign leaning against the wall. Tarnished lanterns glimmer on scattered end tables. The cushioned wicker sofa and chairs are comfortable with pillows and throws. A beach-grass wreath hangs on the door.

And suddenly, there's Kyle—holding a plate and standing in the doorway.

"Hey, Bradford," Jason says.

"Barlow." Kyle steps onto the porch, his leather slippers scuffing on the floor. He must've worked a long day because he's still in his black work pants and black tee. Looks tired, too. "Where you been, man?" Kyle asks. "Had a cinnamon cruller out for the past two days at the diner." He sits in a chair and bites into some deluxe sandwich he threw together tonight. "The crullers got stale and *I* ended up eating them," he goes on around a mouthful of food.

"Well, to tell you the truth … Where I've been is why I'm here," Jason begins.

That seems to quiet both Kyle and Lauren. On the dimly lit porch, they sit up a little straighter and carefully watch Jason as he talks. As he fills them in on Shane's Monday night phone call. As he relays the news about the devastating loss of Shane's crewmate and good friend. As Jason tells them, too, that he paused his life to get to Maine. That he and Maris thought it important—Shane sounded in rough shape.

"Jesus," Kyle says. "I had no idea."

"I know. And Shane was so torn up when he first called," Jason explains, "I couldn't even get out of him what *exactly* was wrong. So I caught a few hours' sleep and hightailed it north that night. Just to be sure he wasn't in some kind of trouble, or needing real help."

Kyle and Lauren's questions start then, as they lean forward.

As Kyle stands, and paces, and sits again.

As they try to piece this Shane scene together.

When did this all happen?
Didn't they just get back to work on the boat?
Was this Shiloh sick?
Did they get him to a hospital?
Were the seas rough that day? Bad weather?
But what about Shane now? Is he doing okay?

Jason answers every question. His voice is low in the night. He tells them it happened Monday. Yes, the lobster crew was back to work after two weeks off the water ... Repairs were done, boat good to go ... Don't know what caused Shiloh's fall ... Could've been sick. Or dehydrated, even ... Maybe his equilibrium was off being on the sea again ... Family's working with the doctors on that one ... Coast Guard rescue boat brought Shiloh to an ambulance onshore ... Seas calm, weather fair.

"When Shane called me Monday night," Jason explains, "he was pretty out of it. Seems Shiloh had *just* died."

"Oh my God, that's so sad. And Shane witnessed it all," Lauren says. "How long were you there, Jason?"

"Booked it out of here Monday night, right before midnight. Made it to Rockport early yesterday morning—Tuesday—and just got back home a few hours ago."

Kyle sets his plate and unfinished sandwich aside. "Why didn't you tell me?" he asks.

"I'm telling you now, guy. I was too busy in Maine and wanted to see what was going on there first. I just got back this afternoon, and swung by here as soon as I could."

"Damn," Kyle says.

Lauren shakes her head. *"Poor Shane,"* she nearly whispers on the shadowed porch.

They all quiet for a few seconds. There's the soft splash of waves lapping, over and over, on the bay across the street. A late-summer cricket slow-chirps.

"That's tough, man. Losing someone like that—outta nowhere. Shit, we know a thing or two about that." Kyle stands, motions for them to wait and goes inside for his phone. When he comes back out onto the porch, he's scrolling the phone's screen. "Wish Shane reached out to me, but I got no messages here."

"I'm sure he'll be in touch, Kyle," Lauren says.

"Well," Jason tells them, "he's pretty busy. Wake was today. Funeral's tomorrow. And he's back on the boat Friday."

Kyle just nods. "Helluva week for the guy."

"Yeah." Jason stands then. "So, listen. I just wanted to fill you in," he says. "Keep you in the loop with your brother, Kyle."

"Can we get you anything? Do you want a beer? Something to eat?" Lauren asks.

"Nah. But thanks, Lauren," Jason tells her. "It's late and I'm beat. Told Maris I wouldn't be long, too."

Lauren hurries to him and gives a quick hug. "Well I'm glad you stopped by, Jason. We *really* appreciate it."

Jason nods, then turns to Kyle. "So that's how things went down in Maine this week. Hard times for Shiloh and his family especially. For Shane, too. And ... you know, Kyle. Give your brother a break. 'Cause I know what you're thinking."

"And what's that?" Kyle tosses back.

"That this is *bullshit*—that Shane called *me*, and not you."

Kyle nods, then. Nods and turns up his hands.

"No, man," Jason insists. "Listen. Shane knew. He *knew* he couldn't call you because you'd be busy with your wife, your kids. School. The new house. The diner," Jason goes on, opening the screen door and stepping out into the night. "Don't take it personal, guy. Don't. It was just easier to unload on me."

―◡―

Okay, here's something else that's foolproof. That works—*every* time. Agitation keeps Kyle wide awake at night. When something's bothering him, words swim in his mind. *What ifs* crowd his thoughts. Visions fill the darkness. Sleep eludes him.

Yep. Foolproof. Agitation equals no sleep.

As evidenced tonight.

Wearing a T-shirt and pajama pants now, Kyle lies in bed. Scratches his chest. Looks to Lauren trying to sleep beside him. Looks the other way, toward the open window. Inhales deeply, breathing some salt air into his lungs to cure what ails him.

He just feels sad, actually. Really sad for Shane. Sad that Shane didn't talk to him, too. They're *brothers*, man.

But Jason's words counter Kyle's thoughts. They play in his mind once, then again. *It was just easier to unload on me.*

"*Well, isn't that what brothers are for?*" Kyle barely answers his own worries in the darkness.

"What?" Lauren's sleepy voice comes to him. "What are you talking about?"

"Shane. I mean, he didn't reach out to me, and isn't that what brothers are for? What brothers do?"

"Kyle. You're barely brothers again after fifteen years—*years*—on the outs. Fifteen years of having *nothing* to do with each other." Lauren reaches over and gives a reassuring pat to his arm. "You and Shane *are* still treading water. You know that."

"Yeah, well." Kyle takes another breath, a frustrated one this time. "When Shane first got here this summer, he effing *hated* Jason. And I at *least* had a heart-to-heart on Shane's back porch. *And* thought we were making headway."

"You are."

"But I could've booked it to Maine, too. And been there for him. Brother to brother."

"No, you really couldn't. Jerry can't *always* be running the diner for you. It's not right for you to put that on him. *And* you have the kids—who need you, too. Evan's working with you on his science project. You help Hailey with her homework. Drive them to soccer and baseball practice."

Kyle sits up then. Sits up, plumps the pillow behind him and turns on the bedside lamp. Shit, if there's one thing he wants right now, it's this: a cigarette. Flicking the ash. Taking a drag. Squinting through the smoke. If any conflicted moment calls for a cigarette, it's this one. So he reaches to his nightstand, picks up the rubber band there and slips it on his wrist. Gives it a good snap, too.

"Oh, no you don't." Lauren sits up beside him and straightens her navy satin sleepshirt. "Don't you *dare* sneak a smoke tonight."

"I won't. It just would've *meant* something if Shane turned to me," Kyle tells her, snapping that elastic again.

Lauren sinks down onto the bed and turns her back to

Kyle now. "Well, I'm siding with Shane—who is very much aware of your *family* responsibilities and wouldn't disrupt them. Which is honorable. And he *knows* you run the diner now, on top of everything else."

"*Eh*. Jason has a job, too. Hell, he's got a TV show."

Lauren just gives Kyle a light slap behind her. "*You* can reach out to *Shane* too, you know."

"Yeah. Yeah, I guess I could," Kyle tells her, then shuts off the light.

"Just call your brother tomorrow," Lauren says, her voice quiet. "You'll feel better after talking to him."

"I will." Kyle settles back down on the mattress. He straightens the sheet over him, glances at Lauren trying to sleep. "Do you think I should go to that funeral, Ell?"

"What?"

"Should I go to Shiloh's funeral tomorrow?"

"No. It's *way* too late now. If it was closer, maybe. But Rockport's *so* far from here, and it's too much to make that drive." Lauren's quiet then. The room is still. Night's upon them. "*Just get some sleep, Kyle*," she whispers. "*You'll see things differently in the morning.*"

Kyle hooks an arm behind his head, but says nothing. He just looks up—barely deciphering the ceiling in the dark of night.

twenty-one

LIFE TURNS SOMETIMES.

And for that, Shane's grateful. Because life went and turned on him again today. This time, though, it turned in a *good* way. It brought Celia here.

After the wake, he and Celia came back to his place. Shane changed into jeans and a tee, hung up his black suit for tomorrow and threw together a quick steak dinner. He's standing at his kitchen screen door now. Celia's just outside, sitting on the deck. She's still wearing her long dress, and has a cardigan over her shoulders. It's late. They'd had dinner, cleaned up the kitchen and decided on wine outside. A three-quarter moon rises out over the harbor. That moon is pale gold tonight. Some of its light falls on the dark harbor waters, and on a stack of lobster traps on the dock. It's a still night, too. There's no breeze, so if he listens hard enough, Shane can hear water sloshing in that harbor. Small waves splash against the boat hulls, the dock posts. Lights shine in the night, too. Boat lights, dock lights. In flickering shimmers, they reflect off the black water.

What it all tells him—the harbor boats, and lights, and lobster traps—is this: Life goes on. Yes, it turns, changes direction and keeps moving. Like the tide, maybe. It comes in, goes out. Washes over you, recedes. Good, bad.

Tonight, good.

So after grabbing a bottle of wine, Shane pushes out through the screen door and joins Celia at the patio table. She's bent over her phone and doesn't look up.

"Texting your dad?" Shane asks while filling their two wineglasses.

"No. I talked to him before. Texting Maris now."

"Maris?" Shane asks as he sits beside Celia.

Celia's engrossed in her thumb-typing. "Letting her know I'm here. In Maine," she vaguely says. "With you." Silence, then Celia whispers out loud the words she's typing. "*Going to funeral together tomorrow. Please don't let on to Elsa, though.*" Setting the phone down then, she turns her attention to Shane. "It felt like Maris and Jason should know—after everything they've done to help."

"I agree."

Celia nods, reaches for her wineglass and takes a sip.

They sit there like that, beneath the illuminated globe lights strung around the deck. Their talk comes easy. Shane tells her again that even though he asked her not to make the trip, he's so glad she's here. Didn't realize how much it would mean to him. When she only squeezes his hand, he tells her more. Talks a little about the abandoned-house filming he did with Jason that morning. For *Castaway Cottage*.

"Seems like a lifetime ago now. *Shit* … time, man."

Celia talks about Aria, and how she's missing her little ray of sunshine, and how the baby's with her pop-pop in Addison.

"My dad's not too happy about this, though."

"This?" Shane motions his hand between them.

"Not about us. But that I'm here on the sly, as though something's wrong with making the trip. Says it's the last time he'll cover for me."

"I can see his point. It's not good keeping things secret like that. Deceiving people."

Celia sips her wine. "But it's not forever," she quietly says. "And this trip? It was an *exception*—because of what happened to you. Because of sweet Shiloh." She leans forward and strokes Shane's arm, running her fingers along a tattoo snaking up it. "You're cold," she says.

"What?"

"You're cold. It's chilly tonight, and your skin's cold. And you're a little hunched."

Holding his glass, Shane swirls his wine in it. "I'm all right."

"No." Celia stands and heads inside. "You sit. I'll get you something to warm up."

***

She's in the house only a few minutes.

But those are enough minutes—quiet, alone minutes—for Shane to feel what this night would be *without* Celia here. That quiet would've expanded for hours. Hours giving his mind free rein to veer to dark places. He looks over when the screen door squeaks and Celia returns to the deck.

"Here you go, sailor," she says, standing behind his chair. "Let me help you on with this." She opens his fleece-lined sweatshirt and nudges his shoulder.

So Shane slips one arm, then the other, into the sweatshirt and feels her lift it around his shoulders, his neck, before she sits beside him at the patio table again.

"Huh," he says, half zipping the warm sweatshirt.

"What?"

"This is the same sweatshirt I used as a pillow beneath Shiloh's head. On the boat, Monday. I folded up the sweatshirt, lifted his head and settled it beneath him. To keep him comfortable. The deck floor, it's hard. And it's always wet on the boat when we're out to sea."

"Oh, Shane. I had no idea."

"That's all right. At least I know."

"Know what?"

He gives a piece of the fabric a shake. "I feel the warm fleece, and the thickness of the sweatshirt. And I know it would've cushioned Shiloh, feeling that soft fleece when he needed it. Beneath his head." Shane gives a regretful smile. "Comforted him, maybe."

Celia stands, then, and walks to a railing facing the distant docks. When she turns, she stays there, at that railing. "Is it better, do you think, to die suddenly like Shiloh did?" she asks. "Doing what you love. Living that life?"

Shane looks at her through the night's shadows. "You mean, instead of dying from something prolonged?"

"Right. In a way that everyone can prepare for. In a way that also draws it all out."

Shane shrugs. "Maybe to go suddenly living a life loved *is* better. But ... not at twenty-six."

Standing there in her long dress, Celia leans her hands on the deck railing. "Age doesn't really matter, though. Because, think about it. As long as you're living what you love, to be suddenly gone? Well, there's no fear that way. None of that awful, extended suffering."

Shane looks long at her. He gets up, too, and crosses the deck. Because he's sure of it, yes. It's obvious with each step he takes. Tears streak Celia's face. Tears that she swipes as he gets closer in the night. "What's wrong, Celia?" he asks.

"*Argh*." She impatiently brushes away another tear. But she doesn't say more until he stands right beside her and leans against the railing, too. First she glances up at that waning moon hanging in the sky. She also takes a long breath of the salt air. "I realize *now*," she finally says, "that's exactly what Sal did."

"Sal?"

She nods. "Sal lived the life he loved till the very end. He kept his valve-replacement surgery a secret from everyone so that he could just *live* the summer he loved. The life he loved. At the place he loved. With the people he loved. His mother, his friends. Me. By keeping his condition secret, he lived without anyone's worry, or fear. And I used to resent him for keeping his illness from me. But now? After today?"

Shane brushes back a wisp of her hair. And only listens.

"After today, and seeing how Shiloh, dear Shiloh, lived to his last *minute* doing what he loved?" Celia turns up her hands in a hopeless gesture. "*Maybe* …" she whispers.

And Shane can tell. She's whispering because that's all her emotion lets her do. Anything else she might sob on.

"*Maybe I wasn't fair to Sal. Even to the memory of him—thinking that he tricked me.*" She wipes more tears away. "*I don't know …*"

Shane moves in front of her and doesn't hesitate. Standing there practically at the Atlantic's doorstep, beneath the September night sky, he takes all of her in his arms and holds Celia close. He presses her face to his shoulder. Strokes her hair. "*Just forgive him,*" he tells her.

And though he imagines she fights more stinging tears, he feels Celia silently nod into his hug.

⁓

"Close your eyes," Shane tells Celia an hour later.

It's been a long day for both of them. They're tired and go to bed early. She's lying on her side beneath the sheet. She's looking at him, too. Jute rope holds back the window curtains, so pale moonlight shines in the room—giving Shane enough illumination to see her eyes watching him beside her. "*Sleep,*" he whispers, reaching over and touching her soft hair.

She nods. Kisses him lightly. Shifts away, tucks a hand beneath her pillow and closes her eyes in exhaustion. Fatigue had shown on her face all evening.

So Shane's glad for that. Glad that Celia simply closed her eyes. It gives him one less thing to worry about. Lord knows, he's got enough already. Plenty of thoughts are taking up worry-space in his mind: thoughts of Shiloh's wake earlier; of the funeral tomorrow; of going back out on the lobster boat Friday—without his friend; of the weeks ahead with the crew adjusting to a new greenhorn, for sure.

Of Celia making the trip safely back to Connecticut. Of his empty days without her.

So Shane lies still in the dark bedroom. No salty breezes come through the window. No distant harbor sounds reach him. Tonight? Everything feels like it's paused. Dangling. Suspended in a moment.

Suspended in the moment he turned around Monday on the boat and saw Shiloh down on the deck. Down and already leaving.

Shane doesn't move in this odd suspended time. Doesn't sleep, either. He just senses the night getting quieter outside the window. Darkness deepening. Seconds ticking past—or not. It's hard to tell. A minute can be an hour. Maybe sleep comes and goes; maybe he's been drifting. If he could, he'd turn over and check the bedside clock now. But he won't move. Won't risk moving and waking Celia.

The night silently settles in. He'd pace the house, too, if he could. If he were alone. Because sleep sure as hell isn't coming anytime soon. He'd sit outside on the deck, maybe. Look up at the stars. Breathe.

But going out on the deck would mean moving off the bed.

He won't do it. Doesn't dare wake Celia. She needs to sleep more than he does. He saw that.

So he stays there in bed. Lies still while locked in some dark time warp.

A half hour later? An hour, maybe? Celia's voice comes to him. Hushed. She doesn't move, either. There is just her voice.

"*You up?*" she asks.

"I am."

No movement on the bed. Stillness.

Until Celia reaches over and gently squeezes his hand. Doesn't let go, either.

"You weren't supposed to come here," Shane says, his voice even in the night. "I know what that took to accomplish."

A few seconds of silence. Then, "Nothing could keep me away, Shane."

A few more seconds. "But why?" he asks back. "Why'd you make the trip?"

There's that silence again. It's like they're in some rhythm, some cadence picking up on the motion of the sea beyond the harbor. Questions, silence. Answers, silence.

"Why'd I make the trip?" Celia repeats without moving. "I thought of you sitting here. In this house. Alone." More quiet. "I didn't want you to be."

Shane only nods. And feels her hand still holding his. More rhythm of silence, words. "Close your eyes, Celia." A pause. "Get some rest now."

Quiet moments pass, then, "*Okay*," comes whispered in the night.

Shane feels the mattress shift as she turns onto her side toward him again. So he looks over. In the pale moonlight, he can make out that her eyes are open. "*You lied to me*," he whispers.

"*What?*"

"You said you were closing your eyes." He leans over, cradles her face with one hand and presses a kiss to her forehead to make her eyes close. And with his touch, they do. She rests.

More silent minutes pass. Even everything outdoors

seems to have shut down. In mourning. Out of respect for Shiloh. There's no clanging bell buoy. No late-returning chugging lobster boat. No whispering breeze. Nothing.

And in that silence now, Shane just feels Celia's presence beside him on the bed. She's been beside him all afternoon. He thinks, too, of what he just told her. That she lied to him.

Hell, she lied to more than just him. He knows it. She lied to other people to get here today. Lied, fibbed, fudged. Call it what you will. She did it.

Celia bulldozed her own day, her own week, her own life, to get here to him.

In the darkness, he turns his head toward her. Whether she's asleep or not, he wants her to know something. To know what *he* feels by knowing all that about *her*. About her lying.

"*No one's loved me in fifteen years*," he barely whispers. The words scarcely make it past his lips.

Stillness, then. He doesn't move. Celia doesn't, either. Not for a minute, at least. One long, eternal minute.

Only her hand moves, then. Whether she can see in the blackness of the middle of the night is questionable. But her fingers begin tracing the skin on his arm as though they're tracing each and every line of his tattoos there. If she *can't* see, then she's damn well got those tats memorized. So he squints through the shadows to look at her face. To discern if she sees.

Or is it all just magic?

A dream.

Her touch a feather on his arm, on his life tonight.

"Close *your* eyes," Celia tells Shane now. When she says it, she props herself up on an elbow, then waits.

Shane looks at her for a long second.

"*Uh-uh-uh,*" she whispers before reaching her fingers to his face and brushing his eyes closed. "It's my turn."

"For what?" he asks back from behind closed eyes.

"It's my turn to write you a note."

"Celia—"

"*No.*" Now she places a finger over his lips. "You wrote a letter to me Saturday night, after we were at the Barlows'. And now it's *my* turn to write back. So ... *shh. And pay attention.*"

There's nothing from Shane, then. Nothing except a relenting smile.

And so she begins.

Celia looks at him on the bed. He's got on a tee with drawstring pajama pants. While looking, she takes a moment to consider where to start.

His arm. Yes. It won't involve moving any clothes. It'll be easy. So after checking that his eyes are still closed, she reaches her hand to his left arm and begins. She *draws* the first word of her note to him. Slowly, slowly, her finger barely traces a long line down the skin of his forearm— right over his tattoos. At the top and bottom of that finger-traced line, she then draws a short cross-line. When she's done, she lifts her hand and waits.

"*I?*" he whispers.

"*Yes,*" she whispers back. But more happens now, too. "Eyes closed," she reminds him as her fingers take the fabric of his tee and tug the shirt off over his head. After tossing the tee aside, she contemplates her next letter.

The Visitor

There is no touch between them until she makes her decision. This time, her finger traces along his left shoulder. Down, and across, then stop.

"*L*," Shane murmurs.

So Celia considers his body and moves to his jaw. Her finger barely draws a circle on it. A shadow of whiskers brushes against her skin.

"*O*," Shane goes on.

She tries to surprise him with where she lands each letter. So his other shoulder gets her tracing touch now. Slight, soft. Two long diagonal lines meet at the bottom.

"*V*," Shane says, eyes still closed.

Celia says nothing. Sitting up now, she squints through the shadows at his tattooed chest. Reaches for it, too. Her finger draws one solitary vertical line, then three shorter horizontal lines evenly spaced off of it.

"*E*." That's it. Shane whispers just that one letter into the dark room.

"*Yes*." Celia shifts on the bed. "Two words done, one to go."

But it'll be good for Shane to wait for it. To distract him from, well, from his world, his life right now. So, still sitting up, she straddles him on the mattress. Lifts one leg to one side of him, settles on his belly and shifts her other leg on this side.

"*One word left*," she murmurs, then sweeps her fingers over his eyes to keep them closed before tipping up his chin and exposing his neck. There, she traces the next letter—this time with her tongue. One long line, then another shorter one at an angle to it.

"*Y*," Shane's husky voice says.

Okay, so there might have been more than his uttered letter. Celia smiles. There might have been a slight moan. She bends low and circles his chest with her tongue. As she flicks it, she feels his hand reach up and slightly touch the back of her head. His fingers toy with her hair as her tongue grazes that next letter on his skin.

"*O*," Shane barely whispers.

The last letter now. Celia straddles him still in the darkness. Damp night air fills the room. Shane's eyes are closed; his breathing, deep. This letter needs some contemplation. Sitting there, she waits. Finally, with both hands running down his arms, Celia bends once more and with the tiniest kisses, begins. She kisses and sometimes flicks her tongue in a long, vertical line down his bare belly. Her hands softly follow that kissed line before she curves those tongue-kisses to the side, and lands her mini kisses in *another* line back *up* his belly.

"*U*," Shane scarcely breathes, almost choking up. "*U*."

Celia nods, though he wouldn't know it with his eyes closed. But she nods, then leans low. Her fingers alight on his face and trace softness there. "*Sincerely* ..." she whispers close into his ear. "*Celia.*"

Shane opens his eyes.

Celia, wearing silky polka-dot pajamas, straddles him. And again, there's that quiet. That rhythm of words and pauses. Comfortable pauses where no talking is necessary.

But there's something he *has* to say now, in the middle of the night, to this woman who just physically delivered her next note to him—one intimate letter at a time.

"Celia," he says, and she just looks at him. Tucks back her hair, too. "That … Well, I swear, Celia. Hell, that was the nicest letter anyone has ever sent to me. In my whole goddamn life."

"*Oh, Shane*," she whispers.

On her way down to kiss him, as she bends low, Shane does it. He slips his hands beneath her silky pajama top and manages to get it off her body. After he does, her arms reach to the mattress. With her hands splayed there on either side of his head, she meets his mouth with that kiss. Her silky hair falls forward; his hands run up the soft skin of her sides and feel the swell of her breasts. But she takes his hands. Takes them and presses them to the mattress. Lies on top of him, too, so that every part of their bodies touch—her legs over his, her hips pressed to his, their bellies together, her breasts to his chest—all while holding his hands to the mattress.

When she kisses him again, the kiss moves from his mouth, to his jaw, to his throat. Little kisses land on his skin, kisses flecked with her tongue, kisses gentle on his body. Kisses until she murmurs near his ear, "It's all true. Every word of my note, Shane. I hope you liked it."

And that's all she says—because her kisses start up again. They move from his ear to his mouth, which is when her kiss deepens.

When her mouth opens to his.

When her hands cradle his face, his neck, shoulders.

When she doesn't stop.

Somehow, during that long kiss, Celia gets his pajama pants off. His boxers, too. There are only murmurs in the dark now. And sighs. Shane's hands lower her silky polka-dot shorts, her panties. Celia whispers something *again*, her voice liquid and almost inaudible.

It takes a minute until it becomes clear to him *exactly* what Celia's murmurs are saying. In the black of night, it's hard to decipher. But he does. Each repeated murmur, between a kiss or following his touch, is the same. Over and over. Any way Celia can say it, show it, express it, she does.

"*I love you*," she says into that long kiss, and whispers again when he nuzzles her neck, her collarbone, and murmurs when his fingers run down her naked body, and sighs when his kisses follow his touches, and tells him when *her* fingers trace a tattoo on his shoulder.

But something changes when he lies on his side next to her on the bed, when he presses her hair back and touches her face, her jaw, her throat. This time, she says it with tears. "*I love you.*"

Says it again and again until he moves fully over her.

Until their kisses are too deep, too long, their touches too greedy, their bodies tangled and warm and wet as they make love and hold on, hold on, hold on.

twenty-two

IT WAS ALL WORTH IT.

Early Thursday morning, Jason stands in front of the porthole mirror in his bathroom. And knows. Yes, it was all worth it. Those shadows beneath his eyes. His hair needing a trim. The still unshaven face he hasn't had time to drag a razor over. It's been a solid two weeks since he last shaved at Ted Sullivan's place, and the whiskers are filling in. Hell, Jason didn't even bring his shaving gear to Maine—that's how urgent it was to get there.

Now, leaning on one forearm crutch in his bathroom back at home, he manages to draw his other hand over his jaw. For a moment longer, he stands there in his tee and pajama shorts. The sun is just cresting the horizon outside the window. The day's dawning. And he looks long at his reflection.

Yes, it was all worth it—the trip to Maine. Worth losing time for a friend. Because now? He doesn't mind what he sees looking back at him from that porthole mirror. And it all boils down to something his father used to tell him. His father would be proud of what Jason did the past few days—being there fully for an old friend. Being present. Helping Shane through.

It comes back to Jason now—the words his father said after the accident ten years ago.

Said to Jason when he struggled in his recovery.

When he wanted to give in to his meds. To his addiction to them.

When he wanted to give up.

You have to live in such a way, his father insisted, *that you can look yourself in the mirror.*

Lord knows, there were times early on when Jason couldn't look. Times when he was failing everyone around him: his father, especially; the woman who—God help her—loved him; failing himself. Those were the times when he turned away from the mirror. From everyone.

But no more.

"I'm trying, Dad," Jason says now with a glance out the window and toward the bluff. "Always trying."

Slowly then, Jason gets his pajamas off and drops them on the bathroom countertop. Sets aside his crutches next, lowers himself onto his teak shower bench, leans forward and turns on the shower. The thing is? He feels good about the week, about the past few days. He's glad he drove to Maine.

So sitting on his shower bench, Jason tips up his head, closes his eyes and lets the spray of water stream over his fatigue now. Fatigue rightfully earned.

twenty-three

"DENIED. DENIED. DENIED. DENIED. DENIED."

As he says it, Cliff stamps the next few ticket appeals lined up across his tanker desk. Sticky notes hang from his computer edge. The phone's ringing. The sound of some construction vehicle—a bulldozer or crane, maybe—makes its way through his tin trailer's open slider window. Oh, he can just imagine the dust rising from whatever cottage is undergoing a renovation now that the Hammer Law's lifted.

But the BOG ordinances are *not* lifted.

So he gets back to it. Gets back to the ticket appeals on his old desk. The Appeals Subcommittee turned them in to him, and this is the violators' last chance. Right here at his tanker desk. Cliff's vote decides the appeals' fate: *Approved* or *Denied*.

He picks up his *Denied* rubber stamper and starts stamping. Because … *really?* Rescind a few parking violations for residents who were *issued* Stony Point parking stickers but *lost* them and now claim to be unfairly fined?

"You have a responsibility for the safekeeping of that coveted sticker," Cliff insists as he stamps *Denied* across the parking appeals. His hand brushes over the next few appeals as his eyes skim the reasons. One is a fine for a small stockade fence—which the resident promises is temporary. *Only until our new hedges grow and fill in*, the offender wrote on their appeal.

"Oh, nice try. That'll take *years*," Cliff mutters, stamping *Denied* on the fence-fine appeal. "The rules—no manmade fences—are the rules."

Next up? A speeding golf cart appeal. Cliff reads the reasoning. Seems company had arrived at the cottage while family was on the beach. Petitioner argues that golf cart sped to cottage to greet guests. "But was there a medical emergency necessitating a speed-limit breach?" He flips over the appeal. Nothing. "Was someone in need of stitches? Or stung by a bee, maybe? Anything requiring help?" He flips the appeal back and stamps it. "*Denied*," he whispers, shaking his head. How most of these ticketed violations can even *be* appealed is beyond him.

He reaches for the next. "Seriously?" he asks, reading Elsa DeLuca's appeal to her tomato cart fine. Reading how the tomatoes were for the good of the community. That she was *sharing* her beautiful Stony Point bounty. That her cart of fresh vegetables would help keep people healthy!

Cliff sits back now and draws his hand down his chin.

And thinks of Elsa and that charming cart she set up to sell her garden goods. How she decorated that cart with whirligigs and seashells and a *Welcome* flag.

THE VISITOR

Cliff thinks of something else, too. Thinks of being at Jason's house last Saturday night. When Kyle tallied the *Cliff vs. Mitch* whiteboard list, the guys turned to Cliff on the deck and let him have it. Told him to put on his boxing gloves, for crying out loud. *Or else that Mitch will beat you to the punch*, Nick warned him.

"*Huh*," Cliff says, still contemplating Elsa's appeal. Well. One way to put on his boxing gloves is to give in to the appeal. To have a heart.

The rules are the rules, I know, Elsa recently told him. *But in life, sometimes people make exceptions. Especially for someone they might care about.*

"That does it," Cliff says, reaching for the *Approved* stamper now. Yes, the one time he caves with the appeals, it's for Elsa.

And even though it goes against his rules-resolve, he stamps her appeal: *Approved*.

Pushes back his chair then, too. Quickly. And a little in disbelief. Because he actually let an ordinance violator get off *scot-free*!

Elsa's *unauthorized* charming little tomato business happened *without* penalty.

Cliff shakes his head. What is his rationale here?

"Love," he quietly admits.

Yeah, and look what love gets you. Broken rules. Tested character. Bended will. "*Ach*," he says, standing and grabbing his gold-stitched *Commissioner* cap. After caving like that, he really needs to step away from all this Stony Point drama.

Step away from the drama of the heart, too.

"Maybe I'm just going soft," he says while taking in the

sight of several appeals waiting to be reviewed. Problem is, he caved to Elsa's. Who's to say he won't cave for the next appeal on the list?

Waving it all off, he grabs his keys and heads out the trailer door. Trots down the four metal stairs there, too. He has to get out of Dodge for an hour—and knows just the place.

Glancing back at his trailer with all of its pending appeals inside, he rushes to his car and speeds off—leaving that Stony Point tin-can trailer in his dust.

⁓

"*Aah,*" Cliff sighs after placing his lunch order and sitting back in his booth. Already his blood pressure's dropping. He knew the Dockside Diner would do that. There's the requisite shiny silver napkin dispenser on his table. Ketchup and mustard bottles are tucked against it. Salt and pepper shakers, too. Not to mention the laminated menu listing every lunch comfort food he could want.

But that's not what does it. Not what calms him down. No, it's this. Heck, from his window-side seat, Cliff feels like he's on a ship out at sea. First there's the fishing net dotted with starfish and seashells draped along the far wall. Vintage anchors lean there, too. Then there's the miniature fishing globes hanging in his window. A window overlooking a sparkling harbor, no less, beyond the little shops across the street. Why, he can practically feel the breeze that comes from sailing that sea.

"Yo, Judge. Got your deluxe burger platter here."

Cliff looks up from his diner-booth musing to see Kyle

standing there. He's got on a long chef apron over his standard work attire: black tee with black slacks. He's also lifting Cliff's lunch off a tray and setting it on the table.

"Kyle. Waiting tables today?" Cliff asks while making room for the food. He moves over the Stony Point Adult Ed Fall Catalog he picked up from a stack just inside the diner doors.

"Nah. Saw you come in, thought I'd say hello." Kyle sets down a glass of cola, too. "So what brings you to these parts?"

"Had to get out of there," Cliff answers in all seriousness, then picks up a napkin. While tucking it into his polo shirt collar, he notices Celia's home-staging course advertised in that adult-ed catalog.

"Wait." Kyle stands there holding that tray and squinting down at Cliff. "You had to get out of—the *beach*?"

"That's right. *You* review ordinance violations all morning and see how fast *you* run."

"You upholding the law there, Judge? Like you're supposed to?"

"Certainly was. Until the appeal for Elsa DeLuca's tomato cart fine landed on my desk." Cliff pulls his lunch platter closer. The cheeseburger is on toasted bread, so he lifts a slice to check out the bacon, lettuce and tomato beneath it.

"Oh, no." Kyle lifts a second plate and soda off that tray, then sits across from Cliff. He moves the empty tray to the edge of the table. "Elsa DeLuca's *appealing* to you? Sounds like you're maybe mixing business with pleasure?"

"Eh," Cliff mutters. He also eyes the sandwich plate in front of Kyle. "Hope that charred thing isn't for me."

185

"It's for me. Figured I'd eat it instead of tossing it in the trash." Kyle taps the sandwich's semi-charred bread. "It *was* for a customer, but I burnt it a little."

"To put it mildly. But, why? Something on *your* mind ... distracting *you*?"

"Distracting me?" Kyle picks up that sliced sandwich and pauses, the sandwich half hovering over his plate. "Huh. Matter of fact, Judge? There is."

⁓

Maybe this is good, Kyle thinks. This running into Cliff here. Heck, he's a former State of Connecticut judge, so he'll listen closely to Kyle's tale of woe. Offer some unbiased, judgelike advice, too.

So while digging into his charred BLT, Kyle unloads. He tells Cliff all about Shane's tough week. Talks about his crewmate Shiloh taking a fall on the lobster boat. About the deceptively calm waters of the Atlantic Ocean that day. About the Coast Guard rescue boat. The waiting ambulance. The valiant efforts to save Shiloh both on and off the water. The devastating death that came next.

"I'm pretty broken up about it. For my brother," Kyle explains, then takes a swallow of his iced soda. "And I'm trying to think of what I can do."

Cliff drags a few French fries through some ketchup. "What do you mean?" he asks.

"Well, I'm not there for him. I mean, Jason went there—"

"Jason? Jason went to Maine?"

Kyle nods. "He's back now. But he went for a day or two."

THE VISITOR

"Sounds serious, Kyle. Is your brother okay?"

"Shane? He's pretty shot, I guess. Shiloh was a good friend. They worked side by side for years. Anyway, Shane called Jason that night. After Shiloh died. And Shane, well … He was in a bad way, you know?"

"Wow." Cliff slowly shakes his head. "Well, that was nice of Jason, making the trip north."

"Yeah." Kyle leans over the table and takes a double bite of his burnt BLT. "So what about me? I'm Shane's brother, and after we fixed things this summer," he says around a mouthful of food, "well, I want to be a *decent* brother. One Shane can count on. And what can *I* do? Send him a card? Call him?"

"Those aren't bad ideas."

"They're not enough, though. Not for Shane and me. I mean, after a fifteen-year rift, we're only just now on speaking terms again. And I feel like I should do *more*, but my hands are tied here." Kyle lifts his soda glass. "Got any suggestions?"

"Well, there's always the usual," Cliff says.

"Hey, Kyle," an older man interrupts as he walks past, check in hand. "Thanks for the grub. Good as always."

Kyle reaches over and slaps the customer's arm. "Good seeing you, Smithy," he calls after him, then turns to Cliff again. "The *usual*?" Kyle asks.

"Sure. Some people send flowers."

"Flowers?"

"Or a plant," Cliff says, taking another bite of his deluxe burger. "You can have it delivered."

"A plant. Sheesh, I don't know. Shane'll be out on the water for days at a time. He'll come back to some plant shriveled out on his deck."

"Well," Cliff goes on, scooping a spoonful of coleslaw. "If Shane was closer, you'd maybe go out to dinner. So you could, I don't know, send him a restaurant gift card?"

"Why? To go to dinner alone?" Kyle asks, dabbing his forehead with a paper napkin from the dispenser. "Kind of defeats the purpose if I can't share the meal with him. Talk at the table."

"Guess so. How about this?" Cliff suggests, downing a few of those ketchuped fries. "Can you drive up there this weekend?"

"Oh, man. It's busier than *ever* here on the weekends. And Evan's got soccer. Hailey has Saturday dance class. I can't leave it *all* on Lauren. Or on my diner help."

"It's tough, then. You're spread pretty thin with your time, Kyle."

"I am." Kyle looks out into the diner. Nearly every table is filled and it's only Thursday. People talk; silverware clinks; the waitresses are bustling. "Between here, and home. House projects, and the kids. I'm *booked.*"

"Okay." Cliff lifts what's left of his burger. "So let's get back to the basics."

"Basics?"

"Sure. What would you do *normally*? If Shane lived *here*, I mean. You'd go to the wake," Cliff says, pointing that hunk of burger Kyle's way. "You might go to the funeral services, too. Or just have a beer with Shane, maybe. Sit out on the rocks, do some fishing and talk about his friend. *That's* why it's a tough situation."

"*What?* Why? I don't get it."

"You can't *do* the normal stuff, with Shane living five

hours away," Cliff concludes, pressing that hunk of cheeseburger into his mouth. "So you have to come up with some *variation* of normal," he says around the food.

"Right." Kyle nods. "*So what would I normally do?*" he whispers to himself. "Got to mull that over. Come up with something normal I can … adapt," he tells Cliff. "I'll give it some thought. Because, you know, you might be onto something." Kyle wipes his mouth with a napkin, stands and picks up that empty serving tray.

"Glad to talk it out, Kyle. If there's anything else …"

"Nah, I'm good. You got my wheels turnin' now," Kyle says, tapping the side of his head. "Thanks for the wisdom, Judge."

⁓

Kyle leaves before Cliff can even say more. He watches Kyle wind through the crowded diner. With that serving tray in one hand, he bends and shakes the hand of a smiling baby in a highchair. Turns and waves to a customer heading out. Grabs a couple of dirty dishes off an empty table. Whistles as he nears the kitchen.

So Cliff scoops another spoonful of coleslaw and turns back to that adult-ed catalog. Reads about Celia's staging class. Flips the page to computer class listings. Another page to keeping-fit activities. And sees something intriguing there.

Something *woo*-worthy for the woman who's softening his ironclad will these days.

Something to impress Elsa.

So Cliff sets down his spoon, moves his dishes aside and

pulls that adult-ed catalog closer. Tunes out the clicking flatware and chatting diner voices around him. Leans over that catalog and really scrutinizes what he's seeing.

Okay. He'll step up his game, all right. Put on those boxing gloves—once and for all.

"*It's a duel, Fenwick,*" Cliff whispers now. Because apparently Mitch is known for his fancy footwork, Southern style—shagging!

Yeah, I can waltz, Cliff thinks. *And slow-dance. But how about this?*

He lifts that darn flyer and squints carefully at the details of one class in particular.

Beginning Line Dancing
For the basic beginner ... just getting their feet wet ... Style, techniques, etiquette ... Different dance taught every session ... Links provided to online instructional videos for at-home practice.

"*Huh,*" Cliff quietly says, sitting back in the diner booth. He can already see himself stompin' and swivelin' and scootin' around that tin-can trailer.

So now? Now he punches one fist into the other hand. Boxing gloves are *on*. Yep, he's going to dance *circles* around the competition.

Because, heck. When opportunity knocks to whirl and twirl his girl, he's got to get down and dirty—and *win* that *Cliff vs. Mitch* dance point.

twenty-four

THURSDAY MORNING FEELS LIKE DÉJÀ vu.

After Shiloh's funeral and graveside service, Keith and Tammy host a gathering celebrating their son's life. The event's happening at the large barn on their property.

Shane arrives there with Celia and thinks he saw this very same sight less than a week ago. Just *Saturday* morning, he arrived at Tammy and Keith's farm for a barn brunch. A stream of pickup trucks and cars turned into the side yard that day. Vehicle doors slammed; farm dogs trotted around the arriving guests; guys from the lobster crews milled about, laughing and talking; the American flag fluttered on the flagpole. Then there was the barn. A banner of flags—lobster flags and fishing vessel flags—was strung over the barn's open wooden doors. Inside that vaulted barn? Tables and tables were set with a brunch feast; clear illuminated bulbs hung from the rough-hewn rafters.

Today, it feels the same. The vehicles streaming in again.

The people walking about. The farm dogs. It feels like déjà vu.

But only until Shane stands at a podium in that barn. Before the food is served, he's one of the last people to offer words of remembrance. Ready to talk *about*—rather than *to*—Shiloh. Shane looks out at the sea of somber faces watching him behind the podium. Rows and rows of rented folding chairs are filled with guests. Behind those chairs, more people are seated at old picnic tables. Shiloh's extended family is there. Friends. Neighbors. And the guys—all from different fisheries. Except instead of seeing them in jeans and tees and flannels and work boots? Today the crews are in black suits, and dark blue, and grays. Neckties hang beneath suit jackets.

Déjà vu? Shane thinks. *Like shit.*

Everything—from the muted lobster crews to the black sash of mourning now strung across the barn's open doors to Tammy's hand clutching crumpled tissues—is wrong.

Wrong, wrong, wrong.

But it's reality.

So Shane takes a breath, adjusts the mic at the podium and begins.

"Here in Maine, there are 3,478 miles of coastline," he says. "And let me tell you, there isn't another mile as torn apart and broken up as the mile *we're* on right here. Right now."

A few people nod. No one speaks. The crowd just listens to Shane's stories about Shiloh.

And Shane's not sure how he gets through it all in one piece, but he does. He finds the truths that all the mourners might recognize in Shiloh—lobstermen or not. He talks about Shiloh's greenhorn days. About how he was put to the test in order to fit in. To sink or swim.

"Shiloh never sank. From the get-go, he was one of us," Shane says. He goes on, too, talking about friendship. About shopping for lobstering gear with Shi. "Oh, man. He'd find those thirty-percent coupons at MaineStay, and we'd make a day out of it. Load up on bib pants and oilskin jackets and boots and sweatshirts for the season." Shane takes a long breath. But says little more. Only that Shiloh loved being on the boat. And on the ocean. That he did his family proud. Another pause. Another long look at the sea of faces. "We'll surely miss you, Shiloh," Shane says, turning his gaze toward the blue sky beyond the open barn doors.

As soon as Shane steps away from the podium, he notices something.

Notices Celia getting up from her folding chair and hurrying in his direction. He figures she wants to maybe walk with him back to his seat. Or tell him something. When he meets her as she steps closer, she gives him a sad smile. "I have something I'd like to say," she lets on.

"What is it?" he asks, taking her hands.

"No. I mean, something to say to everyone here."

He looks at her for a second, nods and steps back as Celia takes the podium then. Standing in the shadows now, Shane just watches her. She's wearing a brown tweed blazer open over an untucked cream-colored blouse and brown skinny pants. Gold chains hang loose over her blouse. Her auburn hair is down. She adjusts the mic and greets everyone. In the vast barn, her voice is clear, but soft, as she begins. Shane stands to the side, clasps his hands and only watches.

"Some people ... some people you know *all* your life. For *years*. From when you were a child, to today. Through every milestone," Celia says at that podium. "And some people? Some people pass through your life for just a few minutes. For only a few sweeps of that second hand around a clock."

With those words, Shane thinks of the watch *he's* wearing. The silver-gray watch Jason gave him to help get through an hour at a time.

An hour.

Minutes.

Seconds.

"I knew Shiloh for only that—for several minutes," Celia explains to the silent crowd. "I met him a couple of weeks ago in the place he loved most. On the docks, near the lobster boats. I was walking there with Shane. The harbor water was lightly sloshing. Some seagulls were crying. The sea breeze, blowing. It was a beautiful morning. And Shane introduced me and my daughter to a friend of his that day—someone *else* walking the docks. It was Shiloh." Celia pauses with a sad smile and pats her heart. "There's so much I'll never forget about the few minutes— yes, *minutes*—that we talked there. No, I'll never forget the twinkle in Shiloh's eyes as he ribbed Shane about his new girl. About me. I'll never forget the way Shiloh spoke to my infant daughter ... and gently, *gently* ran a finger along her cheek as he said hello to her. And told her about all the lobsters out in the sea. I'll never forget either his way of *listening*, of looking directly at me when I told him a little about myself. Scarce sentences about my home. My work. And I'll never forget the way Shiloh's hair lifted in the salty breeze. And his absolute ease standing there on the docks. And especially? When he left? I'll never forget the way he turned back and called out to Shane, *I'll be in touch when the captain calls, bub*."

When she says that, when she speaks of Shiloh's nickname for Shane, she looks at only him. From the shadows in the barn, he nods and waits for her to go on.

"So I just wanted you all to know," Celia says then, "that in only a few minutes—eight or ten, tops—I could see, and will never forget, that Shiloh was a great friend to someone I love. And *because* of those few minutes, I'll always miss Shiloh … in my own way."

Okay, that does it. Shane fought his emotion all morning. At the funeral, at the cemetery. He held it in. He stood stoic. But hearing Celia talk with such tenderness about friendship and love, it chokes him up. The knot in his throat stops him from even talking. Apparently he's not alone, either. When she leaves the podium to a round of applause and heads his way, Shane sees something. Her words got to others, too. Because there's Tammy and Keith intercepting her and hugging her and talking close. Shane catches up with them right as Tammy's taking Celia's hand and leaning to her.

"Shane showed me a picture of you last weekend. At our barn brunch." Tammy reaches out and touches Celia's hair, her shoulder.

And Shane sees. Tammy's desperately seeking any

connection to Shiloh, *any*, during this difficult day. And here's one she was unaware of.

"You're as *beautiful* in person," Tammy's saying. "I'm *so* glad my Shiloh got to know you, too. That you were in his life, even briefly."

"The honor was all mine," Celia assures Tammy and Keith as she briefly clasps their hands.

"Listen." Shane comes up beside Celia. "I wanted to ask you both something," he mentions to Shiloh's parents.

"Shane," Keith says. "Thank you for your kind words earlier, about our son."

"Absolutely. I'll miss Shiloh tremendously. Which is why I wanted to run this by you."

"What is it?" Tammy presses.

"Well, I see that Alex is here. And of course, he's not set up for giving tats. But I asked him earlier, in the parking lot, if he had his gear with him. And he *does*. So with your approval, Keith. And Tammy … We'd like to set up a table for tattoos."

"*Today?*" Keith looks around at the crowded barn. "Well, I don't know if that's appropriate."

"Keith," Tammy says, clasping her husband's arm. "Hear Shane out."

Celia takes Shane's hand then. "*Shane*," she whispers. "*Are you sure?*"

"I am. Because Shiloh was a great friend of mine, and this is a way of keeping a promise I made to him."

"A promise?" Keith asks.

Shane nods, and tells him how he and Shiloh were going to get a tattoo at the barn brunch this past Saturday. It was going to be Shiloh's first, as a lobsterman. "But I got called away to Connecticut, and had to leave the brunch early," Shane explains. "And Shiloh? I talked to him late Sunday when he had supper at my place—which is when he told me he never *did* get a tat at the brunch. Said that after I left, he, well, he chickened out ... and the boys? Oh, they gave him hell. So I promised Shi, *next time*. We'd both get inked next time Alex was set up. And so—"

"*This is next time*," Tammy whispers. Her eyes are filled with tears, too. "And you want to fulfill that promise?"

"I do." Shane looks toward the front of the barn, where a couple of guys are moving an empty table closer to the open doors. Sunshine streams into the space; a small line is already forming; Alex stands back with a carton in his arms. "And some of the boys want to join in, too. In Shiloh's honor. So," Shane says, nodding to the cleared table, "with your permission?"

∼

Celia and Shane don't go to the tattoo table right away. Shane wants to make the rounds and talk with some of Shiloh's extended family. Wants to see some of the fishermen, too. And his neighbor Bruno is over at the food table, so they head that way first.

But they don't make it there easily. Guys that Shane's worked with over the years stop him. Slap his shoulder. Talk lobstering.

> *Where the hell's this crazy industry headed?* one of them says.
> *Canada*, another answers. *To colder waters.*
> *Get outta here. You don't believe that bullshit, do ya?*

It ain't BS, brother. Climate change is coming for us in Maine. Eh, that's just a rumor—no?

Regardless, sock that dough away while the good times last, boys, says another.

The barn is noisier now. People are chatting. Socializing. Catching up. Remembering Shiloh together. Shane also points out to Celia some of the decorations left over from Saturday's brunch here. The clear illuminated bulbs hanging from the rafters. The burlap-wrapped jars filled with sand and seashells. The lobster flags and fishing vessel flags strung beneath the black sash draped across the open barn doors.

"Who'd have thought they'd be used again like this?" Shane asks, shaking his head.

Celia agrees as they take their place in the food line now. A buffet is laid out on two long tables, and people slowly fill their plates. Shane steps ahead and tells Bruno to save him a seat, then rejoins Celia. But right as he gives her a plate off a stack there, a noise rises. It's a little alarming, this sound. Jarring. Something about it gets people to quiet. To look around for where it might be coming from. Shane and Celia look, too.

When Celia sees it first, her heart breaks. She nudges Shane. It's Tammy, over to the side of the barn. What started as one sob ... erupts. Waves of those gasping sobs rise right out of Tammy's body. The sound's almost fluid, the way one sob follows another, over and over and over. The grief in that sound is painful. Every heart, oh Celia knows it, *every* heart in that vast barn breaks all over again— right with the mother who lost her only son. It seems the finality of that just now caught up with her.

The Visitor

Celia loops her arm through Shane's as he watches with concern, too. Watches Keith lead Tammy into the nearby shadows. Tammy's body is defeated: her head, bent; her shoulders, hunched; her chest, gasping. All the while, those plaintive sounds bubble up, again and again. Someone brings her a glass of water.

"Get it together, Tam," Keith says, gently taking his wife by the shoulders, wiping her face. "Get it together. *Come on*," he softly—but adamantly—encourages her quivering body. "You can do it."

As Celia's watching, though, she's unexpectedly alarmed by something else. It's Shane. He pulls away from her and tears out of the barn. Wordlessly—and quickly—he walks straight out into the sunshine and leaves Celia behind. There's almost a ferocity to the suddenness of his departure.

Celia just stands there, glances to Tammy, then watches Shane leave. He doesn't look back. Doesn't stop walking, either. It takes a long moment for Celia to get past the abruptness of it all. So after glancing once more to Shiloh's mother collecting herself over in the shadows, Celia turns and heads out of the barn.

To what, she's not sure. The glaring sunlight doesn't help. Celia stops outside the big double barn doors, shields her eyes and squints around the yard. But there's no Shane in sight. So she walks further out into the yard and glances toward the farmhouse in the distance.

No Shane there. Not on the porch. Not going through the door.

So Celia looks around from where she's standing in the middle of the sloping backyard. The only person she notices is Shane's captain. He's standing in the shade of a maple tree in the side of the yard and having a smoke there. Celia looks at him, hesitates, then heads back toward the barn. On the way, though, she looks back at the captain. It's obvious by his stance that while he's smoking, he's watching something. Something off a ways, beside the barn. So Celia veers around over in that direction.

And stops.

There. Beside the barn. Wearing his black suit, Shane's standing alone and somewhat pacing. His suit jacket's unbuttoned. The sleeves are shoved up. The ground around him is all unkempt grass and weeds. There's a long garden table there, too, against a rudimentary lean-to hut tacked onto the barn. That wooden table is covered with clay pots and trowels and shovels. A few piles of potting soil are mounded there. Celia makes it all out, quickly, before looking first back at the captain out in the yard, then again at Shane. Shane's dragging a hand through his hair now, and doesn't stop that pacing. *Just* as she's about to call his name, to get his attention, he makes a move that stops her. Both his hands grab hold of that long, heavy garden table. He takes hold of it and roughly flips it. Flips it right back so that it crashes into the side of that garden lean-to. The clay pots fly in every direction before shattering to the ground. The trowels and shovels soar into the air before also clattering down. With the force of Shane's table-flip, those mounds of potting soil are obliterated into nothing more than scattered dust. The table itself ends up tipped on edge and leaning askew on the ground, too.

It's like a bomb went off outside that run-down hut. Some angry bomb.

Celia, well, she steps back. And looks around. She half expects a crowd to rush out from the barn after that racket. But the barn's so large, so vast, so filled with people and noise that no one notices.

Well, maybe one person does. Because a movement catches her eye. It's Shane's captain from the boat. He's stamping out his cigarette while fully watching Shane. But the captain doesn't walk toward him; doesn't step in to intervene. He just silently turns away, veers around in a wide path and heads back toward the barn entrance.

When Celia looks to Shane again, it's obvious he didn't see his captain there. Didn't see his captain witness what he just did.

But Celia? Celia saw the captain. She saw Shane's garden-table breakdown. Saw his rage.

She saw it all.

―

Shane squeezes his eyes closed at the sight of clay pot shards and askew tools and scattered dirt. It's too much, too much—seeing the destruction he just wreaked on the farm here.

Seeing the destruction of Keith and Tammy inside.

Seeing the destruction Shiloh's death inflicted on their lives.

Seeing Tammy just *lose* it. Lose it to her deep sorrow.

Shane's anger at it all knows no bounds today. So he breathes—long, fast breaths.

Tips his head up to the God damn beautiful sky.

Looks at the gardening detritus at his feet.

Tears off his suit jacket and tosses it aside when he can't get a decent breath.

Jumps when someone's taking his arm. He whips around and sees that it's Celia.

"*What the hell are you doing?*" she hisses at him while giving that arm a yank.

"Nothing." He looks long at her. At her hazel eyes visibly upset. At her hair blowing in the soft breeze. At her hand still clutching his arm. At her blouse and her gold chain necklaces and her tweed jacket and her worry. "Nothing, I'm doing nothing," he tells her—then leans close. His jaw is clenched. His mouth is dry. His voice, hoarse. "What the hell do I *ever* do? Nothing. What the hell did I do Monday? Nothing. Did I notice anything off with Shiloh? Did I notice he was maybe off-balance on deck? I saw him, Celia. Saw a missed step or two. And chalked it up to—nothing. To being off the water for two weeks." He takes her by the shoulders now and gives a slight shake. "Did I ask Shiloh if he was okay? No, I asked nothing. I moved on to the next string. The next haul while a third crewman baited traps. Could I have saved Shiloh? Who knows?" The closer Shane tugs Celia, the more his voice drops. "Instead, I crouched beside him when the damage was already done and could do ... *nothing*. Told Shiloh to keep his eyes open. To breathe. To stay with us." Shane stops then. Burning tears run down his face. He looks up at that fucking blue sky once more—as if there's some answer there. Still gripping Celia close, he looks through his tears at her. "Okay, Celia? *Okay?*" he asks, his words angry;

his grip on her tight; his bent posture, rigid. "I told Shiloh to stay with us, and he *left*. Left. Left his mother in there practically on the *floor* with unimaginable sorrow. So … what was I good for?" Shane lets go of her, swipes his face, takes another shaking breath. When his voice comes next, it's low and emotionless. "Nothing."

⁓

Celia doesn't speak.

She steps back, though, her eyes never leaving Shane's. Not until she takes a few *more* steps back and the wide barn entrance suddenly comes into view. So she knows—Shane's breakdown was also out of view from anyone *inside* the barn. She looks away from him now and sees Alex. He's all set up with his tattoo gear just past the barn's wide doorway. Inkpots are spread out. Gauze and napkins, too. Some guy's sitting at that table. The man's suit jacket is off, his shirtsleeve is rolled up, and Alex is bent over that exposed arm with his tattoo pen.

Celia doesn't look at Shane again. Watching Alex, she just straightens her blouse, her blazer.

And walks away.

Shane's anger is about more than Shiloh; there's no denying that. It's about so much, and Celia can figure what some of it is. It's frustration at the distance between here and his Connecticut life; frustration at his still-hidden relationship with her; frustration at undeniable changes ahead in the lobstering industry—the only livelihood he's ever known; frustration at a fifteen-year mistake with his brother, Kyle; at losing a friend this week; at potentially losing everything—herself included.

Well, Celia's not going to stay on the sidelines and watch. Because she can't tolerate Shane's recklessness. Not in *her* life; not with the baby. So she walks steady toward the front of that barn.

Until Shane grabs *her* arm from behind.

"Celia. What are *you* doing?" he asks.

Celia glances over her shoulder at him. He's right there, close. "*I'm not listening to this*," she says between clenched teeth. "*Not listening to you anymore.*" Then? Then she pulls her arm out of his hold and keeps walking. "So I'm going to Alex's table and getting a tattoo."

"No, you're not."

"*Yes*, I am." She doesn't look at Shane. But Celia feels his presence hurrying along beside her. "*You're* not going to tell *me* what to do," she insists, looking only straight ahead.

Again Shane takes her arm, this time stopping her stride. He turns her to him, takes her other arm, too, and backs her up against the barn's outside wall. She feels the barnboard press against her back. Feels the crunch of scattered clay pot shards beneath her shoes. Feels her hair mussed against that dried-out barn wall.

"Celia." Shane steps closer, his hold unforgiving. "That's bullshit, that tattoo crap."

"I want one," Celia tosses out, her voice flat. She doesn't push back physically. She just lets Shane press her there against that barn wall.

"You do *not*, and you know it. It's not your style, Celia."

"*What do you know about style?*" she hisses back. "About *me*? You've known me for what? Six weeks, give or take?"

"Jesus. Are we seriously going *there*?" he asks.

But the whole time, Shane doesn't look away. He bends close to hold her eye. Which is why she can see more now. She sees something and it's not so much anger. Hell, Shane's afraid. He's really afraid. These past few days reminded him, without mistake, how easily someone can slip away. Walk away. Turn away. Die. Leave him for no good reason. It's not the first time that's happened to him, either. Maris walked away from him years ago. Kyle pretty much left him for dead for fifteen years. And now, this. Shiloh's unexpected death seems to have scared the daylights out of him.

"*Listen*," Celia whispers. "Maybe you *don't* really know too much about me. But people here, today? They can see *plenty* about *you*, Shane Bradford. And is this what you want them to see? You want them to see you turn on everybody because of what happened? Turn on Tammy and Keith with your rash behavior out here? Turn on *me*?"

Shane looks away, shakes his head, then looks back at her.

"Shane," Celia quietly says, still pinned to that barn wall. She moves her hands to take hold of his forearms. "It's not that you can't feel things. But *staying* angry? It's not good, let me tell you."

Shane doesn't speak. Doesn't back away, but doesn't speak, either. He only manages a difficult swallow.

"Anger," Celia says, nodding to the garden table mess around them, "does *nothing*. Nothing to help. Anger's just a wall that nobody can penetrate. Remember that day last month when I got caught in a rainstorm while walking past your cottage? And you took me in? I had an angry breakdown in your living room. I told you about Sal keeping his dirty little secret from me to get what he wanted. It was pouring rain out, and *I* poured my angry *heart* out. To *you*. Do you know, Shane? Do you know the only thing that finally made that anger subside?" She squints at him. "*Do you?*" she whispers.

He only shakes his head. Still holds her pinned there, too.

"*Letting the light in,*" she whispers, her eyes filling with tears now. Those tears streak her face. She gasps a small sob, too. "*Letting Aria in, my sweet, sweet Aria. Letting her beautifully into my life.*" Celia hesitates, looking at his shadowed face, his troubled eyes, before continuing there—against the barn, in the midday sunshine. "And letting in one more person. Just one." She gives Shane a teary, sad smile. "*You.* And I *can't* stand by you like this."

"Celia," Shane finally says, his voice low. Regretful now, even.

"Let go of me," Celia tells him then.

Shane does. He drops his hands, steps back and nods at her. So she collects herself, brushes back her hair and walks away. She heads around to those big open barn doors. But before turning inside, she gives one look over her shoulder. Shane's moved down to that lean-to hut. He's scooping up his suit jacket off the ground there, and trying to right the flipped garden table.

So Celia looks no longer. She steps inside the barn instead and gets in line for her tattoo.

⁓

Shane does the best he can. In his grief, in his regret, in his embarrassment, he tries to right the mess beside Tammy and Keith's barn. Once the garden table's back in place, he picks up the random shovels and garden tools and sets them on that table. The shards of broken pots will have to be raked up later.

For now, he's got something more important to do.

Grabbing his black suit jacket off the table, he slips his arms into it, lifts it over his shoulders, straightens his tie, clears his throat.

And walks around to the barn's double doors.

In the nick of time, too. Only one person's ahead of Celia in the tattoo line. So Shane calmly comes up beside her. Without touching her, he leans close. "*I'm so sorry, Celia,*" he whispers.

Celia looks up at him. Her eyes are gentle. She understands.

So Shane puts a hand on her shoulder and bends low. His eyes drop closed as he presses his mouth to her hair. "*Please forgive me,*" he quietly begs.

Yes, begs.

Celia looks at him again, touches the side of his head, brushes her fingers across his hair—and nods.

Shane moves right beside her then. And when the guy in front of them takes a seat at Alex's tattoo table, takes off his button-down and shoves up his tee sleeve, Shane nudges Celia aside.

"I know what you were doing here, Celia, and you don't have to. *I'll* get inked," he tells her as Alex finishes up with a small tat on the guy ahead of them. "I promised Shiloh that he and I both would, next time. Let me keep my promise."

"There's the man," Alex calls out, motioning Shane to the table. "Thought you took off."

"No," Shane says. "Just had to step away for a few."

"Got it." As Alex changes into clean disposable gloves, he asks Shane, "What'll it be, guy?"

Shane takes off his jacket and drapes it on the chairback there. Starts unbuttoning his shirt, too. And looks back at Celia as he takes his seat at the tattoo table. "Any suggestions?" he asks her.

Celia nods, then pulls up a chair beside Shane's. She sits with him, runs her hand over his arm and leans close. "*Bub*," she whispers.

Shane tips his head, looking at her.

"You'll hear Shiloh's voice whenever you see that nickname," Celia softly explains, then sits back in her chair to watch.

Before Shane preps for his tattoo, though, he leans over. Puts an arm around Celia's shoulders, pulls her close and kisses the side of her head. Presses that one kiss there for several seconds.

Then? He finishes unbuttoning his white shirt and takes it off. Sitting there in only his T-shirt and dress pants, he sets his arm on the table, points to a spot above his elbow and nods for Alex to begin.

twenty-five

BACK AND FORTH. BACK AND forth. Up and down. Back and forth.

By late Thursday morning, Elsa and her floral-print rubber clogs have practically worn a path between her Sea Garden and the stone garden shed. First she removed any remaining tomato stakes and her cherry-tomato trellis. All of those supports got sprayed with a bleach-and-water solution before being rinsed off with her garden hose. Now the wood stakes and crisscross trellis lean against the stone shed.

Next up? She's back at her garden. It's time to pull out any withering plants and weeds. "*Hmm. Where did I put my floral kneeling mat?*" she whispers while looking around. "*Ugh,*" she finally says, realizing she left it in the shed. One more back and forth will do her in. So instead, she looks down at her striped tee over cropped jeans and clogs, shrugs and does it. She drops to her knees—dirt stains be damned. Pulls cloth gloves out of her garden apron, too, and starts yanking and tossing plant debris.

Row by row, Elsa works her way across the garden—sans her cushioned knee mat. There's a hint of autumn in the September air. The sun shines warm on her back.

Until a shadow falls over her.

When she looks up, Cliff's holding a bag and standing at the garden gate.

"There you are, Elsa," he says, opening the gate and walking to a nearby bench. "I was looking all over for you."

Elsa sits back on her haunches and tucks an escaped strand of hair behind the rolled bandana on her head. "Cliff. What are you doing here? Shouldn't you be working?"

Cliff sets that bag on the bench and turns to her. "Just a quick visit, some of which *is* work-related," he says, then motions to her knees. "You're covered with mud, you know."

"Yes, I know." Elsa looks at her mud-stained jeans, kneels in the dirt again and tugs out a few weeds. "I forgot my garden mat in the shed."

"But you ruined your pants!"

"I'll worry about that later." She tosses the weeds in a debris pile and sits back again, squinting over at Cliff near the bench. He's pulling paper plates, napkins and what looks like a plastic knife out of that bag he brought. "What in heaven's name are you doing?"

Cliff looks back at her. "Had an early lunch at the diner. Kyle packed this dessert for me." Cliff lifts some wrapped-up morsel from that bag. "Poor Kyle."

"What do you mean, *poor Kyle*?" Elsa asks. "What's happened now?"

"You haven't heard?"

"Heard what?"

"About Shane."

"Shane? I thought you said Kyle."

Cliff walks into the garden and extends a hand to help Elsa up. "Come sit on the bench and I'll fill you in."

Elsa sits with Cliff then, and is riveted to this story finally reaching *her* through the Stony Point pipeline. Cliff talks about Shane and his crewmate friend Shiloh. And a tragic fall on the lobster boat. And the unknown of what came first: Shiloh's fall, or some medical issue that *caused* his fall. Cliff takes off his *Commissioner* cap, sets it on the bench and goes on.

Sadly, the kid didn't make it … Shane's really upset … Called Jason that night … He made the trip north … Kyle feels for Shane … Wants to reach out to him.

"Oh, *my* heart breaks for Shane, too," Elsa says. "And for that dear Shiloh and his family. They lost their son—and so young. Even younger than my Sal was."

"I know. And for Shane? *Everyone* here seems to feel some of that loss. Kyle especially. And he wants to do something for his brother."

"So do I. I'll get in touch with Shane. Send him a nice card with a note."

"He'd like that, Elsa." Cliff picks up that wrapped food now. "But that's not why I'm here, actually."

"Wait. Is that a brownie?" Elsa asks as Cliff unwraps some pastry and sets it on a paper plate. She leans closer. "One of those delectable, loaded *fudge* brownies Kyle sells?"

"It sure is." Cliff drops the knife through it and slices it in half. "And Elsa, while you have a piece of this brownie, well, I want you to know …"

"Oh, *Marone*. What else?"

"Well, *this* is the work part of my visit." Cliff drops a brownie half on the second plate. "I want you to know that *I*, along with the Stony Point Board of Governors, have agreed to rescind your tomato cart fine."

"*What?*" Elsa lightly slaps his arm. "I'm shocked! On what grounds?"

Cliff reaches into his pants pocket and pulls out her folded appeal—stamped *Approved*. "On what grounds?" he repeats, then hands her the form. "On a caring heart that's gone somewhat soft, I guess."

"But—"

Cliff stops her when he also gives her the paper plate holding her fudge-frosted brownie.

Sitting there in the warm sunshine, with her muddied jeans and gardening-mussed hair, Elsa just shakes her head with a small smile that she feels all the way down to *her* heart.

Oh, and she darn well peels off her dirty gloves, *lifts* that loaded brownie, cups a hand beneath it and digs right in.

This little shotgun cottage hangs in limbo—unlike his life.

Because it's lunchtime … but Jason's work can't stop. Lunchtime just means he gets to squeeze in eating *with* the work. Like he knew it would, that two-day Maine trip caused a pileup from here to what feels like eternity. So he sits at an old picnic table in the shotgun cottage's side yard. His lunch cooler is on the table. But a finished blueprint is anchored down, too. Beside his dinging phone. Still, he first unflattens the foil wrapping from his turkey sandwich on a hard roll and uses the crumpled foil as a plate. Dumps a bag of organic chips on it, beside the sandwich oozing mayo and mustard and fresh tomato juices and shredded lettuce. Sets a nectarine off to the side. Sips from a bottled water.

And eyes that cottage-in-limbo here at White Sands Beach.

It looks the same as the last time he was here, and for one reason. The reno work's been waiting on *him*. Waiting on this finished blueprint for the portico revised to a full-on screened-in porch. So for now, the empty cottage's brown shingles are *still* tinged black from the sea damp. The window-trim paint is *still* faded. That one loose shutter *still* hangs askew. Jason blows out a long breath. Because he knows it's more of the same inside, too. The paused interior demo leaves nothing more than dried-out and exposed laths and rafters. Construction work couldn't move forward until today; the supplies couldn't be ordered.

Yep, in limbo.

As opposed to the *Planner* app on his phone. After taking a double bite of that sandwich, Jason adjusts his brimmed cap and scrolls that app. Rolling down the screen are all the jobs he's already completed today: returned phone calls to contractors; new client contract-signing, this one right at Stony Point; quick stop at the tiny Beach Box reno over on Ridgewood Road; portico-to-front-porch redesign work in the barn studio—for *this* very shotgun cottage.

"*Check, check, check, check,*" Jason whispers. He looks up at the stalled cottage now, then at his blueprint. His design actually extends the peaked roofline several feet to accommodate the new porch. The whole look is open, airy and casual. Shaded, too.

More important, his clients Austin and Nina just signed off their approval.

The reno can move forward.

So he returns the rolled-up blueprint to its tube. Next, he picks up his phone and swipes photos of the *new* project he signed on earlier back in Stony Point. It's another small ranch the owners want to enlarge. But there's no *way* zoning will allow the footprint to be expanded on the quarter-acre lot, so all Jason can do is go up.

With a limited budget.

After downing a handful of those organic chips, he toggles from the photos to answering emails on his phone. While doing so, he finishes his sandwich with a few hefty bites. Pulls up his afternoon schedule. Looks at it, and reaches for his nectarine. Shifts on the picnic-table bench seat.

Decides to pause working for as long as it takes to eat that nectarine. A few minutes, tops. So he turns around on the bench seat and leans his elbows back on the slivery tabletop. Nudges up his cap. The sun still shines warm this late in September. A sea breeze rustles the leaves of a nearby tree.

Slacking on the job? Jason hears whispered—and tips his head. But, nothing more. *Was* it Neil? Or was it only Jason *wishing* his brother were here to pick *up* the slack. When they worked together before the crash, Barlow Architecture was busy as hell getting off the ground—and Neil kept them flying.

"*More like keeping my energy up,*" Jason whispers back, then bites again into the dripping nectarine. *"Trip to Maine threw a monkey wrench into my schedule."*

Quiet seconds pass.

It's good you went, he eventually hears. Or that breeze picks up. *Life first, then work.*

It's true. Jason knows it. Putting life first means having no regrets. And he has none—even being up the wazoo with work since his Maine trip. Worth it.

So—nectarine done—he pulls up his *Planner* app and sees what's next in his day. A stop at the Fenwick cottage with Trent. But if he leaves here now, there's enough time beforehand to visit the site of that *new* job he signed on. He'll look again at that ranch on the too-small yard; look at the sun's illumination; study any trees; examine varying views.

Okay, so he packs up his lunch, adds that next stop to his *Planner*, calls the contractor for *this* shotgun reno to give him the green light, and heads to his SUV.

First up? He'll swap his SUV for Maris' golf cart and drive *that* between his two Stony Point jobs—the ranch and the Fenwick place. The golf cart's a helluva lot easier to maneuver around all the construction vehicles there now that the Hammer Law's lifted. So after loading his lunch gear into the SUV, he climbs in the driver's seat, starts the engine and gets on with his day.

In limbo, like hell, he hears whispered as the tires spin some over a gravelly patch.

All Jason does is give a slight salute to the sky above, then drives off—trying to just keep up with the passing hours as he heads out.

Shane won't look.

He can't bring himself to. Driving home after Shiloh's memorial gathering at the barn, Celia's sitting beside him in the pickup. She's quiet for a stretch. And he feels it—feels her eyes on him now. He knows it—knows she's looking at him—but he watches only the road.

How can you feel it? Feel a *look*. But shit, he does. It's almost tangible as the pickup rolls along the coast now. Is that how much Celia means to him? So much that he senses her gaze? Or is it something else? Is it that her quiet during the past few miles seems somewhat ominous? Like maybe her quiet gaze is preceding something difficult to say. Preceding another looming goodbye as she'll have to drive home soon, too. Maybe it's one goodbye too much. Because how many times can they do this? How many goodbyes can they manage? Can you build a relationship around goodbyes? His mouth goes a little dry, then. But still, he doesn't look. Just drives, not letting on that he *knows* she's staring him down.

The road curves right along with the winding coastline. Distant views of the Atlantic Ocean break through from time to time. The air is heavy with salt today. Shane slows for a stop sign. Signals for a turn. Motions a driver to pull out ahead of him.

Does *anything* but look to the right. To Celia.

Maybe it's because he's already feeling her absence, before it's even here. Oh how he needs to get back to work. Get on that damn lobster boat, line up pots, pull up strings, measure, bait, keep, toss—over and over again. Stay damn busy to fill the coming void. To distract from the loss. To just move on. Tomorrow. A day away. Work tomorrow. He glances at his watch.

An hour at a time.

So he'll do it. He'll fill this hour with Celia. Finally, he glances across the truck's seat at her. She's sitting sideways, kind of leaning against the door there. And facing him. Her expression is calm. And beautiful. Her sunglasses are propped on top of her head, so he sees her eyes. They're locked on his.

"What?" Shane asks with a small laugh.

"I'm really glad, Shane."

"About what?" he asks, not looking at her anymore. Those couple of seconds were distracting enough.

"I'm glad that I was here today. And got to share this time with you." She reaches across the seat and briefly squeezes his arm. "I know it's really sad. But Shiloh was special to a lot of people, me included. So thank you for not turning me away when you saw me yesterday. In the funeral home parking lot."

They're on his street now. Shane drives a few blocks before he looks at her again. "I would never turn you away," he tells her. "No matter the circumstances."

She smiles then. Just a small smile as they pull into his gravel driveway. The stones crunch beneath the tires. And when he shuts off the truck, the warm engine clicks as they sit there.

Because this is it.

She has to leave. It's early afternoon already and she has a long drive ahead.

Now? Now her voice breaks the muffled silence. "Walk the docks with me? Before I go?"

Her visit's coming to a close. Celia leans on some weathered dock railing fifteen minutes later. Shane's by her side. They look out at the harbor and to the distant sea beyond. They talk. Their voices are quiet. Words come easy here, beside the ocean.

"I'm sorry, Celia. Truly," Shane tells her. "About what happened outside the barn."

Celia just looks at him. Sees his tired eyes. The shadows on his face. Sees the past few days' sadness there.

"It's just that ... hearing Tammy broken like that *in* the barn, with people all around ... just *broken* ... it got me so mad. She *never* deserved that kind of pain. Nor did Keith. And *especially* not Shiloh. So seeing all that go down? Well, it really shook my faith."

"In God, you mean?"

"Yeah. Because, well ... I'll never understand His intent in weeks like this one."

"I know." Celia touches his face. "Some things in life are beyond comprehension. Try as we might."

Shane looks at her right as a wind picks up off the water. "You're cold," he says—instead of anything else.

"Little bit." Celia's dress flutters; she wraps her arms around herself.

"Here." Shane slips out of his black suit jacket and drapes it over her shoulders. "Better?"

Celia nods. The jacket is warm from his body. That warmth touches her. Calms her.

"I'll be out *there*," he says, nodding to the harbor. "On the boat. Tomorrow."

"Are you okay with that?"

"I am. It'll help everything—being busy again. Having a

purpose. It'll help me to move forward. Maybe I'll better understand things, too, out on the ocean." He takes a long breath of the sea air. "I'm actually thankful the captain's getting right back out."

"I'll be thinking of you." Celia leans into him. "*But, Shane?*" she whispers then.

"I know." He turns to her now. Touches her hair, her face. "You have to go."

She only nods.

"Come here." His hands cradle her neck as she steps as close to him as she possibly can. In that moment, his thumbs stroke her jaw, her face. He looks away, then at her again. This time, he leans low and kisses her, right there on the dock.

And Celia's not sure she's ever felt a kiss like this one. A kiss of emotion, pure emotion. Of love, and tenacity, *and* goodbye. She feels her breath catch in that kiss—but doesn't let it stop her. Someone also walks past them as she and Shane embrace. As that black suit jacket of his envelops her. As his arms hold her even closer. As their bodies press together and the kiss doesn't let up. Shane's hands reach around her neck. His fingers lift her hair. That kiss is like one long inhale, necessary for them to go on.

The kiss is such that even after they pack up her things, and he helps her into her car a short time later, and even after she wishes him a good trip out on the sea tomorrow, and even after he tells her to call him at every rest stop, and even after she glances in her rearview mirror while driving away from his shingled house and sees him just standing there—not waving, not moving—the kiss is still there.

Even when she gets on the highway, and leaves Maine,

leaves the sea air and call of the gulls far behind, she has to raise her fingers to her face, touch her lips and look again in her mirror ... though a hundred miles have already passed.

twenty-six

NO ANSWER.

Kyle's sitting in his pickup outside the diner. He waits a few minutes there before trying Lauren's cell phone again. She must be busy with something. The kids, maybe. He checks his watch—it's late afternoon already. Could be she's getting dinner ready. He remembers what she called to him this morning when he was already out the door headed to work.

"The kids' tubes are still out in the backyard! You've got to get them rinsed off and put away for the winter."

She trotted to his backing-up truck then, so he stopped and waited. "Don't worry, Ell. I'll take care of it when I get home," he'd told her.

"Okay. Make sure you rinse them first." She waggled a stern finger at him through his open window. "I don't want to store them away all salt-coated."

Kyle nodded, grabbed that waggling finger, pulled her

close and gave her a kiss before taking off.

And it'd been so busy at the diner, he never checked in with her again all day.

The diner's *still* busy, too—not unusual for a Thursday. Three cars have pulled in during these few minutes that he's been sitting in his truck. One couple heads to the outdoor patio; the other two groups of people go inside. Good thing Rob's covering the stoves.

"*He'll be swamped,*" Kyle says under his breath, then lifts his phone and tries Lauren again.

Still no answer. So this time, he leaves a voicemail.

"Hey, Ell. You're probably mixing a pot of something or other for dinner. Just letting you know I'll be late today. Have to make a stop for my brother first. Won't be too long."

Yeah, Kyle thinks when he drops his phone on the passenger seat. *And this'll be good.*

It all started when Cliff talked to him at lunch today. The commish gave him ideas of what he might do for Shane. Got the gears turning in Kyle's noggin all afternoon.

Until everything clicked.

Until he knew *this* was it. With an assured nod, Kyle turns on his truck, pulls out of the diner parking lot and heads to his destination.

It all feels right.

As Kyle cruises down Shore Road, and passes the gas station, the dollar store and a mostly empty campground, he knows. This will say the most, mean the most, to Shane.

Shit, nothing's worse than a loss like the one his brother's feeling right now. Kyle drives the curving road as it turns a little more rural. The next few miles are wooded. Tall trees line the roadside. Long shadows fall across the pavement as he drives along. Up ahead, the stone train trestle comes into view. Any other day, he'd be hitting his blinker and whistlin' a tune—happy to be turning home.

Today, he drives straight past that trestle. What is it they say? You leave beneath the trestle with one of three things: a ring, a baby, or a broken heart. Well, Shane sure as hell didn't actually *leave* with a broken heart. But that heart did break post-departure. Kyle glances at the trestle fading in his rearview mirror. Gives a sad shake of his head, too.

But he drives on. Rural gives way to coastal again on Shore Road. He passes a vast marsh stretching out to Long Island Sound. The September grasses sway golden in the late-day sun. There's a bait-and-tackle shop up ahead. The police station. A couple of take-out seafood joints. All of it's a blur as his eyes are set on one, and only one, landmark.

At least it's a landmark in the lives of anyone living at Stony Point. Because hell, what is a landmark, anyway? As he drives along, Kyle knows. It's some object, or structure, marking a locality or event, maybe one of historical interest. *This* landmark more than fits that bill—marking the milestones of the gang at Stony Point. Weddings, christenings, funerals. Masses and brief stop-ins pleading for help, or asking for mercy, or getting down on knees and thanking the good Lord above. Oh, haven't they all pulled into this parking lot during either the highest of highs, or when feeling the lowest of lows.

Ain't that the truth, Kyle thinks, remembering the

desperate times he's hit the blinker like he is right now before pulling into St. Bernard's Church. Okay, so *he's* not the desperate one today. But maybe this visit will help his brother. Maybe it'll lift Shane, somewhat.

―⁓―

There's a first time for everything, and right now is a first for Kyle. Standing in St. Bernard's parking lot, he eyes the low-slung church. Over time, the damp sea air has weathered the church's cedar shingles to a driftwood gray. A few cars are parked near the entrance, too. Kyle hesitates some, glances at his truck, then straightens his black tee over black work pants. The clothes are a little rumpled after a day behind the stoves.

"*Heck*," he whispers, running a hand through his hair then, before crossing the parking lot and pulling open the church door. "*God won't care.*"

Inside, late-afternoon rays of sun shimmer through the church's stained-glass windows. That light casts a reverential glow on the wood pews, the holy statues. A priest is talking with someone beside the altar. Their low voices hum in the vast space. Someone else kneels in a pew on the far side of the church.

Before doing what *he* plans to, Kyle stops in a pew, too. He drops onto the kneeler, rests his folded hands on the pew in front of him, closes his eyes and whispers a familiar prayer. "*Hail Mary*," he begins, "*full of grace … Blessed art thou … Holy Mary … Pray for us sinners … Now and at the hour of our death … Amen.*" The words come rote, but he means every one of them as much now as he ever has. Blessing himself then, he pushes up off the kneeler and walks to the candle stand in a side alcove. There's an offering box there, and he drops a few dollars in it before turning to the flickering bank of candles.

Yes, this is a first.

Oh, he's lit plenty of candles before. The very first time was at his father's funeral fifteen years ago. The candle then wasn't for his father, though. It was for Shane. In the ensuing years when he and Shane no longer spoke, when he never even uttered Shane's name, Kyle stopped in here and lit candles every so often. *Every* one of those candles was for Shane. If Kyle'd been thinking about him; if he wondered if his brother was safe on the winter seas; if Kyle had a childhood memory or wondered if Shane was even alive. *Any* random thing might get him to stop in and light a candle.

But always for Shane. Never for Lauren or his kids. Not for Neil when he died. Never for Jason when he lost half his leg. Only Shane's been at the receiving end of Kyle's lit tapers.

Except today.

Yes, today's a first.

Now he lifts a taper, touches it to the flickering flame of a burning candle, and pauses. Finally, he does it. He lowers that burning taper's tip to the wick of a white candle off to the side.

Lights that white candle for another lobsterman.

For Shiloh.

For Shiloh, who was out on the Atlantic Ocean with Shane when some unfathomable event occurred, costing Shiloh his life. Some unfathomable event that brought the crew to its knees—as though in a church—as they tried to save the guy.

Kyle drops his head for a moment, then. The church is quiet now. In that muffled silence, he only imagines the sounds on the ocean this past Monday. The desperate pleas on that lobster boat. The yells for help. The curses, the rushing footsteps. They surely weren't peaceful, comforting sounds.

Looking at the candles again, Kyle takes his taper and sets the tip to the flame of Shiloh's candle. Once the taper's burning, he lowers it to another candle behind Shiloh's and lights that one, too. For Shane. After blessing himself again, Kyle pulls his cell phone from his pocket. He backs up and carefully takes a picture—a close-up—of Shiloh's candle flickering in the candle stand beside stained-glass windows glimmering in the afternoon light.

Once Celia left that afternoon, Shane went back inside his house. He changed out of his suit pants and into jeans. But he kept on the white button-down and wears it loose and untucked over those jeans now.

So. If he's got to get through an hour at a time, he's ready to fill the next.

This one is a distracting hour. Shane lands on the couch and turns on the TV. Minutes tick past on a cable news network. There are breaking stories; an analysis of the financial markets; world news. Ten minutes here, five there, eight there. Commercials, national weather. Sixty minutes are soon done.

The Visitor

He checks his watch, shuts off the TV and goes out to get his mail. "*Okay*," he whispers, thumbing through the envelopes. The next hour is all set. He'll pay his bills—some from today, some that accrued during the past few days when his mind was elsewhere. He gets out his checkbook and postage stamps. Sits at the kitchen table. The only sounds come as he tears open the envelopes. Pays the electric bill, the cable bill, an insurance premium. Rips checks out of his checkbook. Loads the envelopes, stamps them, double-checks his account balance. Twenty minutes are left, enough to fill with a trip to the post office. He'll be out on the boat again tomorrow, so might as well get the bills sent off now.

Bill-paying hour filled and complete.

The afternoon's passing, too. By the time he returns from the post office and answers Celia's check-in call, he knows just how to get through the next hour.

With cooking.

A decent meal will be good. He'll be up and at 'em early on the water tomorrow. The morning's due to be cold; the captain's due to keep the crew haulin'. And hell, after this week, Shane's energy needs a boost. So he spends the next sixty minutes in his kitchen. It's late afternoon, and the light is on over the sink. Sea air drifts in through the screen door. All the while, Shane peels carrots; puts a few potatoes in the oven to bake; slices an onion; gets some pork chops out of the fridge. His knife clicks over and over again on a plate as he cuts up the onion. Every single sound seems amplified in the muffled quiet of his empty house. The silverware drawer rattles; the tap water runs; the refrigerator door slams; the applesauce jar pops open; pans scrape on stove burners; the gas pilot clicks as he ignites the stove flame; butter sizzles in the pan; frying onions hiss. As they do, Shane carefully sets the wooden table he and his father made with a place setting for one. Dish, silverware, napkin, glass, salt-and-pepper shakers. He cooks the pork chops next and by the time they're done? The hour's gone.

Eating and cleanup fill the next hour until, finally, there's only one thing left. And for this last chore, he's immensely glad. Glad and relieved.

It's time to get things ready for work tomorrow. Lunch bag set on the counter for the morning; duffel filled with lobstering gear; alarm clock set; work boots, jeans, tee and flannel shirt laid out.

This is what he's waited for all week. This getting back onto the boat.

Back to routine.

Back to purpose.

Back to crossing the creaking dock at the crack of dawn.

Nodding to the resident squawking seagull.

Tossing his full duffel aboard ship.

Feeling the sea beneath him.

His hands busy, busy.

His mind busy, too.

Captain's buoys and baited traps set in the ocean.

More buoys snagged with the gaff.

Trap lines attached to the hauler.

Dripping pots lifted from the sea and emptied.

The sun rising, the day—a *normal* day—passing.

Tomorrow, tomorrow.

His life will start moving again tomorrow after it stalled last Monday afternoon.

THE VISITOR

But first, another hour's done at home, an hour of work prep.

Thanks, Barlow, Shane thinks as he takes off the watch Jason gave him Tuesday. It worked. Shit, Jason knew. He knew Tuesday morning when he sat on Shane's deck with a beer or two and told the story of his father's pewter hourglass, and how it got Jason through his recovery ten years ago.

That's how you'll get through the day too, my friend, Jason told him as the sun rose higher that morning. *An hour at a time. And we just got through one.*

"Got one more now," Shane tells himself as night settles outside his windows. This time, he lands in front of the TV again. This time, it's just to crash. To wind down before sleep. Okay, and to be distracted by his cell phone when it dings with a text message. Thinking it'll be Celia, he reaches for it on the coffee table and is surprised.

It's not Celia. It's Kyle.

Yo bro, Kyle writes. *Heard about your week, and about Shiloh. Really sorry, it's tough.*

"*Kyle,*" Shane whispers as he types the words. "*Thanks, man. Been a helluva few days.*"

Seconds later, another text ding from Kyle. *You must be beat.*

Shit, yeah, Shane types. *Funeral earlier today. Huge turnout. Long day.*

I hear you, comes from Kyle. *Hey, got something for you, too.*

"Okaaay," Shane says, clueless as to what it might be. Holding his phone, he waits. Some entertainment show is on the TV. The hosts gab; celebrity clips play. Finally, another text-message ding. Shane looks at the phone screen and sees a photograph of a flickering white candle. It looks like it's on a candle stand. He can make out stained-glass windows nearby.

That's for Shiloh, Kyle's text reads. *You know, to light the way for him on his next journey.*

Shane pulls the phone closer.

Another text comes from Kyle. *Lit that a couple of hours ago. At St. Bernard's.*

Shane shakes his head, thinking of that familiar coastal church. He hasn't been inside it in *years*—not since their old man would take them Sundays way back when they were kids. Whenever they were on summer vacation in that little rented blue cottage, they made a stop at that church.

Really means a lot, Shane types back. He looks toward the window to the dark night sky outside. *More than you know*, his fingers pluck out on the phone.

Good, comes Kyle's text back. *And hey, one's burning for you too, bro.*

Shane's at a loss for words with that. A loss for any words—spoken, typed.

Shit, some candle in some weathered, gray-shingled church is burning right now.

Flickering to help get him through.

twenty-seven

ABSENCE MAKES HEARTS GROW FONDER?

Or, Jason thinks, absence means someone's hiding out. Or hiding something. Or doesn't want to answer prying questions. Doesn't want to reveal that they've been up to no good.

Yes, each one of those answers *could* apply to Elsa DeLuca. Jason's sure of it—especially since neither he nor Maris has seen hide nor hair of Elsa since last weekend. She's been as absent as can be. So after filming wraps at the Fenwick place Thursday, he swings around to the Ocean Star Inn, parks Maris' golf cart at the curb and crosses the inn's grounds—heading past the inn-spiration walkway to the side yard. It's dinnertime, after all. Surely Elsa will be cooking up something good. He gives a few taps on her kitchen side door.

"*I'm right here*," Elsa's muffled voice makes its way to him. "*Come on in.*"

So Jason does. He opens that door and steps into the inn's kitchen. Late-day sunlight streams through the huge garden window holding Elsa's red herb pails. The dark hardwood floor glimmers; two copper pots simmer on stove burners; Elsa—wearing a long tee over black leggings—sits on an upholstered stool at her massive white marble island. A rolled bandana holds back her brown hair. A few bangle bracelets are set aside on the island as she works on … *something*. Because she's ensconced—yes, *ensconced*—in some project demanding her attention. All she manages is the *briefest* glance in Jason's direction.

"Jason," she says without looking his way again. "Nice to see you."

"Elsa." Jason moseys over to that island. A pair of jeans is laid out atop a big towel there. He walks past Elsa, grabs a biscotti from beneath the glass dome on the island and grabs a stool, too. "I was in the neighborhood," he says, then gets up and finds a small plate in the cabinets. "Thought I'd stop in and say hello."

"Oh." As she talks, Elsa's bent over those laid-out jeans. She's working her arm back and forth, back and forth, over what looks like soiled denim. "I'm glad you did."

While he's up, Jason also gets a glass from the cabinet, then heads to Elsa's huge, double-door, stainless-steel refrigerator and pulls out a milk carton. He gives it a hefty shake and fills his tall glass with the frothy milk before sitting at the marble island again.

All while noticing how Elsa's task is distracting her from even talking. So while sitting on his upholstered stool, Jason dunks his chocolate-chip biscotti in the cold milk and starts digging for dirt. "Haven't seen you in a few days,

Elsa. You staying out of trouble this week?"

"Best I can," she promptly answers, all while her arm's going at it on those jeans.

"Which *means*," Jason muses around a mouthful of milk-dunked biscotti, "there might be *some* trouble?"

"Depends on who you ask."

Jason eyes Elsa—still rubbing something on that dirty denim. There's also a big basin of water on the marble island.

"By the way, I heard about Shane," Elsa goes on, still not giving Jason more than a glance. "And his friend Shiloh."

"Yeah. His friend, his crewmate. They worked together on the boat." Jason dunks more of his sweet biscotti. "I just got back yesterday from a *trip* to Maine, actually."

With that announcement, Elsa turns her attention, briefly, to him—her fisted hand hovering above the marble island. "Cliff mentioned that," she says before resuming with her dirty jeans. "He heard it from Kyle at the diner. The situation with Shane sounded dire?"

Jason nods. He tells her, too, a little about Shane's frantic Monday night phone call. And how he and Maris both thought it wise to check up on him. That Jason spent a day in Rockport and saw how the death devastated Shane. Learned how Shane valiantly tried to get Shiloh to hang on.

"But nothing worked," Jason says. "Poor Shiloh was here one day, and gone the next."

"*Ach.*" Elsa sits back, sets down her busy hands and shakes her head. "The ways of life … It's just terrible sometimes."

Jason lifts the last of his chocolate-chip biscotti—dripping milk—to his mouth. "Don't we know it," he quietly says.

Elsa just looks long at him, pats her heart, then gets back to her task. She leans forward over her marble island and starts rubbing those muddy jeans again.

"Wait." Jason squints at her hand and leans closer. "Is that a *potato* you're holding?"

Elsa stops rubbing the denim and lifts what looks like a partially peeled potato half. "Yes. As a matter of fact, it is."

"And what are you doing with it?"

"I was working in the garden this morning," Elsa explains. "And my knees got all muddy. I remembered that Kyle once told me to rub an uncooked potato half on dirt-stained jeans. Said to give a good rubbing, then soak the jeans in cool water before putting them in the washing machine."

"You mean, a *potato* gets off all that muddy crud?"

Elsa nods. "Sort of. Kyle said that some *acid* in the potato dissolves the dried muck so that it comes right out in the wash. Thought I'd give it a try after seeing how dirty my jeans got today when I cleaned out the rest of the garden."

Jason grabs a napkin and wipes his mouth. "Why don't you just save yourself the aggravation and use those attachable knee pads?"

"Oh, Jason," Elsa says, then *tsk-tsks* as she gets back to potato-rubbing. "I use knee *mats*. Knee pads are so *not* my style."

"Why not? We use them on construction sites all the time."

"Exactly. And ... *hellooo*." Elsa lifts the back of her potato-clutching hand to brush away a strand of hair fallen in front of her eyes. "I wasn't going to look like a ... well, like a *dork*."

"A dork?"

"Yes." She slides the dirty jeans closer and shifts her potato-rubbing to the other knee. "You know. Dorky. *Unstylish.*"

"But who would even see you?"

"Oh, you'd be surprised. So, no. I do not garden in *construction* gear," she says with a bristle.

"Of course not. *What* was I thinking?" Jason brings his crumb-covered plate and empty milk glass to her big farm sink. "And I've *seen* your renowned foam mats. Why didn't you just *use* those today?" he asks over his shoulder. Setting down his things, he walks back to the island and leans closer to the dirty jeans. "Because this isn't like you, getting those knees all muddied."

"Listen." Elsa's arm is going at it, rubbing back and forth a little rougher now. She's bent close to the mud stain. "I was all over the place in my Sea Garden this morning. Up and down, this way and that. It just would've been too cumbersome to keep moving that cushion from here, to there, and over yonder."

All this she says without looking at Jason. But he notices a change while standing in her grand kitchen filled with golden sunlight and copper pots and sweet biscotti. Elsa's getting really aggressive with that raw potato. He watches her going at those jeans with gusto. The potato juices are smearing right into the now-damp mud.

"Something happen with Mitch this week?" Jason quietly asks. "Or Cliff, maybe?"

Elsa abruptly stops and, through another fallen strand of hair, squints at Jason standing there. "*What?*" she asks.

"I *said* ... Did something happen with Mitch or Cliff this week?"

Now? Now Elsa sits back on her upholstered stool. She tips her head, too, all while really clutching that potato half. "Why do you ask?"

"What else except your beaus would get you that riled up?" Jason's backing toward the door to leave now. "Because you *were* getting awfully aggressive with that spud."

"What? *Aggressive?*" Elsa lifts her hand and looks at the practically finger-indented potato. "*Ohhh ... You ... you,*" she says—and yes, she does it. Lurching from her seat, she throws that grimy, half-peeled potato right at him!

One-handed, Jason snatches the spud in midair and lightly tosses it in the trash—all while laughing and then heading out the side door.

───

As Jason cruises off in the golf cart, he notices Celia's guest cottage beyond the inn. The shingles are honey-colored beneath the late sunlight. The eaves are edged with a gingerbread trim. Two wicker rockers are on the front porch. Really, it could look straight out of a fairy tale. But there's a deception to that charmed appearance. Because Lord knows, a fairy-tale life around these parts is nearly impossible these days. Slowly passing her house, Jason also sees that Celia's driveway is empty; her car, gone. Can't say he's surprised, not after Celia texted Maris last night. Of course Celia was going to get herself to Maine—come hell or high water. So she must still be there, or is on her way home at the very least—because Shane's back to work tomorrow. But Celia surely attended Shiloh's funeral today.

THE VISITOR

Must've met his family, too. Must've witnessed the sad grief all around.

Fairy tale, like shit.

At least, not for Shane and Celia right now.

So ... Jason does it. After being away for a couple of days, he decides to take a ride around Stony Point. To check on everyone else. With all that went down in Maine, he feels a little bit like a sentry now. Like he wants to take a half hour and cruise the beach streets here just to be sure everything else is right with their world.

Driving the golf cart past the marsh, with its sweeping golden grasses and blue water inlets, all starts out fine. Life is as it should be. There's a white egret standing on the banks of the marsh. Dragonflies flit above the grasses.

Further down the street, he approaches the Gallagher house. The old Dutch colonial's yard backs right up to that marsh. He catches sight of Matt standing at his smoking grill, no doubt getting some juicy steaks sizzling for supper. Jason sounds the golf cart horn, and when Matt waves from the grill, Jason waves back and drives off.

All good, there.

He goes up and down a few more sandy beach roads. American flags flutter on tall, white poles. Whirligigs—one a blue jay with flapping wings, another of leaping dolphins—spin in front-yard gardens. Yellow marigolds spill from porch pots. Curtains in cottage windows waver in the sea breeze. A motion catches Jason's eye, then. It's Cliff. He's using a push mower to cut the grass at the Stony Point Beach Association trailer. So Jason pulls to the curb and waves him over.

"Jason!" Cliff calls out, tipping up a brimmed cap he's wearing. "Nice to see you."

Jason nods and reaches out to shake Cliff's hand. "Just wanted to tell you something."

"Everything okay, I hope?" Cliff asks.

"Sure, sure. It's just that, well …" Jason points to the little patch of grass around the trailer. "You missed a spot, Commish," he says before peeling out so that a bit of sand sprays up from his golf cart tires.

Jason keeps driving, this time toward the train trestle. Figures he'll circle around the whole place to check on *everyone*. The tended cottages on his route, and the fired-up grills, and the chugging lawn mowers are a good indication so far that all's well here.

But the sight of the guard shack gets him skidding to a stop.

"*What the hell?*" he whispers. Because the once-staid Stony Point guard shack has turned into a kaleidoscope of colors. Every time he's driven past it this week, there's yet another peel-and-stick paint sample tacked up. Each shade, though, is nicely arranged and cohesively stacked—light to dark. Varying shades are grouped by color family. Rows of colors are numbered. And … what? Jason gets out of his golf cart and walks closer. Is that a voting box nailed near the shack entrance?

Nick pokes his head out of that shack. When he spots Jason skidding and muttering and walking over, he ambles out.

"Hey, dude," Nick says. He's in full security uniform threads—epaulets and all. "What's happening with you this fine Thursday?"

Jason crosses his arms and stands there, taking in the multicolored shack. "This your doing?"

"Yeah, man. Come on," Nick says, motioning him closer. "I'll give you the deets."

Well, Nick's got the paint-color conundrum down to a science. There are reasons supporting each shade. Sunlight variables are noted. Popular preferences are indicated.

"Are those *ballots*?" Jason asks, pointing to a wire basket hanging beside that voting box. A pile of loose white papers fills the basket.

"Sure are."

"Give me a couple, would you?"

"Definitely. Every vote counts, and it's *your* responsibility to cast one for your desired color." Nick lifts out two ballots. "One for you, one for the Mrs. And remember," he says as Jason takes those ballots and heads back to the golf cart. "You can't be carpin' about the final color if you don't vote!"

Okay, so Jason drives off relatively caught up on any Stony Point happenings. After his two-day sojourn to Maine, all seems decent. Maybe not a fairy tale—but pretty darn close.

There's just one more stop to make. So he heads up Hillcrest Road and veers over to Sea View, where the cottages face Long Island Sound beyond. Glimpses of the sparkling water are visible as he passes the stately homes there. But he keeps driving, following Sea View to the far end where it forks onto Bayside Road. Railroad tracks run along a raised bank further back off the road here, behind a few blocks of smaller houses. And across the street, past some wild dune grasses, is the bay. Jason slowly drives toward the Bradfords' silver-shingled house. Blue shutters frame the windows. A white wrought-iron bench sits in a

239

fading flowerbed beside the screened-in porch.

And there, he sees what he's looking for.

Or *who* he's looking for.

Kyle must've just gotten home from work. He's standing outside in his black tee and black pants. A garden hose is coiled at his feet; the hose's nozzle is in his hand. Jason pulls the golf cart right onto the lawn and slowly drives to Kyle. He's actually spraying off the kids' beach tubes and rafts leaning against the side of the house.

"Got a sad sight going on there, Bradford," Jason tells him, parking nearby.

"Yep." Kyle keeps spraying, the gentle stream of water rinsing all the sand and salt off the inflatable tubes. "Going to deflate them and pack them up till next year."

"Ah, summer. Another one gone."

Kyle nods, sets the hose down and turns the tubes around. When he picks up the hose again, he resumes spraying and talking at the same time. "Still got Friday night fishing tomorrow, though. We on?" he asks.

"You bet." Jason starts steering the golf cart to head out. "Later, guy," he calls as he slightly accelerates across the lawn.

"See you then, loser," Kyle calls back. Does something else, too. Kyle turns that spraying hose nozzle in Jason's direction and gives him a good dousing in his golf cart.

So ducking, Jason swerves that cart out of the cold spray. But Kyle did the damage: Jason's hair is damp; his shirt, water spattered. Laughing then, he discreetly flips Kyle the bird before getting that skidding golf cart on the street again and heading back to Sea View Road.

Heading home.

THE VISITOR

But there's one more cottage he notices before he gets there. A little beach bungalow a stone's throw from Long Island Sound. The shingles are weathered from the salt air. The trim paint is peeling. There's a narrow walkway made of boardwalk planks running through some scrubby beach grass alongside the place.

It's Shane's rented bungalow. And it's empty. His pickup truck isn't in the driveway. The windows are all closed. The whole place is buttoned up tight. Who knows when Shane will even be around these parts again? He missed a lot of work the past few weeks; said his captain's got a helluva quota to catch up on.

And Shane also told Jason he's counting on that. Said that being back on the water is what he needs now. That there's nothing like working out life, working out your head, miles from land.

Yeah, for Shane? The sea definitely calls.

Jason gives the deserted cottage a last look. He catches sight around back of the sparse, open-air porch with the sloping roof. There's the grassy area, too, where he and Maris, Celia and Shane had their lobster dinner—two weeks ago, now. Turning away, Jason steers his cart down Sea View Road toward his gabled house on the bluff. A roof peak is visible in the distance, beyond the row of tall shrubs lining his side yard.

But still, Jason slows.

Slows and gives one more look back at that empty beach bungalow beside the sea.

twenty-eight

CALL IT WHAT YOU WANT, but Jason thinks this might be another version of paradise.

Late that afternoon, he walks into his house on the bluff, sets his duffel on the kitchen counter, stops right there, closes his eyes and deeply inhales. Which is when it hits him—an incredible aroma coming from their new, stainless-steel oven.

Paradise.

He has to do it, though. Has to see this to believe it. To believe that his cooking-insecure wife accomplished this feat. He walks to the stove for a look. Yes, there's a roaster chicken in the oven with sliced potatoes. A pan beside it is filled with seasoned tricolor carrots. *And* there's a fresh loaf of some farm bread on the kitchen table. Place settings are arranged there. Wineglasses, too.

"Maris?" Jason calls out when he walks back to the counter and unloads his work duffel. He sets his phone and tablet near the charger. Empties out his lunch sack. Rinses the thermos. Sets the two guard shack paint color ballots on the table. They can discuss *that* hot topic over dinner. Speaking of which. "Food smells *amazing*, sweetheart," he calls again.

"Been such a crazy-busy week," Maris' distant voice calls back from another room. "So we'll have a good supper together, babe."

"Sure will," Jason tells himself. There's a pile of mail on the counter, so he picks that up and thumbs through the envelopes. The electric bill came. An architectural magazine. A few pieces of junk mail.

"Be out in a sec," Maris' distracted voice calls again. "I'm in the laundry room, doing some ironing."

Jason glances that way, then tosses out the junk mail, drops his keys in the basket near the door, brings Maddy a bowl of fresh water out to the deck where she's fenced in, and goes back inside. Maris must still be ironing, so he heads to the laundry room.

And stops in the doorway—surprised to see her wearing only her skinny jeans and a black bustier bra as she irons a shirt. Amused, he crosses his arms, leans against the jamb and silently watches. When Maris flips the blouse she's ironing, she catches sight of him standing there.

"Jason! You weren't supposed to see me like this!" she scolds while giving a puff of steam to that blouse.

"Why not?"

"Well … Because I'm not …" She presses the iron along the fabric. "It's just that I wanted to look nice for supper. And then I noticed there were all wrinkles in my shirt!" Another puff of steam rises from the iron. "And since nobody was around," she goes on, throwing him a quick smile, "I whipped off the shirt to touch it up."

Jason still only watches her in that black bra. It's got a plunging satin neckline, and a wide, scalloped edge is all black lace. Black lace gently crossing Maris' bare torso as she stands there pretty much topless in her jeans. "Well," Jason remarks with a grin, "my job's half done."

"What are you talking about?" Maris doesn't look at him, though. With her brown hair down and tucked behind an ear, she just presses out some troublesome wrinkle.

"Your top's already off," Jason explains as he walks up to her at the ironing board and wraps her in his arms from behind. "Now on to the undergarments."

"Jason Barlow!" As she says it, Maris is setting the hot iron on its rest pad. Shutting the iron off, too, and unplugging it. That done, she reaches for her nicely pressed blouse, but stops. She doesn't move. At all.

Oh, Jason knows why, too. He can tell by the way she drops her head as he brushes aside her long hair and runs his fingers across her bare shoulders, leaves a few kisses on her neck.

"*Jason,*" she whispers now before turning to him.

"*Shh,*" he whispers back, then cradles her face, leans down and kisses her—right there at the ironing board. Right there as she forgets about her spread-out blouse. Right there as she stretches up and meets his kiss, too. Her lips are soft on his; her fingers skim his whiskered jaw.

As they kiss, and as he nuzzles her neck, and as she slips her arms around his waist, he slowly backs them out of the room. They maneuver backward through the kitchen next, all while kissing and touching and as Maris unbuttons *his* shirt. He continues walking backward through the room, his hands holding his half-dressed wife and tugging her along with him. Tugging her along between those hands of his stroking her collarbone, moving down that plunging bustier's neckline, over the curve of her breasts, across the delicate lace on her skin.

Another step backward, and another, is managed. A pause for a kiss, then—deeper this time. Until more steps resume. They sideswipe the table, almost trip on a chair, but make it to the dark, paneled hallway. Maris' fingers have already lifted off his button-down and dropped it on the floor. Now her hands are busy tugging his tee up and over his head—as though her hands just can't stop.

"*Jason*," she murmurs into his kiss, then moves her mouth to his jaw, his shoulder. "*How will we make it up the stairs behaving like this?*"

He glances over at those steep steps, then turns back to her. His hands slip down along her bare sides. Her skin is so soft. And that black lace bra? Hell, it's tormenting him. "How much longer does the chicken have to cook?" he asks, his voice husky.

"Twenty minutes," she murmurs into another kiss.

"*Huh. We'll have to take a detour to beat the clock,*" he whispers, then pulls her into the living room instead of up the stairs. "*This should give us enough time.*"

"*Good idea,*" she whispers back once standing at the couch.

Before they go any further, though, Jason sits on that couch. Maris does, too, whispering and leaving kisses on his shoulder as he quickly unzips the long custom zipper on his pant leg's inner seam. That done, he rolls the silicone liner and sock down his thigh and pulls his stump out of his prosthesis. After getting the sock and liner off, he sets it all aside—prosthesis, liner, sock—and turns back to Maris, still half dressed. Still waiting. Still murmuring little nothings to him as she idly strokes his skin.

All talking stops then. There's not a *minute* to waste before that chicken is ready to come out of the oven—and they both damn well know it.

So there's a bit of a race for them as Maris reaches down and unbuckles his belt.

And as Jason gets her jeans off.

And as they lie back on the sofa while her mouth opens to his in another long kiss.

And as they rush, and push down her silky bikini panties, and unzip and get his pants off. His boxers, too.

Until that kitchen timer is *so* close to beeping that Jason just moves over her on the couch, and lowers himself, and leaves that sweet bustier *on* her as he brings his mouth to her throat, her neck, her breasts. His touch is insistent, her whispers nearly insatiable as she tussles with her panties tangled below her knees, as they wait for no oven timer now, wait for not even each other, in the shadowed room.

⁓

It's a night of gluttony.

Every moment seems beautifully pushed to excess. Even getting dressed afterward is thrilling as they pick up pants and underthings from the living room floor, and shirts from the hallway floor, and, yes, end up back where it all started—lifting Maris' wrinkle-free blouse off the ironing board. Jason's on his forearm crutches now, so

Maris helps him dress—holding a pant leg here, a shirtsleeve there. And she sits beside him in the kitchen, where *he* puts that blouse on *her* before loosely buttoning it up.

And Maris loves it. They need this.

A half hour later, the kitchen's recessed lights are dimmed. Food and flickering candles are askew on their new antique-gray pedestal table. The roasted chicken's been carved and forked and salted and is about to be eaten. The baby potatoes cut in halves were drizzled in olive oil and roasted to perfection. Flecks of chopped parsley dot those small gold potatoes. And the tricolor carrots? They're lightly caramelized on the edges and seasoned with rosemary, thyme and parsley. Everything is arranged in their vintage blue-and-white serving dishes. Tarnished silverware glimmers beneath the candlelight. Crystal wineglasses sparkle.

And they can't stop talking now, instead of touching and whispering and kissing.

But as Jason reaches to scoop some potatoes, Maris moves aside her dish. She gets up, too, and grabs their lost-time log from the kitchen island. Sitting again, she opens that journal. "I want to log this before we eat," she says, jotting a few lines for her latest entry. "So I don't forget."

"Pass that over to me so I can see what you're writing," Jason says, setting down his fork and reaching for the journal.

"Read it out loud," Maris softly says. "*To* me."

Jason looks at her for a long second, then opens the journal to the latest entry. His voice is low as he says the first word. "Ironing?" He glances at her with a shrug then.

"Keep reading," Maris tells him.

"Oh. *I* get it." He looks back to the journal page. "*Ironing*," he repeats. "Written beside a winking smiley face and a scrawled heart. Thirty minutes retrieved." Again, he looks at her across the table. "Might be the best thirty minutes of the day."

"*Might* be?" Maris asks, adjusting the collar of her freshly ironed blouse.

"Well I don't know yet, because this dinner's giving *those* thirty minutes a run for their money. The food's *incredible.*"

"Food for which you've *certainly* worked up an appetite, babe." With an easy wink, Maris grabs the journal back and returns it to the island. "Anyway, Elsa gave me fresh herbs from her garden window," she says around a mouthful of carrots once she's sitting again. "She's so happy I'm doing more cooking now that I have a new kitchen."

"Me, too." As he says it, Jason's forking a few slices of chicken breast and setting them on his plate. He cuts a piece and drags it through drizzles of olive oil. "Met up with a new client today," he tells Maris as he lifts the fork to his mouth. "Right here at Stony Point. They have a small ranch cottage they want to expand."

"Oh, which one?" But she's too busy slicing her fork through a tender potato to look up at Jason across from her. She just listens as he goes on, telling her it's the old white cottage on the corner.

"Problem is," he's saying, "the property's small lot size. Zoning won't let me expand the cottage footprint, so I'll have to build *up*—with a *very* limited budget. But I have an idea that might fit their money constraints."

"What do you have in mind?"

The Visitor

"I'll show you once I get some drawings firmed up." Jason lifts his wineglass and takes a sip. "Want to change up the design on this one."

They talk more then, while stabbing potatoes and carrots onto their forks. While buttering a slice of the warm peach-raspberry bread Maris picked up earlier at the farm stand. While refilling a wineglass. Jason tells her what's coming down the pike for him—including more CT-TV meet-and-greets at local fairs. Maris tells him that she rescheduled her editing consultation with Mitch. Moved it to next week. They contemplate guard shack paint colors, agreeing on none and leaving their ballots blank. Meanwhile, amidst the talk and dining, the sun's just about gone down. Maddy's inside now and lying sprawled out at the screen of the open slider. Salt air drifts into the room. A robin holds on to its song, chirping a few notes from the big maple tree in the yard.

Jason sits back in his chair, then. Takes a long breath. Clasps his hands behind his head. "*Just perfection*," he says.

"What is?" Maris asks him. "The food?"

"No. Well, yeah. That *too*," he answers, sitting forward and picking up his fork again. He drags a hunk of chicken through dregs of vegetables on his plate. "But sitting here with you at the table like this? After we almost didn't make it this summer? And after last weekend with the whole deer thing?" He raises his fork to his mouth. Chews some as he's ruminating on this. "Then there was the sadness with Shane this week, too," Jason adds before taking a swallow of wine. "So, yeah. Sitting at this beautiful table after all that … life can't get much better."

Maris looks at him sitting there. His dark, wavy hair

needs a trim. His whiskers are a light beard now, having gone unshaven for two weeks. His crutches lean against the chair beside him. His smile comes easy. Any shadows of fatigue seem to have faded. So she does what says it all. She reaches across the table and simply squeezes his hand.

Jason squeezes back, and they eat more. It's that kind of dinner, one that necessitates picking—the food's *that* good.

"Think Celia's still in Maine?" Maris asks.

"Not sure. After filming at the Fenwicks', I took a golf cart ride around a few streets on my way home. Celia's place looked empty. No car in the driveway. But she could be in Addison, too."

"Yeah." Maris sips her wine. "At least Shane wasn't alone these few days."

"No, and that's good. Because, you know ... he lost a brother, in a way."

"With Shiloh."

Jason nods. "That's how the crews are, on the boats. They're a brotherhood. The guys are tight."

They quiet then, she and Jason. They linger there and kill the bottle of wine.

"It's funny," Jason says, motioning his fork to the shabby white frames hanging beside the table.

"What is?"

"I felt like I got to see a side of *my* brother up north that I didn't really know."

As Jason mentions Neil's visits with Shane, and the long-ago talks they had, and the abandoned mansions they once explored, Maris looks at the wall of Neil's framed bandanas. They're stretched taut behind glass. Each faded

The Visitor

bandana is swirls of varying blues and whites—the colors of the sea.

The sea that Neil loved.

⁓

Later, much later in the night, Jason can't sleep. Can't quiet his thoughts. He eventually leans over, kisses Maris' shoulder and tells her he's going for a walk with Maddy. It takes a few minutes to get dressed and swap out his forearm crutches for his prosthesis, but he does it. It beats tossing and turning in bed. Downstairs, he grabs his sweatshirt, whistles for the dog and heads out. Some pale light falls from the waning moon. And a certain quiet is everywhere. Walking in the night's shadows, the only sound is his footstep on the gritty road. In no time, though, he's on the beach—walking the hard-packed sand below the tideline. It feels good beneath his gait, that small coastal stretch of earth. Always has. Walking comes easy here in the night. His mind relaxes.

And he'll take it.

The dog runs ahead of him now, her nose to the wet sand. To Jason, the day—with all its normalcy—is all he seeks. Restoring cottages, checking in on his friends, his family, time spent with his wife, time spent by the sea … How sweet that kind of life is, doesn't he know it—especially after the past few days in Maine.

"You there, Neil?" he quietly says into the darkness then. Over the Sound, that waning moon rises higher. Just a swath of its light falls on the water. The salt air is still.

But no answer comes.

So he keeps walking. Maddy turns back and sloshes through the shallows toward him. Her paws prance and splash through the cold water. But there's more. There's some whisper of sound in that splashing, too.

I'm here, Jay.

Jason strains to listen. The whispered words are either his brother's, or else it's just the gentle splash of the water fooling him. Or wishful thinking tonight. His brother's been on his mind.

Jason stops there on the packed sand—just in case. He drags a hand through his hair. Small waves lap on the beach, steady. Steady. The salt air is a little misty; the night, cool. Standing there beside the sea and looking up at the dark sky, Jason asks a favor—just one—in the calm night.

"Look out for Shane on the water tomorrow, would you?"

twenty-nine

FRIDAY MORNING AT DAWN, SHANE'S glad to be back on familiar turf. Glad to be walking the docks. Glad to hear the dock boards creak beneath his booted feet. Glad to be carrying his duffel packed with work gear and a sack of food—sandwiches, fruit, snacks. Glad to be headed to the lobster boat.

Everything's the same, you'd think at first. Just another day in Rockport, Maine. Another day on the job. Against the morning damp, he's got on his newsboy cap and a canvas jacket over his flannel shirt. Gloves, too. While walking, salt water splashes at the dock posts. The sun hasn't crested the horizon yet, and wisps of fog rise off the lapping harbor water. He sees that mist in the dock lights' illumination. Up ahead is the little coffee shed. Its windows glow from inside. Someone already got the first pot of the day started.

And that's when things change. When Shane knows the

morning is *not* the same as it's been for years. That the familiar *normalcy* of everything is deceiving. Because typically? Typically *Shiloh* pushes out through that coffee shed door right as Shane approaches. Shi would be holding two steaming cups of fresh brew.

Here you go, bub, he'd say, handing Shane a cup.

And they'd stop there at the railing. They'd talk about the day ahead. Look out at Rockport Harbor as the horizon lightened with the rising sun.

So as much as everything *looks* the same, it's not.

Shiloh's long gone from ever walking these docks again. He's six feet beneath the earth now.

Shane stops for a few moments outside that coffee shed. He drops his duffel, leans on the railing and faces the Atlantic beyond. The sky's still dark; the sea, darker. But Shane senses it. Smells it. Hears it. Before turning to get going, to get on the boat and get working, he tips his cap at dawn's sky over the sea.

Moving on then, he's good to go. He acknowledged Shiloh, or his spirit, or his absence, even. There's nothing more to be done except get busy on the boat. Haul those pots. Feel the sea beneath him. He's thankful for the distraction of his workaday life. So he picks up his duffel and walks further out on the dock. Several coiled ropes are piled against one dock post. The resident ornery seagull is perched on another.

"Good to see you again," Shane greets the bird—which grumbles and ruffles its feathers in response. "I'm back to work," Shane tells it, tipping his cap as he walks past.

Still, his step is slow.

Still, this isn't easy.

Shiloh's absence will be tangible for the boys on the boat—himself, included.

Shane shifts his grip on his duffel as he walks along. He breathes the salt air.

And he stops once more.

Just leans his arms on another railing, bows his head and closes his eyes for a long moment.

"Hey there, Shane!" a voice suddenly calls through the dusky morning.

He looks off to the right and sees his captain sitting in a skiff floating nearby. It's just a simple rowboat, really, with a few sparse benches. There's a small outboard engine, too.

The captain's paddling closer now, so Shane looks past him to see if the lobster boat is tied at the dock. It's not. It's moored out in the harbor's open water—which isn't unusual. Sometimes the captain does that and transports the crew there in his old skiff. He uses those few minutes of rowing to pep-talk the boys. Or start a busy day with quiet reflection. When the rowboat pulls close to where Shane is on the dock now, the captain motions him aboard. So Shane drops his duffel in the boat and hops on.

"Morning, Captain," he says as he sits on a bench.

"Shane." The captain dips the oars back into the harbor waters and gets the skiff moving. When he leans back and slowly lifts those oars, the water *drip-drips* off of them before he dips them in again. Pulls back on them. Lifts them again in a slow, steady rhythm that keeps the boat moving.

"Don't you just want to *motor* out to the boat?" Shane hitches his head toward the small engine lifted out of the water.

"Not today." The captain keeps rowing, but noticeably slows down. "Need to loosen the kinks this morning," he tells Shane while rolling a shoulder. "Feels good paddling."

Shane says nothing. Further out, he can decipher the granite shoreline edging the harbor. In dawn's light, the shadow of tall pine trees rises beyond that long granite ledge. When he looks to the captain again, Shane's a little surprised at the way he's being watched right back. The captain's got a short, grizzled beard. His face is leathery from a lifetime out on the water. And his eyes stay locked on Shane—who looks from the captain, then back to the docks they're leaving behind.

"What about the rest of the crew?" Shane asks, not seeing any of the guys waiting on the dock. "Don't you have to pick them up?"

"They're on the boat already," the captain answers, his voice somewhat gruff.

"Oh. Didn't realize I was late." Shane shoves up his jacket sleeve and checks the watch Jason gave him. Figured he'd wear it today, just in case. But he also knows that being busy hauling lobster pots, and bullshitting with the boys on the boat, and getting out on the Atlantic is the *only* Rx he truly needs. "So who'd you get to fill in for Shiloh? Your nephew?"

"For now. Till I can find a greenhorn looking for work."

"At least you've got a full crew."

"Ayuh. And the reason I'm picking you up solo like this is that I want to catch my deck boss up on things. Let you know the day's plan."

"Sure it'll be busy as hell." Shane glances to the lobster boat further out in the harbor. Beyond it, the sun is just cresting the horizon. Time to get to it. To get the boat chugging out to sea. "And don't worry, Captain. I'll keep the boys in line. We'll be all right. Get the job done for you. Keep those pots filled."

The captain just nods while still slowly paddling. The oars dip into the seawater and slosh some.

"Quite a season we've had," Shane quietly goes on. "A lot of setbacks."

"Ayuh. Like none we've seen in years."

"All those pots needing fixin' after they took a beating in that storm earlier in the summer. Then the busted fuel pump." Shane squints across the rowboat at the captain's face. Something's up. Something's going on here; Shane can feel it. The captain's not saying much.

"Shiloh, too," the captain adds to the list. "We lost a good one." He says nothing more then. He just lifts those heavy oars, holds them aloft while they *drip-drip*, then slips them back in the sea and pulls on them again.

"Yeah, we did. Rest his soul." Shane adjusts his newsboy cap, lifting it a little. Damn, his pulse quickens, too. His heart's beating faster as the captain rows even slower. "Seas look calm today. Nice day to get out there," Shane says, looking toward the deeper waters. The sun's rising higher now. That light falls on the orange and yellow leaves of the sugar maples further down the coastline. There's no mistaking fall's upon them. It's even in the air, that telltale chill. "Heading into the season of bad weather," Shane remarks. "Calm today, but conditions can turn on a dime this time of year."

"Nothing we're not used to."

"No." But Shane gets a funny feeling. Starts perspiring

now. Something's *really* not right, not with the sparse words coming from the captain.

And Shane doesn't want to know about it. He just wants to get to work; wants to keep his mind and body busy. Wants to throw the gaff hook—whip it for all he's fuckin' worth—to snare the pot lines; wants to lift those dripping traps, to manhandle them right off the hauler; wants to measure the damn lobsters, to band the keepers and fling the rest out to the mighty sea; wants to rebait those empty traps with sacks of stinking herring; to heave those pots back over the gunwale. Wants to keep moving, moving, moving.

To *exhaust* himself.

To be dead on his feet.

To be so damn fatigued, he can't *think* anymore.

To be so depleted, he can heal some.

So he presses the captain for what he needs—to *move*, damn it. To board the lobster boat so they can head out to sea and begin hauling. "Well ... we're ready to get to it," Shane says, leaning his elbows on his knees. "To get working, Captain."

"We are." The captain stops, then. Stops talking *and* stops rowing. He lifts the oars fully out of the water, takes a long breath, and hesitantly resumes their conversation. "But Shane ... well ... listen up, now."

Again, Shane tips up his newsboy cap. A bead of perspiration trickles down his face as he eyes the captain. "I'm listening." As he says it, the harbor water jounces the boat around. "You got my ear."

"Good. Because I'm going to tell you something, Shane." The captain looks long at him. "And you're *not* going to like it."

The Visitor

Shane shifts on the bench. Straightens his wristwatch. Beyond them, the sun rises over the Atlantic. Gulls swoop overhead. Seawater sloshes against the sides of their idled skiff, too. Shane turns and sees the boys waiting on the lobster boat. They're just silhouettes standing on deck. When Shane turns back to the captain, he knows. This solo trip was intended for what's coming—coming right this second.

"Now, Shane," the captain goes on. "Try to—"

Shane holds up a hand and interrupts. His heart's pounding. "I'm going to encourage you, Captain, to stop your words. Stop right *there*, damn it." Shane leans back a little on that narrow bench seat. He crosses his arms in front of him and squints through the dusky light at the scruffy captain. The leather work gloves on his hands holding the oars are as worn and tough as the man's expression. A faded thermal sweatshirt is pulled up close around his shoulders in the sea damp. This old salt is a guy who's spent his life fighting the Atlantic, fighting for lobstering territory, fighting for his livelihood. And he never lost any of those fights.

Well, Shane's ready to fight him, too.

"Shane—"

"I *told* you, Captain. That's *enough*," Shane warns him. "Because there's something *I* have to say, first." The only sound then is that water lapping against the stilled rowboat.

Until Shane continues—with no bullshit, no fear. He has to. It's the *only* way to keep a grip on his life. "And when I'm talking, *you* better listen up, sir," he tells the captain now, then drops his level voice low. "And listen up, real good."

The beach friends' journey continues in

STAIRWAY TO THE SEA

The next novel in The Seaside Saga from New York Times Bestselling Author

JOANNE DEMAIO

Also by Joanne DeMaio

The Seaside Saga
(In order)
1) Blue Jeans and Coffee Beans
2) The Denim Blue Sea
3) Beach Blues
4) Beach Breeze
5) The Beach Inn
6) Beach Bliss
7) Castaway Cottage
8) Night Beach
9) Little Beach Bungalow
10) Every Summer
11) Salt Air Secrets
12) Stony Point Summer
13) The Beachgoers
14) Shore Road
15) The Wait
16) The Goodbye
17) The Barlows
18) The Visitor
19) Stairway to the Sea
–And More Seaside Saga Books–

Also by Joanne DeMaio

Beach Cottage Series
(In order)
1) The Beach Cottage
2) Back to the Beach Cottage

Standalone Novels
True Blend
Whole Latte Life

The Winter Series
(In order)
1) Snowflakes and Coffee Cakes
2) Snow Deer and Cocoa Cheer
3) Cardinal Cabin
4) First Flurries
5) Eighteen Winters
6) Winter House
–And More Winter Books–

For a complete list of books by *New York Times* bestselling author Joanne DeMaio, visit:

Joannedemaio.com

About the Author

JOANNE DEMAIO is a *New York Times* and *USA Today* bestselling author of contemporary fiction. The novels of her ongoing and groundbreaking Seaside Saga journey with a group of beach friends, much the way a TV series does, continuing with the same cast of characters from book-to-book. In addition, she writes winter novels set in a quaint New England town. Joanne lives with her family in Connecticut.

For a complete list of books and for news on upcoming releases, visit Joanne's website. She also enjoys hearing from readers on Facebook.

Author Website:
Joannedemaio.com

Facebook:
Facebook.com/JoanneDeMaioAuthor

Made in United States
Troutdale, OR
05/30/2023